The Tellurian Trinity

Part 1: The Aura Stone

NEIL BARCLAY

Printed in the United Kingdom. First printing 2016.

ISBN-13: 978-1537502267
ISBN-10:1537502263

Cover illustration by AJ

The Aura Stone will blaze thrice bright,
When from the shadows they appear,
With strength to face the final fight,
To light a path away from fear.
Born of water, air and fire,
United in truth, together as one,
To lead us from the eternal mire,
The Tellurian Trinity will come.

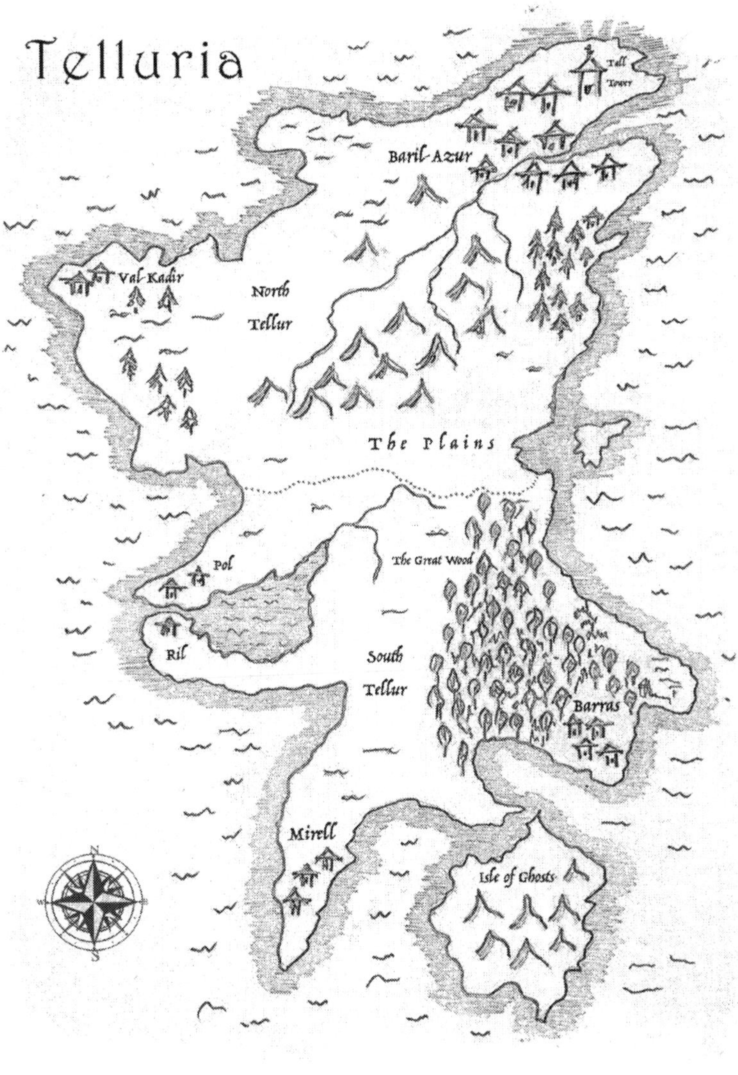
Telluria
Tell Tower
Baril-Azur
Val-Kadir
North Tellur
The Plains
The Great Wood
Pol
Ril
South Tellur
Barras
Mirell
Isle of Ghosts
N
S

1

"I'm not going and that's that!" Freddie cried, drawing his knees up to his chin and trying to put on his best 'just you try and make me' face!

"Oh Freddie darling, don't be like that, please", his mother begged, "it's only for a week and you love Aunt Mags, don't you?"

He was determined to make this as difficult as possible. How dare she send him away at the beginning of the school summer holidays! OK, Aunt Mags was one of his favourite aunties, but she lived in the middle of nowhere and her house stunk of cheese!

"But I'll be bored to death and I won't be able to play with any of my friends... and I won't have any of my stuff and... and... I might as well just die!" The words came out a little sharper than he intended.

"Oh Freddie, stop being so dramatic!" said his Mum.

That just infuriated him even more! Dramatic? Why did she always say that?

Every time he got upset she would tell him that he was being dramatic. He didn't even know what it meant, but obviously it had something to do with screaming and shouting. It just wasn't fair! He'd been away at boarding school all term and finally the holidays had arrived and on the first day she was sending him away again!

"Why can't I come with you?" he asked.

An awkward silence hung between them for a moment. Eventually, his mother spoke.

"Of course we would love to take you, but Daddy has to go again for his work and this time, I'm allowed to go too. I only found out a few days ago."

"Where are you going?"

"It's a place called Barcelona, in Spain. It's very beautiful and I've always wanted to see it and, well, I didn't want to miss this chance."

"Sounds horrible," he snapped, "Daddy can just go on his own."

Mary Bright had had enough. "Well, I

am going with him and that's final. It's only for a few days. Aunt Mags is really excited that you are coming to stay with her and I'm sure you'll have a lovely time."

There was no point pushing it any further. His Mum had made up her mind and he suspected that despite all the 'dramatic', he was never going to get his own way. He'd just give her the silent treatment for the rest of the day and when she dropped him off at Aunt Mags' house, he'd make her feel really guilty! With any luck, she'd be so upset that it would completely ruin her silly trip to Bartyloona or wherever it was!

Mrs Bright stood up. "Right then, I suggest that you go up to your room and pack whatever you want to take. I'll do your clothes. You just put some toys and books and things in your backpack, OK?"

Freddie thrust his hands into his pockets.

Mrs Bright reached over to ruffle his hair, but quick as a flash, he jumped up, swerved to avoid her hand and ran upstairs to his room.

He hoped that a good slam of the door would teach her a lesson! However, he failed to spot the Batman slipper lying in the way. The door rebounded sharply, the handle striking him firmly on his funny bone.

"Ouch!", he yelled, clutching his elbow and falling theatrically onto his bed.

"Are you alright?" his Mum called.

"No I'm not," he groaned, "In fact I'm really dying now and it's all your fault!"

"Well, just make sure you die quietly and don't make too much mess... then pack your things and we'll be off after lunch. OK?"

No reply.

Mrs Bright allowed herself a wry smile. "Right then, what's next?"

~ ~ ~

True, Mary Bright did feel a little uncomfortable... maybe even guilty... about the timing of her visit to Barcelona with her husband. But she really needed a break and more importantly, they desperately needed some quality time together, just her and Martin. It seemed as though they'd barely seen each other recently and if nothing but for the sake of maintaining a loving, healthy marriage, when Martin broke the news she simply could not turn it down. Her husband worked for the Foreign Office, which meant that he had to spend quite a lot of time away from home. Mary too led a busy working life as a partner in a city Law firm. In fact, it was mainly due to their demanding work obligations that they had decided to send eleven-year-old Freddie, their only child, to boarding school last year.

"But I just can't imagine not having him here all the time," Mary had said, struggling to get used to the idea when Martin had first suggested it.

"I know, I feel the same way too," he'd

replied, "it will be difficult and a bit strange at first... but Chartsfield is a wonderful school... and Freddie will soon settle in. It really is for the best, you know."

At the time, Mary worried that they had come to the decision without fully thinking it through, but Freddie's first year at Chartsfield had just come to an end and, thankfully, he was loving it! The facilities were excellent and, on the few weekends that he came home, he was forever telling them stories about all the exciting things he was doing. Football, rugby, swimming, tennis, a residential trip to a castle in Scotland and endless tales of all kinds of antics that he got up to with his friends in the boarding house!

One week away, that's all it was going to be, and then all three of them would be jetting off to America for the holiday of a lifetime! Disneyland, New York, Las Vegas, the Grand Canyon... she was sure that her little boy's disappointment with his Mum wouldn't last too long after that treat!

Upstairs, Freddie packed a few of his

favourite things in his backpack and added a couple of books that he hadn't yet read from his bookshelf.

He was a clever boy… 'Bright by name, bright by nature!' That's what his Dad always said! He was popular at school, both with his peers and his teachers. He had a boldly handsome face, topped off with a shock of wavy, dark brown hair, which fell casually on his forehead. His inquisitive, raisin-brown eyes showed intelligence and independence of spirit… qualities that, as his father had also said on more than one occasion, 'he would go far with'… whatever that meant?

He was just about to select a third book when he remembered that Aunt Mags had a library room in her house. He'd spent hours looking through all her books when he was last there at Christmas… or was it the Christmas before? Anyway, he thought, and what about all those other rooms too, many of which he had never even been in? Aunt Mags lived in a great big house in the countryside... and the garden seemed to go on and on forever! Maybe it wouldn't be so bad after all to spend a week exploring?

He started to feel a little guilty for the way he'd spoken to his Mum earlier. He'd wanted to ask her if his friends Peter and Tom from his last school could come over for a sleepover, but before he got the chance, she had ruined his plans. Maybe he had overreacted... just a bit! Perhaps that's what being dramatic meant? Anyway, he had a whole seven weeks holiday ahead of him, so midnight feasts with Peter and Tom would just have to wait until next week.

2

"Where's my lovely boy? Where is he? There he is!"

Freddie had barely stepped out of the car before Aunt Mags was upon him, enfolding him to her bosom in an embrace that seemed to squeeze the very life out of him!

"Let me look at him," she chortled, crudely grasping the sides of his head between her enormous hands. "My, hasn't he grown!"

Why do grown-ups always say that? Obviously I've grown! I'm a child! We all do! Keeping his thoughts to himself, he gave her his best 'I'm fine thanks, but please leave me alone' smile and mumbled a gruff 'hello.'

Aunt Mags then turned to his Mum and threw her arms around her in an equally passionate crush!

"It's so lovely to see you," she cried, "... and how lucky am I to have this little rapscallion all to myself for a whole week?"

"Oh Mags, you're a true saviour!" said his Mum, "it's so kind of you to look after Freddie for us." Tactfully she began to prise herself from her big sister's grasp.

Aunt Mags was a prim looking woman in her fifties. She was a good few years older than her sister. She had thick, sandy hair and honey-coloured skin. Her face, although work-hardened, still retained faint traces of beauty from her youth.

When their mother died at the relatively young age of forty-eight, Mags, being the eldest and by far the most capable of all the siblings, had naturally assumed the maternal role in the family. In truth, it had never left her! She had never married. In fact, Mary couldn't recall even hearing about a single boyfriend in all those years!

"Why do I need a family when I've already got the best one?" This was one of Aunt Mags' pet phrases that she always pronounced with pride at every family gathering!

"And a man about the house? Tish tosh!

He'd only get in the way!"

Mary felt very lucky to have her, in more ways than one. Freddie would be more than safe with dear Aunt Mags.

~ ~ ~

Miss Margaret Cherry was affectionately referred to as 'Aunt Mags' by just about everyone who had the pleasure of knowing her, related or not!

She lived in a beautiful little village in Kent called Shadoxhurst. The area consisted of mostly wooded countryside and farmland, with the Whitewater Dyke (a tributary of the River Stour) rising nearby. The history of the village was well documented, particularly up to the end of the 18th century. Historical records revealed a unique and rather peculiar claim to fame for the village. The Reverend Charles Rolfe (1800-1877), who worked as the rector at the local church for thirty-nine years was directly descended from John Rolfe of Heacham who married Chief Powhatan's daughter, Pocahontas, on 5th April 1614 in Jamestown, Virginia in the USA. That's the very same Pocahontas who many years later was immortalized in the Walt Disney Company's animated feature film bearing the same name!

After an early lunch, which consisted of a delicious bowl of Aunt Mags' homemade red lentil and coconut soup, and the tastiest crusty white bread you could wish for, Freddie waved goodbye to his Mum. Obviously, this was after yet more hugs, kisses and tears (his Mum's) and numerous instructions to 'be a good boy', 'make sure you help Aunt Mags' and 'don't forget to brush your teeth!'

"Right then, young man," Aunt Mags sighed, closing the front door behind her, "now the fun begins!"

Freddie really loved his Aunt. She didn't behave like other grown-ups. She didn't seem to care about all those silly things that parents normally moan about.

He'd noticed that after lunch, Aunt Mags had quickly piled up all the dirty soup bowls, plates and spoons and dumped the whole lot in the sink saying, 'that lot can wait until later!' It would have been a bit different at home!

'Now, before you leave the table,' his Mum would have said, 'clear all the dishes and put them in the dishwasher... and mind that you rinse them first... and make sure you don't put them in upside down like you did last time!'

Aunt Mags leaned forward and, as if she were passing on a secret, whispered, "Do you fancy a bit of exploring this afternoon?"

"Oh yes please," he replied with a sparkle in his eye, "I love exploring!"

"Good," she continued, "well, there's this windmill, you see, only about seven or so miles down the road."

"What, a real windmill," he exclaimed with disbelief, "with big arms and wind and stuff?"

Aunt Mags smiled. "Yes! Four big arms!

And wind! And oodles of stuff too! And, it all works! They even make their own bread there... not as good as my own of course, but if we're lucky we might be allowed to try some."

Freddie wasn't too bothered about tasting the bread, but the thought of seeing an actual real windmill with its four gigantic arms going round and round in the sky filled him with pure excitement!

"Right, young man," said Aunt Mags as she led him into the hallway, "I'm just going to powder my nose and then we'll be off."

"What's that?" he asked.

"What, powder my nose?"

"No, I know what that is. I'm not stupid! I mean that, up there, on the wall?"

Freddie pointed at the large, oil painting of a handsome man in full military uniform, hanging in the hallway.

"Oh, that!" she exclaimed. "Do you like it? I had it framed recently. That fine gentleman is your grandfather, my dear late father, Rear Admiral Horace Cherry. A true war hero, my lad. I'll tell you all about him when we get back."

Freddie curiously rubbed his fingertips along the engraved, brass plate underneath the painting.

"What do these words mean? It doesn't make sense!"

Aunt Mags looked at the inscription she'd read a hundred times before and began to read aloud.

'If our strength fails, at least one stands up for pride and gain, or the cards I deal will lose the jewel, leaving me lost. If in doubt stay calm, apply the mind.'

"But what does it mean?" he repeated.

Aunt Mags looked for a moment as if she were weighing the question.

"Not a clue my duck! My old Dad was a funny fellow. Sadly he went a bit doolally toward the end. Maybe that explains it? Anyway, we're going to be late! Come on, let me through and whilst I'm having a quick widdly-woo, you can go and sit in the car!"

Freddie smiled and rushed out the door.

Before he knew it, they had both set off, chugging along the road toward Ashford in Aunt Mags' trusty old 1969 Morris Oxford, the only car she had ever owned since learning to drive nearly forty years ago! Freddie noticed that the road they were on was called 'Tally Ho Road,' which made him laugh. He looked at Aunt Mags in the driver's seat, both hands firmly locked on the steering wheel and her nose almost touching the windscreen! Tally-ho indeed!

After only about fifteen minutes he spotted a sign announcing that they had arrived in 'Willesborough.' Sure enough, as they rounded the next bend, the windmill came into view up ahead.

Freddie couldn't hide his astonishment! It was much bigger than he had expected. The bottom part was made of a reddish brick with windows just like a house. About half way up there was a white metal platform that ran all the way around the middle.

"Look, Aunt Mags," he said, pointing forward, "the windmill is wearing a giant iron belt!" They both laughed.

The next part of the structure was made of wood and painted a dazzling white. The shape reminded Freddie of pictures that he had seen in history books at school of the pyramids in Egypt. By far the most striking section was the very top. It actually looked like someone had balanced a shed on the apex of the pyramid, and from this shed there sprouted four enormous wing type things that were all turning, lazily and effortlessly in the wind.

"Wow! It's amazing!" he gasped, mouth agape and eyes wide open, firmly fixed upon the magnificent machine before him!

Aunt Mags parked the car by the roadside. "I thought you'd like it," she affirmed, with a satisfied smile.

Taking his hand, she led him to the entrance where they were met by an old man with a bushy, white beard. Freddie thought he looked just like Father Christmas!

"Well, good afternoon,' the man said in a warm, gravely voice, "Welcome to Willesborough Mill."

Aunt Mags smiled as she fished around in her purse and then placed a few coins in the wooden donation box near the door.

"Why, thank you ma'am," the old man said, "It all helps to keep this magnificent, historic building all shipshape and Bristol fashion!"

Freddie didn't understand what he was talking about, but the old man seemed pretty happy to see them nonetheless.

"You're very welcome," replied Aunt Mags, "what a beautiful windmill you have here!"

"We certainly do," he beamed. "My name is Alfred and I would be delighted to tell you a little bit about it if that would please you?

Aunt Mags looked at Freddie and they both nodded. Whenever he went visiting places with his Mum, like when they went to Hampton Court last year, Freddie always preferred to be able to explore on his own but his Mum always insisted on joining one of the boring guided tours! Once, she even made him wear headphones listening to someone with a very posh voice rambling on about all sorts of things he couldn't care less about! It was much more fun hunting for hidden passageways, trying to open secret, locked doors and peering around every dark corner in search of ghosts!

However, Alfred seemed like a friendly old man, and Freddie really wanted to find out how a windmill actually worked.

"Right," Alfred began, "you're standing in what is known as a white smock mill, which was built almost one hundred and fifty years ago in 1869."

"What are the big arms called?" Freddie asked.

Alfred laughed. "The 'big arms,' young man, are actually called sweeps. Some people call them sails, but in this part of the world they're known as sweeps. We'll have a good look at them a bit later."

They both followed him up a narrow, wooden staircase into a small, cramped room full of the most amazing bits of metal machinery Freddie had ever seen. He thought about the boxes of Lego he had back in his bedroom and decided that as soon as he got home he was going to build his very own windmill, with working sweeps and all!

He listened carefully as Alfred explained that they were standing in the Cap of the mill, where all the action takes place. Pointing at a long, wooden plank, (which was called the wind shaft), he showed them how it was attached to the sweeps outside and also connected to the giant wooden wheel above their heads. This was called the break wheel, and when the wind blew on the sweeps, it turned the break wheel, which in turn, made the shaft go round to drive the mill. Freddie was fascinated!

Next, Alfred led them into another wooden room full of brown sacks.

"Oh, what a lovely smell!" Aunt Mags declared, filling her nostrils with the sharp, earthy aroma of the grain.

"This is the Bin Floor," Alfred said, "where all the grain is stored. When we are ready to make bread we pour it down this shute, down to the stones, ready to be milled."

For the following twenty minutes or so, Alfred continued to show them around, pointing out all kinds of extraordinary devices that all had their own job to do to make the mill work. Freddie tried to learn all the names of the machinery parts... quant, shoe, stone nut, bed stone... but there were far too many to remember!

When they arrived back at the start, Aunt Mags asked Alfred if she could buy a bag of their strong wholemeal bread flour. She fancied having a go at making some bread with it back in her own kitchen (to see if it was better than her own, although she didn't say that to Alfred!)

"Certainly, ma'am," Alfred replied, "if you just wait here a tick I'll go and get some for you."

Freddie didn't want to wait. "I'm just going out to look at the sweeps again. See you outside!"

"Of course, my duck," she replied, "I'll be out in a mo." Aunt Mags felt pleased that the windmill trip had been an early success in their week together.

Freddie ran around the side of the building and stood right in front of the windmill, gazing up at the four huge sweeps as they turned slowly in the cool summer breeze. He noticed that there were strings of multi-coloured flags tied between the outer ends of the sweeps and wondered if they helped it turn faster... or were they just put there to make it look pretty?

As he stood there trying to count how many seconds it took for one of the sweeps to turn all the way round in a complete loop, something to his right caught his eye. Moving slowly toward him across the grass he spotted a woolly, dark circle, a bit like a shadow. He looked up thinking that a cloud or an airplane... or even a flock of birds...

must be passing overhead, but to his surprise, the sky was clear blue with not a cloud in sight... and no planes or birds... nothing.

The dark shadow continued to move closer and was now only a few feet away. His body felt like a dead weight as he tried nervously to edge away from it, but he could not feel his legs. It were as if he was glued to the spot. He glanced up at the windmill and saw that the sweeps had stopped turning. He looked down at his feet and saw to his horror that he was now trapped, right in the centre of the darkening mass. Everything went silent.

Panic-stricken, he opened his mouth to scream, but his throat tightened and no words came out. Suddenly, the ground beneath his feet began to fade away, revealing a vast black hole in its place. For a terrifying moment, he hovered in mid air, standing above... above... nothing!

And then it happened.

He began to fall.

3

The man slowly paced the wooden floorboards, his footsteps sending eerie echoes down the castle corridors.

He had a hawkish face, with depthless, jet-black eyes, peering out from arrogant, sallow features. Casually, he pushed back a wayward strand of hair, as stiff and black as a raven's wing, and fixed his eyes on the Stone.

An uneasy feeling gnawed at the back of his mind. It was glowing again, and that meant only one thing.

The heavy, wooden door creaked opened at the far end of the room. The outline of a young woman stood framed within the archway. She walked slowly toward him, her bare feet sending up little clouds of dust from under her black, velvet robe.

The light from the Stone lit up her thin, intense face. Her skin was porcelain-pale, but her small, olive-black eyes sparkled like two shrewd chips of quartz. The man turned toward her and stroked her long black hair, which hung in two thick shiny braids down to her waist. Their eyes met without blinking.

"It is happening again," she whispered, her words floating hauntingly in the air.

"Yes," the man replied.

They stood in silence, transfixed by the Stone, which stood on a wooden support in the center of the room, glowing. A bright shaft of white light emerged from it, penetrating clean through the castle wall and away into the distance.

"Another has come," she hissed.

"Yes," he replied, trying to steady his shaking hands, "there is another."

Her dark eyes grew wild. "Have you alerted the North Riders?"

He moved his head slightly. It might have been a nod. "I told them not to return empty-handed."

She walked soft-footed toward the window and looked out into the darkness.

"This time, nothing must go wrong."

She felt his hand on her shoulder.

"Thalia, my dear sister, do not worry," he said, his tone cold and firm, "this time we are prepared. Everything is in place. Merek knows what must be done."

She turned to face him, her gaze alarmingly direct.

"Then all will be well, will it not, dear Tarin?" She drew her lips in a tight smile.

He felt a shiver run across his shoulders. He must not let her down. Not again.

4

Freddie opened his eyes. He was lying on his back amidst thick green undergrowth. Gazing up he could just make out glimpses of blue sky, peeking through the thick cloak of branches above. His body ached all over.

For a moment he lay still, his mind a blank, then slowly he sat up. He was in a forest of thick trees that grew close together.

His heart began to hammer in his chest. He remembered standing in front of a windmill... what was he doing... counting? Counting what? Counting how long it took for the windmill to turn? Yes.

He glanced around fretfully, trying to orient himself, but there was no windmill in sight. Nothing but thick, dense forest.

He rubbed his eyes, desperately trying to clear his head. Aunt Mags! He had been with her, hadn't he? She must be here too!

"Aunt Mags?" he shouted, "Aunt Mags, where are you?"

Silence.

He scrambled to his feet, not knowing whether to run or hide.

A sound from behind made him jump nearly out of his skin. Footsteps... panting... the sound of someone, or something, running toward him.

Freddie froze. A figure of a man suddenly appeared on the track up ahead, breathing heavily with rib-stretching gasps. He was quite old, with shaggy, soot-grey hair, strands of which were clinging to his sun-seared face with sweat.

Spotting Freddie, the old man stopped dead in his tracks, a mix of fear and surprise on his face.

Their eyes locked across a sudden ringing silence.

Then the man spoke, his voice trembling with fear. "Quick, lad! Quick! There's a hunt. We've got to get away from here."

Freddie didn't know what to do. He tried to speak, but panic once again welled inside him.

The man grabbed Freddie's arm and shook him roughly. "Come on lad, we must go, now! Follow me."

Letting go, the old man set off again, darting away into the trees.

Freddie glanced back up the track. Another sound... this time, horses hooves and wild dogs barking furiously. And angry voices... shouting!

"Wait!" he cried, starting to run. "Wait for me!"

Freddie spotted him a short distance ahead, dodging and weaving between the trees and branches like an expert. Like someone who had taken this path many times before. Every so often the man would look back and beckon frantically for him to keep up... run faster.

That was one thing Freddie could do very well. At school he was the fastest runner in his year, winning the Victor Ludorum athletics trophy in his first Summer Sports Day at Chartsfield.

He had almost caught up when he

glanced hurriedly over his shoulder to see if they were still being followed. Suddenly, a dazzling, bright light almost blinded him. Instinctively, he raised his hands to cover his eyes.

And then... darkness.

~ ~ ~

For a moment, Freddie lay still, his mind a blank. Slowly he sat up, pushing away the heavy clogging sleep. He thought he must have been dreaming. A familiar aroma of freshly baked bread filled his nostrils. He must be at Aunt Mags' house, in the kitchen, as she busied herself preparing tea. But Aunt Mags didn't have a bed in her kitchen!

As his eyes strayed sleepily around the unfamiliar room, Freddie realised that he was in some kind of small, wooden cabin. The heat from a small fire crackling in the corner spread a gentle warmth throughout the room. Propping himself up, he gave a short gasp, wincing at the sharp pain in his head.

"Aah, the little tyke's awake." A soft, gentle voice came from behind.

Carefully, he eased himself up a little more and peered over the back of the sofa. Two people stood quite still, staring down at him.

They were as old as Aunt Mags and both wore the same long, brown smocks, tied at the waist with green cords. The man had untidy grey hair and a long, narrow brown face, deeply seamed. The woman had a friendly, heart-shaped face etched with a network of tiny lines. Her hair was a cobweb of silvery gold and her slightly protruding coffee-brown eyes fixed him with curious interest.

"That's going to hurt for a few days," the man exclaimed with a smile, "he didn't half come a cropper out there!"

It was the same man from the forest. The one he had been following.

"Poor little mite," said the old woman, "but he's safe now, yes he is."

Freddie was struggling to make sense of it. To make sense of everything! The events of the past few hours – since he'd been at the windmill with Aunt Mags! What was happening?

"Where am I?" he stammered nervously, "Who are you? What am I doing here?" Questions whirled in his brain as he tried to steady his nerves.

The old man smiled. "You're here, that's where you is, here, with us. Safe."

"And that's all you need to worry your little head with for now," the old woman continued, "let's get some tasty food inside him... he must be famished? Look at him, young stick of a rake he is!"

They were right. He was starving! Gradually, his doubts and fears began to subside. Something deep within was telling him that he could trust these two strangers.

"Now, young man, I think it's time you told us your name," the old woman said, as she ushered him into a chair at the table.

"Freddie. Freddie Bright."

The old woman thrust out her arm and shook Freddie's hand vigorously. "Well now, Master Freddie Bright, I'm Gunda and this here is my brother, Hadwin. And we are very pleased to make your acquaintance, yes we are."

The old man, Hadwin, took his turn and shook Freddie's hand with equal enthusiasm, so much so that Freddie thought his arm might actually fall off!

Gunda set a plate in front of him and placed upon it the biggest slice of pie he'd ever seen!

"Thank you," Freddie said, wide-eyed.

"You're very welcome, young Freddie, now tuck in and enjoy!"

He took a tentative mouthful. It was delicious. He'd never tasted anything so good! Gunda and Hadwin sat opposite and watched, glancing at each other occasionally to exchange a wry, secret smile as Freddie devoured the whole lot.

"Better?" asked Gunda, smiling tenderly.

"Yes, thank you," he replied.

Gunda turned to Hadwin. "Well, I say! Good manners and all! Aren't we lucky!"

Hadwin gave a gruff laugh.

As Freddie was scraping the final crumbs of pastry from his bowl, the door opened and a young, china-skinned girl appeared, carrying a bundle of firewood. Freddie guessed that she was about the same age as him.

She had large, green eyes under golden brows and lashes, a pert nose and a faintly rosy mouth. Her hair was long and wheat-coloured, glistening with golden streaks and hanging loose over her shoulders. She wore a similar style of smock to Gunda and Hadwin, but hers was pale yellow, tied at the waist with a white cord. But there was one thing about her that struck Freddie more than anything else. She was the prettiest girl he had ever seen!

"Here we are," she said, closing the door behind her, "these will get us through the night."

She hurried over to the fireplace and tipped the bundle of wood into a large wickerwork basket.

"Ah, my sweet pet, thank you," said Gunda, giving her a warm hug.

"Oh, do we have a guest?" the girl exclaimed, excitement adding a sparkle to her eyes as they rested on Freddie sitting at the table.

"We most certainly do," Hadwin declared as he stood up, "a very special guest to boot! Freddie, this is Myla. Myla, meet Freddie Bright!"

"Um, hello," Freddie stammered, feeling his cheeks flush red as he rose from the table to greet her.

Myla walked over to him and shook his hand. "Pleased to meet you, Freddie Bright!" Her smile was warm and welcoming.

"Come along, Myla my dear," said Gunda, "sit yourself down and have some pie."

"Oh, thanks," she replied cheerfully, "what is it?"

Gunda scoffed. "Why, pidwen of course!"

"Yummy," Myla smiled, tucking in heartily.

Did she just say pigeon, Freddie thought? Pigeon pie? Yuk!

"Nothing better than pidwen," Gunda exclaimed, a look of pride on her face, "isn't that right, Hadwin?"

"Oh yes my dear, nothing better," Hadwin smiled and winked at Myla.

Gunda poured four mugs of hot, sweet tea and pulled four stools around the fireplace.

"How's that head, Freddie lad?" Hadwin asked.

Freddie felt the lump on his forehead, which seemed to have gone down a bit.

"Not too bad now, thank you," he replied, "I don't really remember much about what happened?"

"Well," began Hadwin, "when we was running through the Great Wood earlier, I looked back and saw you run slap bang right into a tree. Knocked yourself clean out, you did."

"So, Hadwin had to throw you over his shoulder and carry you all the way back here, so he did," added Gunda.

"Were you running from *them*?" It was Myla who asked the question. Freddie noticed a shadow of fear touch her face.

"Aye, lass," Hadwin nodded, "it was them again."

"Who's them?" asked Freddie.

The others looked uneasily at each other for a moment.

Eventually, Gunda spoke. "There's bad folk out there, Freddie, evil, bad folk. They brings nothing but suffering and misery."

Myla, noticing Freddie's slightly confused expression, reached over and placed her hand on his.

"Don't worry, you're safe now," she said,

softly, "and that's what matters."

But Freddie wanted to know more. "But those people chasing us... the dogs? And I can remember a blinding light?"

Myla looked up sharply. "A light?"

"Yes," Freddie continued, beginning to remember what had happened in the forest, "I looked back and there was this really bright light ... it was almost like it was following me!"

Myla glanced eagerly at Hadwin, who in turn looked at Gunda, noticing the wide grin on her face.

Myla couldn't hide the sudden tremor in her voice. "Is he... you know, is he... the one?"

Gunda nodded.

Freddie met Myla's gaze. She was positively beaming at him.

"Um, would somebody mind telling me what's going on?" he asked.

Hadwin leaned back and smiled. "I know right now this all seems very strange to you, my lad, but soon you'll learn all about why you're here. Don't worry... we will look after you. You are very special to us."

Freddie was just about to ask what he meant by 'special' when Gunda stood up.

"My goodness, the moon is up. Time for sleep. Plenty of time for more talk in the morning."

Hadwin nodded in agreement, standing up and stretching his weary limbs.

Gunda led Freddie through a small wooden door into a bedroom that had three single beds. Myla followed.

"That'll be your bed, my lad," said Gunda, "there, under the window."

"And this is mine," Myla smiled, jumping on to the bed on the opposite side.

He would normally have thought it a bit weird to share a bedroom with a girl! But tonight, after everything that had happened, he was secretly pleased not to be left alone. Furthermore, he liked Myla. She seemed really friendly and fun.

"Right then, you two," said Gunda, leaning against the door. "Straight to sleep!

No nattering 'til the early hours!"

Myla cast a cheeky grin at Freddie. "Yes, we promise."

"Goodnight then, see you in the morning."

"Goodnight," they replied.

As she closed the door, her mouth curled into an unconscious smile as she listened to the giggles coming from the room.

'Now we have two,' she thought to herself, her grin widening, 'now we have two!'

5

The thick, black cloud wore a face of pure evil. Freddie's legs turned to jelly. It felt like he was running through quicksand. He glanced fearfully over his shoulder. The dark mass was gaining on him, a sneering figure of death.

Rounding a corner, he came face to face with a towering black windmill. He had to get inside. He knew he would be safe inside. But where was the door? The sky darkened, plunging him into blackness. Frantically his fingers clawed at the brickwork, probing for a way in. But it was too late. The leering monster fell upon him, slowly opening its jaws of death.

"HELP!" Freddie screamed, "SAVE ME!"

"It's alright, Freddie, everything's alright. You're safe now."

He opened his eyes and sat bolt upright. His whole body was damp with sweat. A line of pain cut across his chest, making it almost impossible to breathe.

"It's only a dream, Freddie, just a bad dream. You're OK."

It was Myla's voice.

"You yelled so loud you woke me up!" She smiled, settling herself onto his bed.

"Myla, it was horrible," he panted for breath, "the cloud... it had a face! It wanted to kill me!"

"It's alright, you're OK now... a bit sweaty, but OK!" Her smile was tender and comforting.

Freddie looked at her in silence for a moment. Moonlight shone through the window, bathing her in a pale blue light. She looked like an angel!

He took a deep breath, trying to steady the shakiness in his voice. "Where am I, Myla? What has happened to me?"

She looked thoughtfully past him out of the window, her fingers playing with the lacework hem of her nightdress.

"This is a different world, Freddie, different to the one you know."

A look of uncertainty crept across his face. "I don't understand. What do you mean, different?"

She looked up and met his eyes steadily for a moment.

"We are in a world called Telluria. We live in a village called Barras, which is in South Tellur..."

"Whoa, hold on a minute," he interrupted, "a different world? Now I really must be dreaming!"

"What I'm telling you is true, Freddie, you have to believe me," she said, her eyes never leaving his. "There's a reason why you're here... why we are both here."

Freddie leaned back and drew his knees up to his chin. This was all getting a bit weird!

"What I mean is..." she hesitated to continue, "...what I'm trying to say is that in this world there is evil. Those men chasing you in the Great Wood? They come from the North. They capture families and take them back to their cities to be their slaves. They imprison their children, threatening to kill them if the grown-ups don't do what they say."

Freddie wavered, trying to take in what he was hearing.

"Is this what Hadwin meant, you know, when he said that I'd soon learn why I was here?"

Myla nodded. "Yes, and there is much more. Things that you will find even harder to understand. Things that you will not believe possible."

Freddie leaned forward, gripping her arm. "Tell me, Myla, I want to know everything!"

"All in good time, Freddie," she replied, gently pushing him away. "There are some things that can't be told. Things you have to see to understand."

He sank back again in confusion. "Things that can't be told? That I have to see to be able to understand?"

Myla noticed his worried look. It was so much to take in. Too much, and far too soon for him. He'd only just arrived! She would have to show him something. It might frighten him, but at the same time, it might help him to understand who he was... who she was. Understand that it was his destiny to be here, just as the prophecy had foretold.

Freddie watched intently as Myla raised an arm and stretched it out toward him, her fingers clenched tightly shut. Slowly, here eyes fixed on his, she opened her fist.

Freddie couldn't believe what he was seeing! Cupped in her open hand was a flickering blue flame!

"How in the..." he gasped, his eyes nearly popping out of his head!

Myla's gaze remained fixed on the flame as if she were in some kind of trance. Gradually, the flame grew larger, lighting the room in a brilliant, white light. Then, as quick as a flash, she closed her fist and the flame disappeared.

Freddie was speechless!

Myla sat for a moment, staring at him,

a small smile of enchantment on her lips.

"How did you learn to do that?" he gasped. "That's the best trick I've ever seen!"

She gave him a mischievous smile. "It's not a trick, Freddie. It's a gift. We have special powers."

"We?" he blurted out. "Do you mean I can do that too?"

She tossed her hair back and laughed. "No, you can't make fire like I can... but, you do have your own special power. You just haven't discovered it yet."

"Really? Me?" he asked, wide-eyed. "What about your parents, Gunda and Hadwin, do they have special powers too?"

"No, they don't," she replied, "... and, they're not my parents. I'm the same as you Freddie. I came here from your world too."

Freddie listened fixedly as she told him how Hadwin had found her two years ago, wandering aimlessly, lost in the Great Wood. She was nine years old then, and the last thing she remembered was standing outside Buckingham Palace with her parents, watching some soldiers in bright red coats and big funny hats marching backwards and forwards. Her father had asked her if she wanted an ice cream and she'd chosen a King Cone. But, after he'd walked off to get it, she had changed her mind and decided that she actually wanted a Funny Face instead. Letting go of her mother's hand, she chased after him.... and then, all she could remember was running into a dark shadowy shape, and then falling, falling.... and waking up in the Wood!

"That's just what happened to me!" Freddie cried, "the dark cloud thing... falling in!"

"I know," Myla replied, her voice taking on a more serious tone.

"You have to understand something, Freddie. You are special. We both are. There are wicked people here who would do anything to find us... capture us... even kill us. You and I know that we come from a different world, but here they say that we are 'The Tellurian Trinity.' There is an ancient prophecy… it says that when the Trinity comes, the evil power will be overthrown."

"Trinity? But that means three, doesn't it?" So who's the third one?"

"I don't know. The third is yet to come."

"But how will we know when he does?" Freddie asked.

"He?" Myla replied, "Or she. We don't know if it will be a boy or a girl. But there is a stone… the Aura Stone… the prophecy also says that it will shine and point the way when the Trinity arrives. That's what happened to you today. It also happened to me two years ago. The Aura Stone… that bright light that dazzled you… it was pointing at you. The North Riders were trying to catch you. It was a miracle that you ran in to Hadwin when you did, otherwise, who knows what might have happened!"

Freddie remembered the beam of light in the forest that had dazzled his eyes just before he hit the tree.

But still he was confused. "So, why

didn't the light follow me when Hadwin brought me back here?"

"I don't know," replied Myla. "Perhaps it only shines for a short time? Or, maybe it only points the way until someone finds you… nobody knows."

"Well," he declared, "that's easy then. We'll just watch the Aura Stone until it tells us that the third one has arrived and then we'll go and get him… or her?"

Myla's eyes narrowed. Somehow he thought it wasn't going to be quite so simple!

"The Aura Stone used to be here in South Tellur, kept in a city called Mirell. But after I arrived, some North Riders came and stole it. Now it sits in Baril-Azur, the capital city of North Tellur, under heavy guard. It's kept in the Tall Tower at the home of Lord Tarin and Lady Thalia, the evil twins who rule the North."

Freddie took a moment to try to piece together everything he was hearing.

"So," he began, checking to see if he understood correctly, "what you're saying is that if this Tarin and Thalia have the Aura Stone, then they will be the first to know when and where the third arrives, giving them the best chance of finding him before we do?"

"Yes, Freddie," she replied, "that's right. And if they do, they will kill the third one, thus breaking the prophecy. That is why the Aura Stone is so important, not only to us, but to them as well."

Freddie drew a deep breath. He knew what was coming next.

She moved a little closer, took hold of his hands, and fixed him with her sparkling, green eyes.

"We have to get it back, Freddie. It's our best hope... our only hope! They will be furious they didn't catch you. Now that you're here, I think we can do it... together... we must protect the prophecy."

Freddie swallowed hard, lifted his chin and boldly met her gaze. "OK!"

6

"You fools! You imbeciles!"

Merek, the chief of the North Riders, was standing before Lord Tarin. He was a mountain of a man who smelled of leather and horse sweat. He straightened his shoulders and cleared his throat.

"We almost had him," he said gruffly, "... he was there... in the light... I saw him. And then the light stopped. And then we..."

"Him?" Lord Tarin interrupted. "What did he look like?"

"It was a young boy, wearing strange garments... we... I... I couldn't see his face. He was running...."

Lord Tarin stood up and kicked his chair against the wall. It shattered into pieces.

"He's one of them," he yelled, "I know it. The Stone has foretold it. And you let him get away." His face was a glowering mask of rage.

Merek stood rooted to the spot,

clenching his fists nervously. He knew how important it had been to capture the boy. He just couldn't explain to his master how, just when they thought they had him, he'd seemed to vanish into thin air. They were so close!

"Two years we've been waiting for this! Two years!" The vein in his forehead swelled, looking like a thick black snake. "This will not go unpunished! You, of all my men, you have let me down... let us all down."

Merek bowed his head shamefully. "My Lord, please," he begged, "give me one more chance? Let me take my best men and search the area. I will find him and bring him to you, I swear!"

Lord Tarin looked him straight in the eye. Merek was his best soldier, a ruthless warrior. It was he who had successfully led the raiding party two years before to capture the Aura Stone.

When Tarin eventually spoke, his voice was low-pitched and very cold.

"One more chance."

Merek felt the relief flood through his veins.

"However..." he added, "if you fail..." the warning was crystal clear in his eyes.

"Yes, sir," Merek replied, straightening his back, "I understand. I will not fail you."

With a curt bow, he turned away and left the room.

From the shadows, a female figure appeared.

"My dear Thalia, I didn't see you there," said Tarin, a little surprised.

She walked up to him and placed her hand gently upon his shoulder.

"Where is your courage, my brother," she whispered, "you should have punished the fool."

Tarin turned away. He knew she was probably right. Had he shown weakness? He still had faith in Merek... but the General had failed him, there was no doubt.

"So, now there are two of them," Thalia continued. "The prophecy is coming true. We cannot just sit here whilst idiots do our bidding for us?"

"Thalia," Tarin began, trying to reassure her, "do not worry. Merek will find them this time. And when he does, he will bring them here and we will make sure the prophecy is broken."

She wasn't sure that it would be so easy, however she decided that any further argument with her brother would be pointless. Merek had already failed once as far as she was concerned. He would fail again.

Turning swiftly, leaving her brother brooding, she headed back to her private rooms. Nothing could be left to chance. There was too much at stake. She could lose everything!

Thalia looked at the overbearing portrait hanging on the wall above her bed. Ludiana's eyes, like chips of emerald ice… flat, hard and passionless, stared back at her. Thalia stiffened under her mother's withering glare. She remembered her chilling, last words, whispered from her deathbed almost ten years before.

'The Trinity will come, my dearest daughter, and they will seek to destroy you. You, and you alone must stop them. Do not hesitate. Act swiftly.'

She had been right. Two of the three, as had been foretold, were now here in Telluria. Everything her mother had built for them was now under grave threat. She was not ready to give it all up.

Thalia walked slowly towards the painting and pressed her hand softly against the cold, lifeless canvas.

"Do not worry, mother dear," she whispered, "I will not let you down."

7

Freddie opened his eyes. It took him a moment or two to remember where he was. The events of the previous day swirled around in his head. He still had many questions to ask, but he wasn't sure he would fully understand all the answers!

Propping himself up on his elbows, he noticed the empty bed opposite. Myla was already up. He thought about the amazing thing she had shown him last night... how she had made fire with her bare hands! And all that stuff about how they were special... what was it she said they were... the Tellurian Trinity? And, the evil twins... the Aura Stone, and how they were going to try and capture it?

The door opened. "He's awake... at last!" Gunda stood in the doorway, smiling.

"Good morning, Gunda," Freddie said, rubbing his eyes, "sorry, is it late?"

She laughed. "Well, let's just say the rest of us have already done half a day's work! But never you mind, young Freddie, you needed your sleep after the day you had yesterday!"

Freddie smiled.

"Here," she continued, "put these on. You don't want to be going out in those funny clothes you were wearing yesterday!"

She laid the garments on his bed. They consisted of a plain blue top with a white stripe and a pair of trousers, which looked far too short. He climbed out of bed and put them on. Finally, Gunda picked up a length of cord and tied it around his waist.

"There we are," she said, a proud expression on her face, "you look just like one of us now!"

He followed her through to the main living room where there was a plate of warm bread and jam waiting for him. Freddie tucked in heartily.

She sat down opposite, watching him.

"Now," she began, "I expect you have lots of things you want to know?"

She could tell from the puzzled

expression on his face that he didn't know where to start.

He began by relating everything Myla had told him... and showed him... the night before.

"But what I don't understand is... well, where exactly am I?"

She had been expecting this question.

"Our world is different to the one you know. South Tellur used to be a wonderful, happy place. That is, until everything changed."

Freddie hung on her every word as she continued his history lesson.

"Years ago, an evil woman came. Nobody really knows from where. Her name was Ludiana. She settled in North Tellur in the city of Baril-Azur, as Myla told you, and shortly after her arrival she gave birth to twins, Tarin and Thalia. Ludiana did not want to live as we live. She wanted more, wanted everything. That's when the hunts began. Whole families started disappearing all over the land and we soon learned that the adults that she captured, men and women, were forced to become her slaves. If they refused, she threatened to kill their children. They had no choice but to obey her."

Freddie drew a deep breath. "But Myla didn't mention Ludiana? Is she in Baril-Azur too?"

"No. She died, a few years ago. At the time we thought this might bring an end to the troubles, but how wrong we were!"

"Tarin and Thalia... the twins?" asked Freddie.

"Yes," she continued, "Tarin and Thalia. They have turned out to be even more evil than their mother."

"Has anyone ever tried to stop them?"

"No," she replied, "not yet."

"Not yet?" He wasn't quite sure what she meant.

Gunda sighed, and looked at him. "Myla told you about the prophecy?"

Freddie nodded.

She picked up a scroll from the table,

untied the black ribbon around it and started to read.

"The Aura Stone will blaze thrice bright,
When from the shadows they appear,
With strength to face the final fight,
To light a path away from fear.
Born of water, air and fire,
United in truth, together as one,
To lead us from the eternal mire,
The Tellurian Trinity will come."

Freddie didn't know what to say, but from what Myla had already told him, he knew what the prophecy meant.

"It's you Freddie," said Gunda, "and Myla, and one more yet to come. You are the Tellurian Trinity, come to save us."

Freddie shifted uncomfortably in his seat. What could he do, an eleven year old boy… from a different world? Oddly though, he didn't feel frightened. Instead, he could sense something deep inside him growing, something strong and powerful. It was like this was meant to happen to him, he could feel it.

"Myla says that we have to get the Aura Stone?"

"Yes," Gunda replied, "we have to be ready when the third one comes."

"But how are we going to break in to Baril-Azur and steal the Aura Stone from under their noses?"

She took hold of his hands.

"Have faith, Freddie. You and Myla will find a way. Remember who you are and why you have come."

Freddie had to speak to Myla. He sensed that there was no time to lose.

"Where is she?"

"She went out earlier with Hadwin. They'll be back soon."

Freddie still had questions.

"Myla said that you and Hadwin don't have any special powers?"

Gunda smiled. "No, we don't. These are gifts for the Trinity alone."

"And last night, you said Hadwin is

your brother? Don't you have children then?"

He noticed a touch of sadness in her eyes and immediately regretted asking the question.

"Since we were very young, Hadwin and I have always known what the purpose of our lives would be. It has always been our duty to find and protect the ones who will come to save us... and now we have you Freddie, and Myla. You are our children."

Gunda brushed away a tear with her sleeve. Freddie just wanted to throw his arms around her and hug her.

"There was someone once," she continued, "for Hadwin. Not for me. A girl he met when he was much younger. They loved one another. They were going to marry."

She dropped her eyes to her lap.

"What happened?" Freddie asked.

"She left him. It was a very sad time Freddie. Very sad. Poor Hadwin took a long time to get over it. Sometimes, even now, I watch him in his chair, his eyes staring into the past. I'm sure he still thinks about her...

about what might have been."

The door opened and Hadwin walked in, followed by Myla.

Gunda jumped up and poured some water into a large copper bowl hanging over the fireplace.

"The wanderers return," she exclaimed, smiling brightly. "Who's ready for a nice hot cup of barley tea?"

Freddie thought that it would be rude to refuse, despite the fact that he'd never heard of barley tea!

Gunda passed the steaming mugs around and, taking a sip, he was pleasantly surprised to find that it was actually quite nice. It was warm and sweet and the taste reminded him of porridge and honey.

Hadwin studied his hands, his face clouded with uneasiness, and wasted no time in getting straight to the point.

"We have just been to speak with Aarun The Elder in Mirell. His brother Joel was recently captured and taken to Baril-Azur, but has managed to send home a message with information that might help us."

Myla sat down next to Freddie. They exchanged a quick glance.

Hadwin went on. "Aarun believes that we must bring the Aura Stone back to Mirell. They almost captured Freddie yesterday because the Stone showed them where he would be... we can't take any risks with the third, there is too much at stake."

"But the lad has only just got here," Gunda protested, "at least give him a few weeks to settle in... to make sense of it all, the poor mite."

Hadwin shook his head. "There's no time. Remember, my dear, it is our duty to protect the prophecy."

Gunda stared wordlessly across at him. She knew he was right.

"Tomorrow night we leave for Baril-Azur. The two moons will be full and provide enough light for us find our way through the Great Wood. It will be much safer to travel under cover of darkness. We should arrive at the city around dawn the following day."

They listened intently as Hadwin outlined their plan to steal the Aura Stone. The mood in the room had taken a far more serious turn.

"The best chance of entering without being seen will be at dawn via the South Gate. Joel has noticed that the guards are often weary after keeping watch through the night. This is the best time to cause a distraction to provide an opportunity to get in unnoticed."

Gunda looked puzzled. "But what if someone else sees us once we're in? Somebody might notice strangers and raise the alarm?"

Hadwin nodded. "Yes, there is a risk. Nobody said this was going to be easy. Aarun has already sent a message to his brother asking him to leave two grey, hooded cloaks and a map of the city outside the South Gate. There is an old barn nearby and he will hide them there."

"Two cloaks," asked Freddie, "but there are four of us?"

Hadwin turned to face him. "It is too dangerous for all of us to enter, Freddie. You and Myla will go in and bring back the Aura Stone."

Freddie felt a chill run up his spine. He looked at Myla and, for the first time, he felt frightened. All of a sudden, his new adventure had become very real.

8

Freddie spent the rest of the day thinking about the dangerous mission they were about to undertake. He hardly slept that night, and when he did manage to drop off, he was awakened by nightmares of ogres and monsters chasing him.

The next morning, Hadwin asked him to lend a hand with getting the pony and cart ready for the journey. He didn't really feel that he could be of much help as he'd never done anything like this before. But Hadwin was obviously an expert and Freddie just did whatever he was told... 'hold this', 'clean that', 'tie these together firmly'... Hadwin's occasional smile and nod of approval reassured him that he was at least doing some things properly.

"Right lad," said Hadwin, loading the last bag onto the cart, "you've done well. Here, I made something for you yesterday."

He reached inside his jacket and pulled out a small pocketknife with a carved, wooden handle and a short, shiny blade.

"Go on, take it," Hadwin insisted, "don't you want it?"

Freddie carefully took the knife from Hadwin's palm and held it up in front of his eyes. The morning sun caught the edge of the blade, making it sparkle.

"Thank you Hadwin, it's brilliant!"

"Aye, it is so," he mumbled, "and mind you look after it and don't go cutting yourself. It's sharp as ice, it is. The blade is made of Mirell steel. You never know when it might come in handy."

Afterwards, Freddie sat down on the woodpile, alone with his new knife and his thoughts. He was finding it quite hard to come to terms with the sudden turn that his life had taken. What with all the strange events of the past couple of days, he had hardly given a thought to his other life. His parents? Aunt Mags? No doubt they would be frantic with worry! Aunt Mags would have got in touch with his mother and father and maybe they were right now on their way back from their holiday. He felt an emptiness in his stomach and his eyes welled with tears.

Myla, who had been gathering wood, noticed Freddie sitting alone and went over to him.

"It's very hard, sometimes,' she said, softly. "I miss my family too... every day... even after two years."

Freddie quickly wiped his face with his sleeve, trying to pretend that he hadn't been crying.

"Don't you wonder if you'll ever go back... you know, to your real home... if it's even possible to go back?"

Myla shrugged. "Yes, I do wonder. When I first came here I used to spend days and weeks wandering around looking for shadows and black holes! Once, I ran into a dark cave, convinced that I would find myself back home on the other side, in my mother's arms. But the only thing I found was about a hundred bats, flapping wildly around my ears. I ran out, screaming my head off!"

Freddie smiled. She had already started to cheer him up.

Myla sat down beside him and placed her hand on his knee.

"I think the only thing we can do Freddie, is to try to see all this as our mission... a kind of destiny. The main thing that keeps me going is thinking that I am here for a special reason... that my being here is a good thing. Something that was always meant to be."

Freddie knew she was right. They were special. Myla had been given an amazing power, and, from what she had told him, so had he... he just didn't know what it was yet.

"That fire thing you can do," said Freddie. "When did you discover you could do that?"

"It was not long after I came here," she replied. "It just happened, one day... I wasn't trying to make it happen. I was playing in the Great Wood one afternoon when I tripped on a log and went flying! I threw my arms out in front of me to break my fall and these flames just shot out from my fingertips!"

Freddie looked confused. "But that was an accident... and now you can control it?"

"Yes," she replied, "but like everything, it takes practice to master the power. You'll soon find out."

Freddie felt both excited and a bit nervous at the thought of finding out exactly what he would be able to do. What if he couldn't learn to control it? What if it turned out to be more of a curse than a gift? He shuddered at the thought that he might accidently hurt someone... maybe even hurt Myla!

Just then, Gunda poked her head out the window and told them that they needed to come in and rest. The journey would be long and tiring, so they needed to be fit and ready. Fruits of all varieties grew in abundance in the Great Wood, but she had still spent the morning making preparations, packing food and water and trying to anticipate any problems that might occur. She knew only too well all the dangers that they might come across and wanted to be ready for anything.

She knew that, for most of the journey at least, they would be protected by the Great Wood, but there were also areas of harsh, barren land that they would have to cross. They would be exposed and might easily be seen. This worried her.

9

The endless ranks of lofty trees stood silent, their tips melting with the moonlit sky. It felt as if the forest was holding its breath. The track was rough but you could make your way along it with care.

They had been travelling for about three hours. Hadwin and Gunda were squeezed in next to each other on the front seat with Freddie and Myla in the back, amongst the baskets of food and provisions that Gunda had insisted they bring with them, just in case!

Neither of them had slept much during the afternoon, both being far too excited about the adventure they were about to undertake. However, they still felt wide-awake and chatted quietly as the old cart bibbed and bobbed along the uneven path.

All of a sudden, Hadwin pulled sharply on the reins and held up his hand.

"Silence," he hissed, "over there. I heard a noise!"

Freddie held his breath. He had been asking Myla about the creatures that lived in the Great Wood. She had said that there were lots of wild animals, but nothing they needed to be too frightened of. Yet, he was frightened. It was dark, save for the mellow bars of moonlight that managed to slip through the dense canopy overhead. Maybe it was some kind of wild boar, or a fox seeking a meal for its young?

They all sat dead still, their ears straining to identify the source of the sound. Freddie could hear nothing but the wild thudding of his own heart.

Gunda turned around and placed her hand on his shoulder. "It's alright, young'un, just some little fox lost her..."

But before she could finish her sentence, suddenly, six enormous, dark shapes bounded from the trees up ahead and turned to face them in the middle of the track.

Despite the dim light, Freddie could clearly make out the ominous sight of five or six soldiers dressed from head to toe in black, each one astride a beast of a horse, panting wildly and kicking up clouds of dust with their heavy hooves.

"Stop right there!" The voice came suddenly out of the shadows.

Freddie froze.

One of the horses moved slowly toward them and came to a halt next to Hadwin. The rider towered over him like a hideous bird of prey, waiting to strike.

Hadwin looked up to meet his gaze, the soldier's eyes leering through the two narrow slits in his black, metal helmet.

"And where are we all going at this time of night?" the man asked, the tone of his voice a mix of mockery and scorn.

Hadwin thought quickly. "We are visiting my brother who lives on the other side of the Great Wood. He has been taken ill so we left as soon as we received news."

The soldier turned to his comrades and laughed, a humourless vicious sound. "Aah, did you hear that lads? The old man's brother is not very well! We must let them pass so that he can go and give him a kiss to make it all better!" His voice was sharp with sarcasm.

A hastily suppressed giggle rang out from the others.

"Hey, Merek! We should also give them all our food and water to make sure they arrive safely," said another, as the others threw back their heads and laughed.

Merek held up his hand to silence them. A shadowy, ironic sneer hovered about his heavy mouth.

Slowly he turned his head toward Freddie and Myla. They huddled together, feeling themselves shrinking from the cold grey of his watchful smirk.

"What's this," he said with feigned surprise, "two young children!"

He leaned closer, his eyes travelling from one to the other until he fixed a penetrating gaze on the boy.

Freddie's heart bounded into his throat.

Hadwin took a deep breath, trying his

best to remain calm. "You've got no business with them. Leave them be."

"Silence, old man!" roared Merek, "you'll speak when I say!"

"But they're just children," Hadwin continued, "they can do you no harm..."

The General wheeled his horse violently toward Hadwin.

"I said silence!"

His voice rose almost to a scream as he grasped the ugly wooden club by his side and brought it down brutally across Hadwin's legs with a sickening thud.

Hadwin yelled out in pain as he tumbled sideways out of the cart. Gunda shrieked and flung herself at the attacker, beating her fists in anguish against the thick, unyielding armour on his chest.

The other soldiers roared with laughter at the comical sight of their leader being attacked by an old woman.

Merek grasped her roughly by the throat and with one mighty, gloved hand, lifted her off her feet, his lips twisting in a cynical smile. Slowly he raised the club, ready to deliver a fatal blow.

Freddie sprung to his feet, his eyes blazing with rage, and yelled with all his might.

"Leave her alone!"

The General paused and looked at him, his lips forming a twisted, ugly grin. "Watch carefully little man, you're next."

Suddenly, Freddie felt a tingling sensation in his fingertips, and without thinking, he thrust his arms out in front of him. To his astonishment, a jet of black smoke shot from his fingertips and cannoned into the General's chest, lifting him clean out of the saddle and sending him crashing into a huge tree behind him.

Merek's body slid down the trunk and slumped to the floor.

The soldiers stopped laughing and gaped open-mouthed, unable to believe what they had just seen. Two of them jumped down and dragged the injured General back to their group, throwing him roughly over the back of one of the horses.

Gunda scurried over to where Hadwin lay groaning and clutching his broken legs, and cradled his head in her lap.

Slowly, Myla rose to her feet and stood next to Freddie, their eyes fixed on the group of soldiers, wondering who was going to make the next move.

"Come on lads, they're just kids. Let's take 'em."

Nobody moved.

Another voice, trying to hide a tremble of fear. "What did he just do… to the General?"

"I said, let's get 'em!" commanded the first voice, and he started to move forward.

Myla raised her arm behind her head and thrust it forward in an action that, to Freddie, looked like she was throwing a stone or something.

A ball of fire exploded on the ground right in front of the advancing horseman, causing his mount to rear up with an ear splitting whinny and send him crashing to the ground. His horse, clearly frightened by the towering flames, backed off and then darted away into the trees.

The soldier slowly and painfully got to his feet and motioned toward one of his comrades.

"Here, pick me up. It's them Trinity kids. I'm sure of it."

The soldier lifted him into the saddle behind him. They exchanged a few anxious words that neither Freddie nor Myla could hear and then the group turned and galloped away, back in the direction that they had come from.

The sleepy murmurs of the Great Wood returned now that the skirmish was over, at least for now, thought Freddie.

Both children jumped down from the back of the cart and ran to where Hadwin lay, cradled in Gunda's arms.

His face was lined with pain.

"I think my legs are broke," he groaned through clenched teeth, "I can't go any further."

Myla looked at Gunda. "We'll have to turn back. We can make a bed for Hadwin in the cart."

Gunda shook her head. "No, I'll take him home. You must both go on together. You have to get the Aura Stone."

Although neither of them wanted to abandon their friends in the middle of the Great Wood, they knew she was right. They simply had to get the Stone, as soon as possible. Turning back was not an option.

As carefully as they could, the three of them lifted Hadwin into the back of the cart, having hastily arranged the blankets into a makeshift bed, to provide some measure of comfort for him.

Gunda turned with tears in her eyes and hugged them both tightly.

"Now you mind how you go and be sure to come back to me in one piece, do you hear?"

They both promised her that they would be careful as they swallowed hard to bite back the tears.

Gunda climbed in to the front seat of the cart and taking hold of the reins, she turned the pony around. Freddie and Myla stood close together, watching as they slowly began to move away toward home. Just as the cart was disappearing from view, Freddie felt Myla's fingers close around his and squeeze his hand.

A sudden warmth swept through him. Whatever fears and terrors lay ahead, he knew that he was not alone. And, standing there in the dark, with Myla by his side, he vowed to do everything in his power to protect her from harm. Everything in his power... yes, and now, he too had his own special, awesome power.

10

Freddie and Myla continued northward, sticking to the well-trodden path. They knew they could quickly disappear into the cover of trees either side should they see or hear anything suspicious. They had to keep up a brisk pace now that they were on foot to make sure that they still reached Baril-Azur just before dawn.

Neither of them felt tired. The incident with the soldiers had given them a renewed sense of confidence and courage.

Freddie thought about how Myla had taken hold of his hand. He really liked her. Despite the fact that he'd only known her for a short time, he realised that he thought of her as his best friend. Strangely, he felt as though he had known her all his life, not just for a few days.

At school, he'd never really bothered much about girls. They always seemed to huddle around in little groups and giggle over secrets and silly stuff. Sure, there had been a couple of girls at primary school that he'd called 'girlfriends', but that just meant that you 'hung out' together. He'd never actually kissed a girl before, apart from his mum and Aunt Mags of course, but they didn't count! He found himself wondering if he'd ever get to kiss Myla?

"I said, what do you think?" Myla was standing in front of him, her arms folded, her face displaying a frown of mild irritation.

"Sorry?" Freddie replied, with a twinge of embarrassment, feeling his cheeks begin to flush!

She looked even more puzzled. "Have you actually been listening to anything I've just said, Freddie Bright?"

"Yes, of course," he blurted out, offering her a small, shy smile, "well, um...., or maybe not." Thank goodness she didn't have the power to read his mind!

Her expression dissolved into a bright, forgiving smile.

"OK, I just asked if you thought we should stop for a few minutes to rest and eat something? I think it's about another hour until we get to the city."

"Yes, sure," Freddie replied, a little too eagerly, "that's what I thought you said."

Myla raised her eyebrows and gave him a quizzical look. Freddie couldn't hide the cheeky smile playing at the corners of his mouth.

After they had rested for about twenty minutes, and devoured the delicious bread and jam that Gunda had made for them, they decided to head on toward the city.

They'd been walking for only a short while when they were startled by a noise behind them. Throwing themselves face down into a ditch by the side of the path, they held their breath and listened. The sound came again, only this time, a little louder. A regular, tap-tapping kind of sound, then a snort.

Myla lifted her head a fraction to peer over the edge of the ditch. Freddie grasped her arm and whispered, "No!"

All of a sudden, she relaxed and smiled.

"It's just a horse, no rider. I think it's the one that the soldier was riding, you know, the one that ran off?"

Freddie sat up and saw the huge, black charger slowly coming toward them. Myla climbed out of the ditch and held her hand out toward the beast.

"Here boy, come on, it's alright," she spoke softly, trying to get the horse to come to her so that she could take hold of the reins that hung loosely from its powerful neck.

The animal stopped dead and eyed her with suspicion. Myla edged slowly forward.

Freddie watched as she gently took hold of the reins and patted the horse's long nose, continuing to whisper calming words into its ear.

The animal let her take control and leaned its head toward her face and licked her cheek. Myla laughed and turned triumphantly toward Freddie, smiling from ear to ear.

"I think we won't have to walk any more," she declared, "your charger awaits, kind sir," and she curtsied before him!

Freddie laughed. She looked so small and fragile, standing proudly beside the enormous, black warhorse that she had just tamed.

They both hauled themselves up onto its back, Myla taking the reins with Freddie behind her, his arms clasped tightly around her waist.

Myla gave it a gentle kick with her heels and they began to move forward.

"I didn't know you could ride a horse," Freddie said.

Myla smiled. "It was one of the first things that Hadwin taught me when I got here. He said that every girl and boy should know how to ride a horse as you never knew when it would come in handy!"

"Well, he wasn't wrong there," said Freddie. He himself had never ridden a horse before, but he wasn't afraid, especially as Myla seemed to know what she was doing. He just held on tight.

"Careful," she exclaimed, "I do need to

breathe you know!"

Freddie relaxed his grip a little. "Sorry!"

Dawn was breaking as they reached the edge of the Great Wood. Ahead of them lay a vast expanse of open, barren land known as The Plains. In the distance, they could just make out in the dim light the shape of what looked like another forest to the right of the mountains. It was as if a giant had carved an ugly gash through the middle of the Great Wood. Out there, they would be exposed for all to see.

Myla spoke first. "This must be the place Hadwin warned us about. We are going to have to move fast before the sun rises. Are you ready?"

Freddie didn't quite know what she meant by 'ready,' but he mumbled his agreement and pulled himself tightly into her back, locked his hands together around her waist, and closed his eyes.

"Just don't let go, Freddie," she said, "whatever happens... don't let go."

And with that, Myla let out a muffled

shout and dug her heals firmly into the horse's ribs. The beast darted forward. Within seconds they were galloping at full speed across the open plain. Freddie hung on to Myla with all his strength as the wind whistled past his ears.

After a few minutes, he opened his eyes a fraction and, squinting to the side, saw the first glimpse of the morning sun appear on the horizon.

~ ~ ~

"It is of no consequence," Thalia said, as she stood up and walked toward the door.

Tarin leapt to his feet. "Of no consequence," he raged, "my best… my most loyal soldier… thrown from his horse by a child?"

Thalia stopped and slowly turned to face him, her eyes as cold as the grave.

""If he *was* your best soldier, he would

have captured the imps and brought them here! But no, instead the great Merek lies flat on his back in his bed, defeated by a child! Now you must think of how we can once and for all bring an end to this wretched curse that has hung over us for so long."

Tarin's fury lay unabated. "They will pay for this! I will tear them limb from limb and feed their flesh to the dogs!"

"Then you shouldn't have to wait too long," said Thalia.

"What do you mean?"

"Obviously they are on their way here. The North Riders said that they were heading in this direction and had already almost reached the edge of the Great Wood."

Tarin stared at her. "Then we must set off at once to find them?"

"No," Thalia replied, "let them come. Once they are inside these walls they will be at our mercy. They will be coming for the Aura Stone, to see the prophecy fulfilled... and we will be waiting for them."

A wicked sneer gradually began to form

on Tarin's lips. "Go on, my sister."

"We will position the guards along the route from the gate to the Tall Tower," Thalia continued, "but they must remain hidden, to make sure the little snakes reach the Stone Room. Once inside, we will bolt the doors and they will be our prisoners."

Tarin looked puzzled. "I like it, yes, but what about the powers the soldiers saw them use in the Wood? The girl hurling fire and the boy... well, how he threw Merek from his horse with such force, without laying a finger upon him?"

Thalia smiled. "Don't worry, dear brother, I have an idea. Remember how the soldiers reported that they both thrust their arms forward to use their power? My plan will, shall we say, make it just a little difficult for them to cause us any trouble!"

11

Their frantic ride finally came to an end once they entered the safe cover of trees on the other side of the Plains. Myla heaved on the reins and the horse slowly came to a halt, immediately seeking out a nearby pool of fresh water.

"Do you think we were seen?" asked Freddie, "we were out there for such a long time!"

Myla tied the horse to a branch. "I don't think so," she replied, looking around, cautiously.

"We will rest here a while to let the horse regain some strength. Then we'll head off in search of the old barn that Hadwin told us about." Myla sat down next to Freddie and stretched out her aching limbs.

Freddie wanted to sound confident and strong, but inside he was feeling increasingly frightened and unsure.

"What if the disguises aren't there? What if that man wasn't able to help us?"

Myla sat up. "Look, we have come this far. There's no going back now. We are the chosen ones, Freddie, part of the Tellurian Trinity. We have been given special powers for situations just like this. They will enable us to defeat our enemies and take the Aura Stone. The one that the Stone is sending next will need us more than ever before. Stop doubting yourself!"

It was a rousing speech and it made him feel a bit better. One day he hoped to be as strong as Myla.

"Here, eat this." Myla handed him a chunk of bread from her backpack. Plain bread or not, he was so hungry, it tasted like heaven! After a few minutes Myla turned to Freddie and placed her hand on his arm.

"OK, are you ready? It's time."

Freddie looked into her soft, green eyes.

"Yes, I'm ready."

Myla smiled, leant forward and kissed him on the cheek. It was a kiss as tender and light as a summer breeze.

"Right then, super hero, let's go get that

stone!" And with that, she jumped up, untied the reins and leapt up into the saddle.

"Come on, what are you waiting for?" Myla looked down at him. He was still sitting with his back to the tree, a dazed expression on his face, staring at her!

'She kissed me,' he thought to himself, 'she actually kissed me!'

~ ~ ~

"Bring him in."

Tarin slouched in his golden throne, Thalia perched anxiously at his side.

"Yes, my Lord."

The servant shuffled backward and opened the oak door of the Throne Room.

"His Lordship wishes to see the Scout," he bellowed.

A young boy who looked no more than fifteen entered. He was small and sprightly with tousled, blonde hair. He walked nervously toward his master.

Tarin eyed him up and down.

"So," he began, "you saw them?"

"Yes, your Lordship," muttered the boy, staring at the floor.

Tarin rose to his feet. "Speak up! I'm not going to bite you... yet! Tell us, what did you see?"

The boy looked up. Lord Tarin and Lady Thalia were waiting.

"I... I was on watch, this morning, as usual, at my post... my usual post that is, overlooking the north Plains..."

"Get on with it you imbecile!" screamed Thalia, as she jumped up from her throne. "We know who you are, you fool... tell us, what did you see?"

The boy flushed red, edging further backward and once again looking down at the floor.

"Two children... a girl and a boy... charging full speed across the Plains on a huge, black steed. It looked like Merek's horse."

"And?" asked Tarin, "what did you do?"

The boy looked frightened and confused.

"Er, well... nothing, your Lordship. Captain's orders was to let all riders pass and to remain hidden."

Tarin nodded. "Yes, good, that's right. How long ago was this?"

"About an hour ago, your Lordship, then they disappeared into the trees."

Thalia took her brother's arm and guided him into a corner.

"That means they'll be here soon," she whispered, "and we must be ready... and make sure that nothing goes wrong. Are the guards in position?"

"Yes," replied Tarin, 'everyone is at their station. They all have orders to let them pass and make sure that they head straight for the Stone Room."

"Good," mused Thalia, "Good. By tonight we will have crushed the prophecy once and for all. The imps will be dead and every man, woman and child throughout the land will bow to us."

"Yes, sweet sister," Tarin agreed, "our dear late mother would be very proud of us."

12

"There it is, up ahead."

Freddie looked in the direction that Myla was pointing and could just make out in the distance a rickety old wooden building, nestled amongst the trees.

Myla spoke in a whisper. "We should tie up the horse here and approach on foot, just incase something has gone wrong. We don't want to walk into a trap."

They dismounted, secured the tether and crept forward, making sure that they remained undercover as they approached the barn. Freddie could see the door which appeared to be broken and hanging loosely from a hinge.

"I'll wait outside, just in case. You go in and check that there's nobody there," whispered Myla.

He sneaked up to the door, peered in through the narrow gap and went in. The floor was covered with straw and the room was empty apart from a few hay bales and a couple of old crates in the corner.

"It's ok," he called out quietly, "there's no one here. Come on in."

Myla stepped inside.

They both looked at each other. Their facial expressions could not hide the huge sense of relief that they felt. So far everything was going according to plan.

Myla began searching in and around the hay bales whilst Freddie headed for the wooden crates in the corner. It wasn't long before he found what they were looking for.

"Here," he exclaimed, "over here!"

Looking down, behind one of the crates, was a small, grey cloth bundle, neatly tied with orange twine.

Myla hurried over to join him as he reached down, grabbed the package and pulled on the string.

It fell open to reveal a small sheet of yellow parchment, folded in half. The grey cloth packaging turned out to be two plain, hooded tunics, about knee length. Carefully, Freddie opened the parchment. There was a crudely drawn map and some writing. He began to read aloud.

'My friends. This map will lead you to the top of the Tall Tower and the Aura Stone. Follow the dotted path. Be on alert, for evil waits at every turn. Put on the cloaks and pull up the hoods. All children in the city wear the same, so you will be hidden amongst the sorrows. May the Gods keep you safe, yours with hope, J.'

Freddie glanced at Myla, who was staring fixedly at the map as if trying to memorize every turn.

"Hidden amongst the sorrows," Freddie repeated, "what does that mean?"

Myla wiped a tear from her eye. "It's as we always believed," she said, "just as Gunda and Hadwin have always told me."

Freddie understood.

"The children are all prisoners, Freddie. Held captive, like hostages, to ensure that their parents obey the masters. They must be so sad."

Freddie could feel the anger welling up

inside him.

"Then we must save them, and bring an end to this misery once and for all."

Myla looked at him, smiling. "Yes, we must. Come on, let's put these on and get going."

Quickly, they pulled the cloaks over their clothes and lifted the hoods. Freddie picked up the map and, peering out of the door to make sure the coast was clear, they both slipped outside into the early morning sun. The map showed them that the South Gate was just beyond the next clump of trees. Provided they could reach the gate without being seen leaving the forest, they had a good chance of going unnoticed.

Peering through the leaves, they could see two guards standing outside the gate, laughing and talking to each other. After a short time, one of them slapped the other on the back, placed his arm around his shoulder and led him inside, out of sight.

This was their chance. They had to move now.

Breaking cover, they both ran as fast as they could toward the gateway, only slowing up as they reached the entrance and, holding their breath, they walked slowly through the gate and into Baril-Azur.

"That was easy!" Freddie whispered.

"Shh!" Myla gestured, "Look!"

They had entered a wide, oval shaped courtyard, with various stalls and old wooden tables around the outer rim. It reminded Freddie of a village market scene back home. But it was far from normal! The air hung heavy with wretchedness and despair. All around, people shuffled here and there, men and women dressed in rough brown cloaks and children wearing the same as Freddie and Myla. Heads were bowed and trading at market stalls seemed to be conducted in whispers and nods.

Myla pointed to a pile of wooden crates just off to their left.

"Quick, follow me. Over there!"

They crouched down behind the crates, hidden from view. Freddie unfolded the map that he had kept hidden up his sleeve.

"We must be here," he said, pointing at a spot on the map. Myla nodded and peered around the crates.

"Over there... on the other side, that doorway in the wall? That must be the Tall Tower. That's where we've got to go." Studying the map, she continued. "It will lead us to this staircase, and at the top, turn right, along that corridor, round the corner to the left, and there… that's the Stone Room."

Freddie followed the trace of her finger, trying as hard as he could to mentally record every instruction, before folding the map again and returning it to his pocket.

"Remember," said Myla, "we walk across the yard slowly, eyes down, just like the others. We mustn't attract any attention to ourselves. Once we get to the doorway, just keep walking. Don't stop. Don't look round, OK?"

"OK," replied Freddie, "just stay close. Stay together, yes?"

They could clearly sense each other's

fear, but they both knew what they had to do. Slowly, they stood up and walked out from behind the crates, back into the courtyard.

Suddenly, they heard a voice, shouting. "Oi! You two!"

They froze.

Glancing up, Freddie saw a huge guard, dressed all in black leather, coming toward them, holding a menacing wooden club in his hand.

"Them crates. You can't leave 'em there. You know where they're supposed to go!"

Freddie stared at Myla. Neither of them spoke. The guard continued to walk directly toward them, shouting louder now.

"Alright, you lazy little piglets, maybe you need a bit of help!" He lifted the club above his head.

Just as he was about to bring it down, he was distracted by a noise behind him. Shouting.... a scuffle... a fight had broken out between two of the cloaked men.

The guard stopped and turned, spotting

the disturbance amongst a whirl of limbs and dust.

He started to run toward them. "Hey, knock it off, you dogs! You know the punishment for fighting!"

Freddie stood motionless, staring at the men fighting. One of them was in a headlock and his gaze met Freddie's eyes. With one free arm, the man seemed to be frantically pointing. Pointing to the doorway across the courtyard and his eyes seemed to be begging Freddie to understand.

Myla was quicker on the uptake.

"Come on, it's a distraction, they're not fighting… they're helping us!"

A crowd began to gather around the fighters. More guards came running to break it up. Freddie and Myla headed straight for the doorway.

Once safely inside, they stopped and pressed their backs to the wall.

"Blimey, that was close!" gasped Freddie.

""I know," said Myla, "I wonder if that

was Joel who started the fight? Or maybe one of his friends?"

"Whoever they were," he continued, "we owe them our lives! That guard was really going for us!"

"Don't forget your power, Freddie," she said.

"No, I haven't," he replied, "but if we use our powers here, in the open, then every soldier in Baril-Azur will be down upon us like a ton of bricks before you can say Jack Robinson!"

Myla looked puzzled. "Jack Robinson? Who's Jack Robinson?"

Freddie smiled. "Oh, nothing. It's just something my Mum used to say."

His Mum? Freddie suddenly realised that in all this time he'd hardly given her a second thought. How long was it since he last saw her? Not long at all, but it seemed like forever!

Myla nodded. "Yes, you're right. We do still have our powers, but for now we must use our heads. Come on, let's keep going.

There, at the end of the passage... the staircase."

Quickly, they made their way along the cold, stone passageway, which led directly to an opening in the wall, revealing a narrow, winding staircase. They began to climb, Freddie first. The air grew darker.

After a while, they both stopped to regain their breath. They were now standing in almost pitch black.

"Does this ever end?" Freddie exclaimed, nervously.

"Not much further, surely," Myla replied. "Remember, at the top, turn right, but make sure you check there's nobody about first."

"Obviously! I'm not an idiot!" Freddie retorted, with a little more sarcasm than was intended!

Myla was silent. After a few moments she said, "I just don't want anything bad to happen to you... to us. Not after we've come this far. I... I care about you, Freddie."

Freddie felt embarrassed for snapping

at her. "I'm sorry, I didn't mean it like that, really."

Myla smiled. "I know, don't worry. This is all a bit stressful, isn't it?"

Freddie laughed. "Yeah, you could say that! It's not something I do every day!"

They carried on up the stairwell, which seemed to be getting narrower as they approached the top. Their shoulders brushed against the brickwork as they pressed onwards and upwards.

At last they spied a glint of light above and soon reached the top. They both held their breath and listened.

Nothing.

Freddie poked his head out and looked both ways. It was an empty corridor.

"I don't like it," Myla whispered, "something's wrong. Surely there would be some guards up here?"

Freddie wasn't sure.

"Maybe, but, think about it... they wouldn't exactly be expecting someone to walk in to the city and steal the Aura Stone, would they?"

Myla conceded. "No, I suppose you're right. Come on. Let's go!"

They turned right, away from the stairwell and walked quickly and quietly down the corridor. As hard as they tried not to make a noise, their footsteps on the wooden floorboards seemed to echo throughout the whole castle!

They rounded the next corner and there it was. The Stone Room! Two huge, heavy oak doors standing between them and the Aura Stone. Myla took hold of the rusty, iron, door-latch with both hands, turned it and pushed hard.

Nothing happened. It was locked!

13

Gunda dipped the cloth in the pool once more and wrung it out. Returning to where Hadwin lay in the back of the cart, she placed the damp towel softly upon his brow. She was sure his temperature was beginning to rise.

"We have to keep going," she said, "we still have at least two hours more and it will be light soon."

Hadwin was finding it hard to speak. "It's no good... the cart... too much pain!"

Gunda sighed. They had left Freddie and Myla behind some hours before, but they'd eventually had to stop as Hadwin's groans had turned to cries of pain with every jar and jolt they passed over. She didn't know what to do. His legs were badly injured and he needed to be seen by the doctor in Mirell as soon as possible. Yet, she just could not put him through this pain any longer. She didn't think he could bear much more. Her brother might be old, but he was a strong man who never made a fuss. He must be in agony! There was only one thing to do.

"I'll have to go on and fetch the doctor to you."

Hadwin started to interrupt…

"No, Hadwin, you great lump of a brother! Just you listen to me, for once! If I set off now and make good speed, I can be back here before nightfall. I'll bring the doctor and some other men to help… we'll figure something out to get you home."

He knew that there was no point in trying to argue with his sister, especially when she was in this mood! Reluctantly, he nodded his agreement.

Gunda placed a bottle of water and half a loaf of bread by his side. She didn't tell him that it was all that was left.

"Now, I'll leave you here. You'll be hidden behind these bushes. Try to stay quiet and make sure you eat and drink regular, especially drink, do you hear me?"

"Yes, don't worry." Hadwin attempted a smile, but his face grimaced with yet another spasm of pain as Gunda pushed the cart off the track to a safer place.

She leant forward and kissed his cheek. He was so hot! She knew she had to get back to him quickly, or… or… she just couldn't bring herself to think what might happen to him!

As quickly as she could, she set off along the track heading for home. There would be a right fork a little further on. She would take that road and head straight to Mirell. Once she had organized help, they would be able to make the return journey much faster with horses. She might even be able to get back by midday if everything went well.

She had been walking for about four or five miles, expecting to find the turning to Mirell soon, when a noise from behind nearly made her jump out of her skin. A familiar, fearful sound. A sound that was a mix of heavy hooves and the clanking of armour.

"Stop there, hag!"

Gunda turned and froze. Two ironclad

soldiers saddled atop two of the biggest horses she'd ever seem came toward her.

"It's her... the same woman," said one soldier to the other.

"Yes, and so it is," smirked the larger one.

"But where are your friends, old woman? Where are your little warriors now?"

They both roared with laughter. Gunda did not know whether to run or cry. If she ran, they would easily catch her. She recognized them as two of the party that they had come across during the night. She thought they would have returned to Baril-Azur with their tails between their legs after Freddie and Myla had dealt with them, but she was wrong. They must have doubled back. Maybe they'd been following her all the time? Maybe they knew where she'd left Hadwin? Oh, Hadwin! Was he even still alive?

Gunda broke down in tears. "Please, spare me. I'm just an old woman who can do you no harm."

This only made the soldiers roar even more.

"Don't blub, you old witch! You're not going to die today! We're going to take you on a little journey. To meet a friend of ours."

One of the men leant down, grabbed her by the scruff of the neck and heaved her up behind him, sideways astride the beast.

Something dug into her stomach, making her cry out.

"Careful with that," mocked the rider, "don't want you damaging my sword, do we?"

The soldiers swung their horses around, dug in their heels and galloped away. Gunda knew that she had to hold on for dear life, even though every stride of the horse caused the handle of the soldier's sword to dig deeper into her belly. She thought she would surely pass out from the pain before they reached their destination, which, to her growing despair, must surely be Baril-Azur.

14

"How are we going to get in?" asked Myla. "I can't just burn it down! They'll smell the smoke and we'll be discovered before we can escape? And you can't just blow it down! Too much noise!"

Freddie stepped back, pulling her with him.

"Stand back. I think I can handle this. It's all about control, that's what you said, wasn't it?"

Freddie fixed his eyes upon the lock and stretched a hand out in front of him. Myla watched as his expression stilled and grew serious. Slowly, as he began to turn his index finger, a thin wisp of dark smoke emerged from it and threaded into the lock. His eyes sparkled, almost as if he was playing a game with her. She glanced anxiously left and right to check that they hadn't been discovered and then, returning to the door, she heard a mechanical clunk.

Freddie lowered his arm and turned

toward her, smiling proudly.

"There, that should do it!"

Her mouth dropped open. "Did you just unlock that door?"

He winked at her, looking like the cat that had just got the cream! "The power of the mind! Come on, let's go in!"

Slowly he turned the handle and the heavy door creaked open. They both slipped inside and quietly shut the door behind them.

The sight that met their eyes took their breath away. The room was lit with a warm, rose-pink glow. The light was coming from the most beautiful crystal they had ever seen, about the size of an ostrich egg, radiating from a pedestal at the far end of the room.

"It's beautiful!" exclaimed Myla.

"So this is the Aura Stone!" Freddie muttered under his breath, his face lit with excitement. They exchanged a quick glance and together stepped forward to retrieve their prize.

They had barely reached the middle of the room when they heard a sound above their heads. Their eyes shot up to see a large black net falling fast toward them.

Freddie grabbed Myla's arm and yelled out a warning, but it was too late.

"It's a trap!"

In a flash the rope closed around them and lifted them off their feet into the air. Before they knew it, they were swinging helplessly, upside down, several feet above the ground.

For a moment they just hung there in stunned silence.

Myla spoke first. "Are you ok?"

"I think so… I can't move!"

"Me neither," she replied, desperately trying to free herself.

Freddie continued to struggle in vain. His arms were well and truly jammed against his body. To their horror, they heard the door open and the sound of footsteps approaching.

"What a pleasant surprise!"

It was a woman's voice. Cold and harsh.

Freddie struggled to see where the voice was coming from. Suddenly, a woman's face appeared beside them. Long black hair, icy-white skin, sharp, pointed features.

"Allow me introduce myself. My name is Thalia, Mistress of Telluria. How kind of you both to come!"

He tried again to wriggle his arms free, but it was no good. The net was so tight it dug into his flesh making any movement impossible.

Thalia circled her prize. "Spare your energy, little man. You and your sweet girlfriend are going nowhere!"

Myla felt icy fingertips brush the back of her neck. Her muscles tensed.

"Don't touch me!" she cried, her voice cracking with rage.

Thalia laughed, an empty, cruel sound, whilst lightly fingering a loose tendril of Myla's hair that hung through the webbing.

"Be careful, little girl." She felt the woman's hot breath on her ear. "You really don't want to make me angry." Slowly she wound her fingers around the strand of hair and started to pull.

Myla shrieked at the sudden pain. Thalia's lips tightened as she pulled harder, "Let go! You're hurting me!"

Freddie tried to kick out in vain. "I swear, when I get out of here, I'm going to kill you, you evil, ugly witch!"

"Yes, yes, yes. Of course you are, boy. And, do you know what?" Releasing Myla's hair she leaned her face close to his cheek. "I'm so scared!"

A surge of anger flowed through him. If only he could free himself, then he'd show her something to be frightened of!

Just then, the door opened. "Well, you took your time! Here, look, a gift for you."

Out of the corner of his eye, Freddie could just make out the shape of a tall, dark man approaching. This must be Lord Tarin, her twin brother.

"Congratulations, my dear sister. So, your plan worked?"

"As you can see, faultlessly." Her expression held a note of mockery.

"Well, almost," said Tarin, "one idiot guard nearly ruined everything. Fortunately, he was distracted by a brawl. Well done. So, what now? Public executions at dawn?"

Myla let out a muffled gasp.

"Oh, dear brother, don't frighten the poor things." Thalia walked around the net, brushing her hand against the coarse fabric as she went. "I don't think so. Public executions at dawn would be far too quick. I have, shall we say, some rather more... entertaining plans for these two little ones."

Tarin laughed. "Thalia, dearest. Sometimes, I think you are more wicked than our dear Mother!"

"Yes," she beamed, "I think you might be right!"

All of a sudden, the room filled with a bright, dazzling light. Thalia's eyes sparkled.

"Quick! The Stone. It shines! The third is coming. How perfect! Go and alert the North Riders to follow the beam!"

"At last!" Tarin exclaimed, heading for the door, "the prophecy will be broken. I'll have every available man following the light."

The sound of her brother's footsteps paled as he ran down the passage. Thalia's face once again appeared in front of them.

"The Gods be praised, my dears! The whole Trinity in one day! Your friend is coming to join you!"

She turned her back and walked transfixed toward the Aura Stone, her body lit up in silhouette by the radiating light. The ground began to tremble as the Stone filled the room with a low, rumbling sound.

Suddenly, Freddie had an idea. With Thalia distracted, this was their only chance.

"Myla," he whispered, "quick. In my back pocket. A knife." He'd remembered the gift Hadwin had given him.

Myla struggled. "I can't move!"

"Yes you can! I can feel your hand pressed into my back. See if you can get the knife!"

Using all her strength, she inched her fingers downward, searching for his pocket.

"It's covered up… your cloak!"

"Then pull it up with your fingers, come on. I know you can do this!"

She began tugging at the material with her fingertips, managing to move it slightly.

"A bit more, come on. Keep going!"

Feeling the edge of his tunic, her fingers searched frantically for the lip of his pocket.

"It's no good, I can't get my hand in! You'll have to breath out, OK?"

"OK?" gasped Freddie.

"Right, here goes, one… two… three!"

Forcing all the air out of his lungs, he felt her hand slip into his pocket, grab the knife and pull it out.

"Got it!" she whispered, triumphantly.

"Great, now, try to cut the net. Be careful, the blade is made of Mirell steel. It will cut through anything."

"OK, I'm trying to!"

"Ouch! Careful!" he exclaimed, "that's me!"

"Sorry!" she replied, as she turned her hand a fraction and felt the knife rest on something hard. With all her strength, she pressed the blade in and felt the cord give way.

"That's it, keep going, keep going," he said, excitedly.

She continued to slice through the webbing, each cut getting easier as the net loosened its grip around them.

Finally, it gave way, sending them crashing to the floor.

Thalia spun around and screamed.

Freddie met her gaze, his dark eyes wild with anger. "Now who's scared?"

The blood drained from Thalia's face as he slowly lifted an arm toward her. The thin jet of black smoke crashed into her chest, lifted her off her feet and pinned her flat against the far wall, arms outstretched.

Thalia opened her mouth to scream for help, but he was too quick. Snapping his fist closed, he watched as her lips sealed shut.

He glanced over his shoulder.

"Quick, Myla, grab the Stone. Let's get out of here."

She didn't answer.

"Now... the Stone! We don't have much time!" His voice trembled slightly.

Myla stood stock still, staring at the far end of the room. It was lit up in a beam of bright white light coming from the Aura Stone. There, huddled in the corner, bathed in the light, sat a frightened little boy of about nine years of age, with dark skin and tightly curled black hair.

"He's here, Freddie, he's here!" cried Myla, her eyes brimming with tears of joy and astonishment.

Freddie turned his attention back to Thalia.

"First, I've got to deal with you!"

Her face contorted with shock and fury. With a flick of his wrist, Freddie flung her to the right, sending her crashing against the wall where she collapsed in a heap on the floor.

The Aura Stone stopped glowing.

They both ran over to the boy in the corner and crouched beside him. He stared back at them, his large brown eyes bright and bemused. He looked like he'd seen a ghost!

Myla took hold of his hand. "Hi there, "I'm Myla! What's your name?"

The boy looked up at her. He had a quiet, oval face. Dark, and rather delicate.

"I'm Seth," he replied, trying to keep his voice steady, "who are you?"

Freddie smiled.

"Well, hello there Seth. I'm Freddie. It's great to meet you, really great! But right now, we've got to get out of here, OK? Trust me. Trust us. You'll be OK."

"OK," Seth replied, an expression of complete surprise on his face.

The three of them jumped up and ran out the door, along the corridor, and started down the narrow stairwell.

They had almost reached the bottom when suddenly, Myla stopped.

"The Stone! We forgot the Aura Stone!"

Freddie turned to face her.

"Look, leave it. It's served its purpose. We are all here now."

"Are you mad?" she cried. "We don't know the half of its power! We can't just leave it there! Who knows what it might do in the future? And, there's no way I'm leaving it for them!"

There was no point in arguing! Myla had the solution.

"Look, you and Seth go on, get yourselves safely out of here, and I'll go back for the Stone. I'll meet you at the barn, OK?"

"I don't like the idea of that," said Freddie, "we shouldn't split up."

"Well, we have to. There are three of us and only two cloaks." Quickly, she took off her grey cloak and pulled it over Seth's head.

"There, now neither of you will look out of place."

Freddie wasn't so sure. "But, what about you? How are you going to get out? You'll stand out like a sore thumb in that yellow dress?"

Myla drew a long breath. “Look, don’t worry, I’ll think of something. Now off you go, quickly! And, look after the little one. I’ll see you at the barn, within the hour, OK?”

Freddie opened his mouth to protest further but she was having none of it.

“In an hour, OK?” she insisted, fixing him with a look that invited no further argument.

For a moment they held one another’s gaze. “One hour, no longer.”

She flashed him a smile, turned sharply and disappeared back up the staircase.

He glanced at Seth, who was looking back at him, wide-eyed and bewildered.

“Right, I guess it’s just you and me, for now. Just stick right by my side, do as I say, and everything will be fine. OK?”

“OK.” he replied, taking hold of Freddie’s hand.

Freddie tightened his grip as they both set off again, down the steps.

15

Lord Tarin raced across the courtyard and burst into the Guard Room.

"Quick, I need all of you, now! The Stone is showing us that the third one has come. What news from the watchtower?"

The guards looked nervously from one to another, confusion on their faces.

"Come on, answer me you fools!" Tarin roared.

One guard stepped forward.

"My Lord, I have just returned from there. I... I saw nothing." He looked nervously at the ground.

"What?" Tarin yelled, "The beam. Have you not seen the beam of light, you idiot?"

The guard shifted nervously. "Forgive me, my Lord, but no... no light has come from the Tall Tower. My men have been watching it constantly!"

Tarin didn't understand. He had seen the Aura Stone light up with his own eyes. Surely the beam would have been visible for miles around? Unless... of course!

"Come with me, all of you. The third must still be here!"

Tarin bolted out the door, quickly followed by several guards, all of them struggling to figure out what was actually going on!

In their haste to reach the Stone Room, nobody noticed the two small, hooded figures slowly making their way toward the South Gate.

Tarin took the steps to the top of the Tower three at a time and rushed into the Stone Room. He stopped and stared at the ripped netting on the floor... and an empty space where the Aura Stone had once stood.

A faint voice came from behind him. "My brother." Tarin turned sharply.

"Thalia!"

His sister was lying against the far wall. He rushed over and knelt by her side.

She struggled to speak. "They got away... not far... find them, dear brother, and kill them."

Carefully he lifted her up. There was a pool of blood on the floor, which must have come from the deep gash above her left eye. She flinched with pain. Her left arm hung limply at an awkward angle. Tarin thought it must be broken.

Without delay he ordered one of the guards to go and fetch her maidservants and then turned back to his sister.

"Don't worry, my dear sister, I will find both of them, and when I do..."

Thalia interrupted. "Three... there are three now. The Stone brought the third here... in this room... a small boy with dark skin... black hair."

Tarin turned to the guards.

"Search everywhere. Do not allow them to escape. I want them alive... but take no chances. They are dangerous. If in doubt... kill them."

~ ~ ~

Myla heard the sound of footsteps rapidly approaching. Quickly she hid behind the door as Tarin rushed in and then ran toward the stricken figure of his sister, lying on the floor at the far side of the room.

Noticing his back toward her, she slipped out of the room, the Aura Stone safely tucked under her arm.

Which way to go? She could hear a loud noise and shouting coming from the stairwell leading downwards, so, turning to her left, she set off running along a narrow passage that had doors on both sides.

Rounding a corner she pressed herself flat against the cold brick wall, held her breath and listened. The sounds had faded. Glancing around she could see two doors a little further on. She ran to the first one and tried the handle. It was locked. Quickly she dashed to the next and grasped the iron doorknob and turned it. The door swung open.

She slipped inside and closed the door behind her. She was in an ornate room, dominated by a large, four-poster bed with gold pillars and silk drapes. On the wall beside the bed hung a huge portrait of a woman with sharp facial features and piercing, black eyes. The resemblance to Thalia was unmistakable.

'This must be *her* room,' Myla thought to herself, a chill running up her spine. She noticed a small cotton bag on the floor by her feet. She picked it up and dropped the Aura Stone inside.

Suddenly, the noise of heavy footsteps and shouting began to grow louder from outside. Doors were being thrown open and slammed.

Myla glanced around the room... two open closets stuffed with dresses... double doors leading to... a balcony! She had to get out, fast.

She ran toward the balcony doors and grabbed the handle. It was locked. The sound of the approaching guards now seemed to be almost at the door.

Myla took two steps backwards, thrust

her hand forward and unleashed a tiny fireball, which exploded into the lock. As the balcony doors swung open, she dashed through and pressed herself hard up against the wall to the side of the doorway.

She was very high up. The sight of treetops swaying in the breeze met her eyes as she held her breath, motionless.

'Don't let them catch me,' she pleaded to herself, 'don't let them get the Stone after all we have done.'

The Stone! She held the bag in front of her. This had been the whole purpose of their mission. To seize the Aura Stone to protect the Trinity. And now, Seth had come. Seth. That poor little boy, he must be so terrified. Perhaps Freddie was right? The Stone had served its purpose now. But, something deep inside told her otherwise. She couldn't explain it, but she knew the Aura Stone had to be protected. She couldn't risk losing it now.

Taking a step forward, she peered over the edge of the balcony. The line of trees was not too far off. Thalia's room must look out over the same forest that they had come through as they'd approached the city.

Grasping the bag firmly with both hands and, summoning every ounce of strength left in her body, she hurled the Stone toward the forest. Her eyes followed its path as it soared through the air and disappeared into a large tree with bright orange leaves. She made a mental note. When she got out of the city, she would retrieve it.

Quickly she pressed her back against the wall again and listened. A door opened. A gruff voice mumbled an instruction.

"His Lordship said search everywhere. That includes Lady Thalia's private quarters. Get on with it."

Myla felt the blood drain from her face and her knees go weak as she pressed harder against the wall, wishing that she could disappear into the brickwork. Sounds of banging and crashing, doors being opened and closed and muffled voices barking orders filled her ears.

The search seemed to last forever. She held her breath. Then she heard a different voice, the words coming loud and clear. The speaker must be standing just the other side of the balcony doors. There was no mistaking who it was, no more than an arms length away from her. Lord Tarin.

"They're not in here. Let's move on to the next room, come on men."

She held her breath as they began to leave. She was just about to let out a huge sigh of relief when a sudden gust of wind blew across her face and the balcony doors slammed shut with a bang.

~ ~ ~

Freddie and Seth walked slowly, keeping their heads bowed low as the soldiers rushed past them, swords drawn in groups of six or seven, running in all directions. The quiet courtyard scene that they had first witnessed upon their arrival was now one of frantic commotion and, thanks to their disguises, they both blended easily into the turmoil. Freddie clutched Seth's hand, pulling him close to his side.

"Not far now, Seth," Freddie whispered, "just keep your head down... eyes on the ground."

The South Gate came in to view. Just a few more paces and they'd be safe, but still Freddie felt worried. How could he have agreed to let Myla go back for the Stone alone? They had been together for almost all the time he'd spent in Telluria, and right now didn't seem like the best time to split up! But there was nothing he could do about it. Turning back would mean certain capture, and that wouldn't be of any help to her!

As they approached the South Gate, Freddie heard a faint voice calling out... a child's voice. He glanced to his right and heard it again.

"Over here... help us."

He stopped. The voice was coming from a tiny, barred window in a small wooden door just to the right of the South Gate. Pressed up against the bars he could just make out a small, dirty face.

A child's arm emerged through the bars and beckoned him over.

Freddie didn't know what to do. They were so close to safety. What if this was a trap set by Tarin should they manage to make it to the gate?

"Please, please… help us?" begged the voice, the little hand frantically pleading for him to come closer.

He glanced back at the South Gate. There was no guard. But it was no good, he had to help.

Cursing under his breath, he grabbed Seth and ran toward the door. It was locked from the outside. Freddie slid the bolt and they both stepped inside, closing the door behind him.

The sight that met his eyes almost took his breath away. He was in some kind of dungeon, a small stone room with one tiny window high up on the far wall. It let in just enough light for him to see what must have been at least thirty children, boys and girls, all crammed in to this single, tiny space. Most were of a similar age to him, but he noticed that some of them couldn't have been much more than four or five years old!

And then he became aware of the smell! It was truly awful and he thought he was going to throw up! He looked at Seth who had covered his nose and mouth with his hands.

"What is this place?" said Seth, a look of horror on his face.

Freddie couldn't reply. He just stood transfixed as thirty pairs of wretched eyes stared back at him, lifeless, soulless. The children all looked so thin and dirty.

Anger welled inside him. "Who could treat children like this?"

The boy who had called through the window grabbed his arm.

"Please, help us?' he begged, the tears that trickled from his eyes making little tracks through the grime embedded in his cheeks. "Take us with you?"

"I...," Freddie hesitated, "I can't."

Slowly, a wretched, helpless sobbing began to fill the room.

"Wait!" said Freddie, "who are you? Why are you all here, in this... this prison?"

The boy looked at the ground, his eyes full of sadness.

"We are the forgotten ones," he began, "our parents are all dead. We are no longer of use to the masters."

Freddie couldn't understand. "What do you mean, no longer of use?"

The boy lifted his eyes.

"The masters made our parents work for them. If they refused, then the masters would punish us, their children."

Freddie began to remember what Gunda had said. She had told him about how families had been taken and the adults were forced to work and obey their captors, or else their children would suffer... it was horrific! It was more than horrific! It was true!

Freddie looked at the poor boy in front

of him. "And the masters have no use for orphans?"

The boy nodded.

"So what happens to you? Do they..." Freddie could hardly get the words out, "do they... just leave you here... to die?"

The boy swallowed hard. "Some of us die here. But most of us get taken away. When the carts come."

"Taken away? Where to?"

"Nobody... nobody knows. Some say they take us to Val-Kadir in the east... others say they just leave us in the mountains... for the wolves."

The boy was struggling to speak. Freddie noticed that his lips were cracked and dry, and his voice was fading to a whisper.

"Don't say any more," he said, placing his hand on the boy's shoulder. "You have suffered enough. Let me think. We have to get you out of here. What's your name?"

The boy smiled. "I'm Sol."

Freddie held out his hand. "Pleased to

meet you, Sol! And my name is…"

"… Trinity," the boy interrupted, "we know who you are. The prophecy has come true."

Freddie smiled. "Well, yes, I guess you could say that! But anyway, for now, you can just call me Freddie."

The boy threw his arms around Freddie's neck and hugged him tightly, almost pushing him over!

"Thank you Freddie. Thank you with all of our hearts!"

"OK, OK," Freddie replied, steadying himself, "we're not safe yet! It was going to be hard enough to get two of us out without being seen… let alone all of us! I need to come up with a plan… let me think for a moment."

Freddie sat down and held his head in his hands. Yes, he could use his power to deal with some of the soldiers… but all of them… on his own? It was a big ask! Maybe he could hold them off long enough for all the children to escape? Maybe he had no other option? He turned toward Seth to let him know what he intended to do.

"Seth, I'll go first... you can..."

Freddie paused and stared at the sight that met his eyes.

The children were slowly moving toward his new friend. Seth stood in front of them, his arms outstretched, his hands cupped together. Freddie watched spellbound as a fountain of pure, fresh water sprung from Seth's hands and tumbled into the open mouths of the children gathering around him. It was an amazing, beautiful sight.

Seth looked at Freddie and shrugged his shoulders.

"I don't know how it happened," he said, "I just wanted to help them and then I felt this sudden urge to put my hands together and... and... water!"

Freddie smiled. Seth had already discovered his special power!

"Yeah," said Freddie, "I was going to get to that bit! Don't worry, we all have these powers... you, me and Myla. She can control fire, whilst I can... well... move things. You must have some control over water, I guess?"

Seth continued to refresh the parched mouths of the children gathering around him. They looked like they hadn't had anything to drink for days... maybe weeks?

Freddie walked over and sat beside him.

"This kind of changes things," he began, placing his arm around Seth's shoulders. "I think we might all be able to get out of here. Listen carefully, this is what we're going to do."

Seth hung on his every word as Freddie outlined their escape plan.

"But what if I can't do it?" said Seth. Freddie could see the doubt in his eyes.

"You can, Seth," he said, "you just have to go with the feeling. When the time comes, you will know what to do, trust me."

Freddie turned to Sol. "Right, I want you to get everyone lined up at the door. Tell the older children to take hold of the little ones and not to let go. Stay here until you hear my call, OK? When I say the word, all of you run for your lives toward the South Gate, and head for an old barn behind the trees, dead ahead of you. We'll meet you there. Got it?"

Sol nodded and immediately began to organize the children just as Freddie had ordered.

He turned back to Seth.

"OK, this is it Seth, remember what I told you. Let's go."

Sol glanced up at the door and watched as they both slipped out, into the open courtyard.

16

Tarin had almost reached the bedroom door when the balcony doors slammed shut. He stopped still. How had he forgotten to check out there?

He rushed over and flung them open. Nothing. It must have been the wind.

As he turned to go back inside, he thought he heard a rustling sound coming from down below. He leaned his head over the edge of the balcony wall.

The girl was about half way down, clinging to a vine that grew up the south wall.

"Stop!" he bellowed.

The girl glanced up, her face flushed with fear. As quick as a flash she swung around, gripping tightly to the vine with one hand and raising the other above her head.

The fireball exploded right in front of him, smashing a gaping hole in the stone balcony, sending him staggering backwards.

Partly dazed, he got to his feet and

picked up a large chunk of jagged stone. Peering over the edge once more he saw the girl frantically continuing her descent. He hurled the rock toward her.

She glanced up again and Tarin watched as she swung herself to one side to avoid it. But she was too slow. The rock crashed into her shoulder with an almighty crack. The girl let out a piercing scream as she desperately tried to hang on to the vine with one hand.

Tarin gave the ghost of a grin as she clung on for her life, slightly swaying in the breeze.

He was about to pick up another rock when, slowly, the girl lifted her head and looked up at him, her crippled arm hanging lifeless by her side. For a few seconds their eyes met. She looked finished. Tarin smiled, his features twisting into an evil leer.

The girl let go of the vine and fell.

~ ~ ~

The sight that met Freddie's eyes was one of complete confusion and panic. There were soldiers everywhere, upturning market stalls, ripping doors off hinges and rushing around, swords drawn at the ready. Strangely, the ordinary townsfolk were nowhere to be seen. In the middle of the courtyard, a mammoth brute of a man stood barking orders. Freddie knew that they had to act quickly. It was now or never. Secretly, he prayed that Seth would know what to do.

"Hey! Fatso! Over here!" Freddie yelled.

The man giving the orders turned with a quick snap of his thick shoulders. Their eyes met. Freddie watched as his broad-carved face twisted in anger.

"There they are! Get them!" His lips moved as if he would spit!

Freddie, feeling his chest tighten, thrust his arms forward and watched as the jet of black smoke struck the ogre, sending him reeling backwards and knocking over several guards behind him in the process.

"Now, Seth!" Freddie screamed.

Seth raised his arms. Nothing happened!

The brute lumbered to his feet, his face red with fury. The soldiers started running toward them.

"Seth!" Freddie shrieked, "do it now!"

Seth's expression darkened, his eyes fixed on the advancing foe.

A savage torrent burst forth from his hands, sending a monstrous wall of water crashing into their attackers, sweeping them off their feet in a tumbling cartwheel of limbs and spray.

Freddie jerked his head toward the dungeon door.

"Now, Sol! Run for your lives!"

The door burst open and Sol tore out, the children in tow as they scampered toward the South Gate as if their lives depended upon it!

Seth continued to swamp their floundering enemy, pushing them further and further back, whilst Freddie picked off any stragglers who managed to stumble to their feet amidst the cascading chaos.

Glancing briefly behind him, Freddie noticed the last child disappear through the South Gate.

"Keep it going, Seth," he shouted, "they're all out. Walk backwards with me toward the gate and when we're safely through, run for it!"

Seth gave a brief nod, his resolve fixed and unbroken.

Edging their way slowly backwards, a thought flashed into Freddie's mind. Should they go in search of Myla? But what if she had already got out… with the Stone? He decided against pushing their luck, hoping with all his heart that he would find her waiting for him in the barn as they had arranged.

As they reached the gate, Seth lowered his arms and the waters ceased. For a moment they both stood motionless, surveying the bedlam before them. It was as if the place had been hit by a tidal wave. Wretched, drenched bodies and fragments of wood and fabric lay scattered all around.

Freddie looked at Seth and they exchanged a brief, silent smile. There was no need for words. They turned on their heels and ran.

~ ~ ~

Myla awoke to find herself lying on the ground in a filthy, darkened room. Gradually the memory of seeing Tarin laughing above her as she clung onto the vine came flooding back. The rock had struck her full on the shoulder causing her to let go with one hand. She had desperately tried to lift her free arm to release another fireball but it just wouldn't move.

Now she was in this rotten prison, their captive. Her hands had been bound tightly behind her back with some kind of rough cord that dug sorely into her wrists.

She couldn't remember how she had got there. The fall must have knocked her out. With great difficulty, she just about managed to lift herself up and rest her back against the cold stone wall. She buried her face in her knees as the tears began to trickle down her cheeks.

The sound of a heavy, iron bolt being drawn back made her look up sharply. The solid oak door swung open to reveal a crooked old man with dirty, unkempt grey hair and a large, hooked nose.

Filling the doorway, he looked down at her as if to sting her with his sneer.

"Get up!" he commanded, his upper lip curling grotesquely.

Myla remained squatting on her heels.

"Where am I? Who are you?" she said

quietly, trying to keep her temper, aware of the ringing bells of warning in her aching head.

"Shut up!" he spat furiously, his words like bullets. "Follow me."

Myla, summoning what strength remained in her battered limbs, pushed her self upwards, her back scraping against the rough stone wall. The intense pain in her injured arm and shoulder almost made her cry out, but she was determined not to give the guard the satisfaction of seeing her in pain.

Following closely behind, she tried to size up her chances of escape. She quickly realised that they were probably non-existent! There was no way she could loosen her hands and, without the ability to use the fire, she wasn't going anywhere in a hurry!

The guard stopped at the end of the passage and turned toward her.

"Up there. Follow me!"

Myla hesitated as she peered into a murky stairwell. She couldn't see the top.

"Now... and don't try any of your funny business," he growled.

She started to take the steps, one by one. The air was filled with the stench of rotten fish as the man puffed and panted in front of her.

The warder stopped at the top and pushed open a heavy wooden door.

"In there.'

Myla recoiled as she squeezed past his sweaty, repulsive body. Once through the door she was met by another guard who ushered her along a finely decorated landing until they arrived at a large, ornate black door.

He knocked three times. As the door opened, the guard shoved her through with so much force she almost fell in.

Quickly gathering her thoughts, she glanced around the room. Lord Tarin and Lady Thalia sat at one end, glaring at her. She noticed that one of Thalia's arms was bandaged and that one side of her face was heavily bruised. Her expression was thunderous, overflowing with bile and hate.

Tarin stood up and walked slowly toward her.

"So," he began, with unconcealed contempt, "the little princess returns! It's been so long since we last saw you!"

Myla stared wordlessly across at him, her heart pounding.

Tarin continued. "And such a shame that you are on your own. How I wish your friends could be here to join in the fun!"

"Oh just get one with it, brother," Thalia interrupted, with savage irritation.

Tarin raised a hand. "All in good time, my sister, all in good time." He now stood face to face with Myla.

"However, I think you can solve that little problem for us, can't you?"

Myla wasn't sure exactly what he was getting at, but she could tell from his mood that whatever was coming wasn't going to be good!

"It's very simple really," he said, circling her slowly like an eagle eyeing its prey, "you are going to tell me where I can find your two little friends. I was most disappointed that they decided to leave... and what a mess they left behind... very irritating."

Myla's heart jumped in her chest. So Freddie and Seth had managed to get out?

"So, what do you say?" His voice was suddenly flat.

Myla swallowed hard, squared her shoulders and met his icy gaze straight on, a blue flame of defiance in her eyes.

"Never."

For a long moment they glared at each other in waiting silence.

Thalia broke the tension. "This is pointless," she announced, her voice taking on a grave note that frightened Myla. "Bring the old woman in and let's get this over and done with. I'm growing tired of this girl's insolence."

The door burst open as two burly guards emerged, half dragging a hunched figure between them. Myla swung around. A sudden icy fear twisted around her heart.

"Gunda!"

Gunda glanced up, her face bleak with sorrow as silent tears streamed down her cheeks.

Tarin stepped forward, grabbed Gunda by the hair and jerked her roughly toward him, spinning her around.

Myla stared in horror as he locked his arm firmly around Gunda's neck, the glinting dagger teasing the puffy, pink flesh of her throat.

"No!" she screamed.

Tarin roared. "Either you tell me right now where your friends are hiding or, the Gods help me, I will slit the old crone's throat from ear to ear. Do you understand?"

Gunda locked her eyes on Myla, her gaze unwavering.

"Don't you dare, my love, don't you dare!"

Myla tried to speak, but the words were locked in her throat.

Gunda sensed from the stricken

expression on Myla's face that time was running out. Summoning all the strength remaining in her body, she jerked her elbows violently backwards into Tarin's stomach.

Tarin recoiled with a howl, dropping the dagger. Gunda wrestled herself free and ran toward Myla. Reaching behind, she started to tug wildly at the binding around her wrists.

"Let's get this off and then you can send these devils back to the fiery hell from whence they came!"

The guards looked eagerly at their master for instruction.

"Leave her! She's mine!"

Myla's eyes widened in terror as he stooped to pick up the dagger and started to move toward them, his face cruelly twisted, full of hatred.

"Gunda, look out!" Myla shrieked.

"Won't take long, my sweet, just can't seem to..."

A haunting silence filled the room.

Gunda suddenly grasped the front of

Myla's dress and looked up at her, staring blankly, her mouth wide open. Slowly, her grip weakened and she slumped to the floor face down.

Myla stared in horror at the dagger buried deep in Gunda's back. Thick, red blood seeped from the wound, rapidly pooling at her side.

One of the guards knelt down and pressed his fingers against Gunda's neck. He looked up at Tarin and nodded. Thalia stood beside him, smiling.

A shadowy sneer hovered above Tarin's heavy mouth.

Myla launched herself at him, trying desperately to free her hands. However, the binding remained fast.

Kicking and screaming furiously, she sunk her teeth into his hand as he tried to fight her off. He cried out in pain.

Thalia stepped back as several guards jumped in and tried to pull her off their leader, grabbing hold of her hair and shoulders.

She continued to struggle frantically until a blinding blow to the head knocked her to the floor.

Tarin stood over her, clasping his bleeding hand. In a fury he leapt onto her, taking hold of her throat with an iron grip. Myla felt his merciless fingers tighten as she fought for breath.

"Stop!" Thalia cried, and with the help of one of the guards, managed to pull her brother off.

Myla rolled to one side, gasping for breath and shivering violently.

Tarin turned angrily on his sister. "Why did you stop me? The girl deserves to die!"

She lifted her chin and boldly met his gaze. "Why settle for one when we can have all three? Patience, my brother, I have an idea that will have them all begging for mercy." Her dark eyes grew wild. Tarin shrank back. She frightened him sometimes.

"Take her back to the dungeon," Thalia ordered, "the rats have missed her!"

The guards grabbed Myla and started

to drag her to the door. She fixed her eyes on Tarin.

"I hate you, I hate you!" she screamed, her eyes blazing with fury.

She continued to struggle all the way back to the dungeon, her heart refusing to believe what her mind was telling her. Gunda was dead?

The guards flung her inside and slammed the door.

She landed with a jolt, face down in the stinking dirt. In the darkened silence, she finally gave in to the compulsive sobs that shook her, and wept as though her heart would surely break.

17

Freddie sat cross-legged on the barn floor, idly chewing on a stick of straw, deep in thought. It was now well over an hour since they had escaped from Baril-Azur and still there was no sign of Myla. He was in two minds as to what to do next. To go back to the city seemed far too risky. Everyone would be looking for them. And, he didn't even know if he would find her there! Maybe she had got out before him, found the barn empty and gone on home?

In the stairwell, she had promised that she would meet him at the barn in an hour, hadn't she? But he'd been with Sol and the children for at least that long... plus the battle to escape... surely, Myla must have gone on without him. It seemed the most likely thing to have happened.

Seth walked over and sat down beside him.

"The children are hungry. How are we going to feed them all? I can give them water, but they need to eat!"

Freddie sighed. "I know. Look, Seth, I've been thinking. Myla must have got out before us and made her way home. I think we should leave. This place could be crawling with soldiers any minute... I'm surprised they haven't come already."

Seth nodded. "I'll tell Sol to spread the word... but what about food?"

"There's fruit in the Great Wood. It'll take us a while to get there, but when we do there'll be plenty for everyone."

Trying to ignore the knot forming in his stomach, Freddie got up and went outside to check that the coast was clear. Within a few minutes, they all set off for home, Freddie and Seth leading the way, the children following in twos with strict instructions to stay in line, and Sol bringing up the rear.

They had only walked a few steps when Freddie suddenly raised his arm and the line stopped.

"What's wrong?" asked Seth, noticing the puzzled look on his face.

"Nothing," Freddie replied, "It's the horse."

"What horse?"

"The horse Myla tied up here, when we arrived earlier this morning. It's gone!"

They looked at each other.

"She must have taken it," said Seth. "If she thought we were ahead of her, she would have taken the horse to catch us up… yes?"

Freddie thought for a moment and then nodded in agreement. It was quite possible. He smiled, patting Seth on the shoulder gently.

"Yeah, you're probably right. Come on, let's carry on."

As they set off again, Seth's foot struck something hard and he fell flat on his face.

"Hey, careful there," said Freddie, "the path can be pretty bumpy… keep your eyes down. Are you ok?"

Seth got to his feet, dusting himself down. "Sorry, I just didn't see that rock. I'll be more careful."

Freddie glanced at the object that had

caused Seth to stumble.

"Wait a minute!" He bent down and picked up a cream coloured cloth bag.

"What is it?" Seth asked.

Nervously, Freddie tugged at the cord around the neck and peered inside. He couldn't believe his eyes!

"What is it?" Seth repeated, getting excited. Sol and the children gathered around. Freddie put his hand into the bag and pulled out the Aura Stone. His expression stalled and grew serious.

"You know what this means?" He bit his lip, trying to keep his voice casual.

They all stared at him.

"It means that Myla *was* here. She went back for the Stone and, well, here it is!"

Seth looked confused. "Yes, but, why would she leave it here?"

Freddie thought for a moment before replying. It was a good question. Why would Myla have risked going back for the Stone, only to leave it in a bag in the forest?

"She must have put it down to untie the

horse... and, well, something must have startled her and she galloped away... I don't know, but without any doubt, she was here, which means she got out!" His face broke into a wide grin.

He returned the Aura Stone to its bag and dropped it into his backpack.

They continued for a while in silence, the troop following dutifully behind, until Freddie decided it was a good time to find out a bit more about his new friend.

"Where are you from Seth?"

"A little village in Shropshire, called Nescliffe. My dad runs the pub there."

"Must be fun living in a pub?" said Freddie, with a smile.

"Yeah, it's OK," Seth shrugged, matter-of-factly, "gets a bit noisy sometimes, but I never run out of crisps!"

They both laughed.

"So, how did you get here, you know, in this place?" Freddie had wanted to ask him this question since they'd first met.

"I'm not sure," he replied, his voice

trembling a little, "I don't really remember much about it."

Freddie wasn't sure if he should continue. "Do you remember a cloud or something, like a dark shadowy shape?"

For a moment he thought Seth wasn't going to answer, but then he nodded reluctantly.

"It's OK," Freddie said reassuringly, "to be honest, I'm still struggling to make sense of all this myself!"

"Tell me what you know," Seth asked earnestly, "please?"

As they walked on, Freddie related everything that Myla, Gunda and Hadwin had told him. It didn't answer all Seth's questions, but at least he now knew a bit more about what was happening.

The sun was creeping toward the horizon when they reached the edge of the forest. Nothing but the empty plain extended before their eyes. Far off in the distance, Freddie thought he could just about make out the leafy treetops of the Great Wood.

He turned to address the group. "We must wait here until nightfall. We'll cross the plains under cover of darkness. Make yourselves comfortable and try to get some sleep. It's going to be a long night."

They started to settle down just off the track amongst the trees. Some of the younger children were crying whilst the older ones tried their best to comfort them. Freddie guessed that their tears fell because they were hungry. He hoped that they might fall asleep to bring at least some temporary relief.

A young girl who couldn't have been any more than five years old wandered over to him. She had a heart-shaped face with large blue eyes, vivid and questioning. Tilting her head to one side, she stopped and studied him closely.

"Are you a king?" Her voice was soft and almost tuneful.

Freddie smiled apologetically. "No, I'm sorry. I'm not a king!"

There was a pause as she observed him

suspiciously. He noticed that her eyes sparkled curiously.

"Well, I think you are a king!" she declared, with an air of proud defiance.

Freddie tried to suppress a gurgle of laughter. "OK, I guess that means I really am a king then! Thank you for letting me know!"

The little girl grinned shamelessly as she swept a deep curtsey and said, "you're very welcome, your highness!"

She knelt down beside him. "Is that your king's crown?"

"Where? Where is my crown?" he replied cheerily, playing along with her.

She gave an exasperated sigh. "In there!" She pointed at his backpack. "It must be very shiny!"

Freddie glanced at his bag. To his astonishment it had started to glow brightly. Quickly he opened the flap, releasing a beam of light, which circled above their heads and then descended rapidly, forming a luminous dome around their party.

He threw his arms around the little girl and drew her tightly to his chest.

Two North Riders raced into the clearing and pulled their mounts to a rearing halt, their hooves plunging into the dust. Freddie held his breath. His heart hammered furiously against his ribs. One of the Riders was looking straight at him. They had been caught. Freddie searched his gravely face for a reaction. There was none.

A voice rang out, loaded with anger and frustration. It came from the other Rider.

“Well, they’re not here. Maybe we should go back and circle around again. They can’t have got far.”

The first Rider continued to stare directly at Freddie, a slight hesitation in his hawk-like eyes. Then he turned sharply to his companion.

“Yeah, nothing here. Come on!”

Freddie watched with disbelief as the two Riders swung their horses and galloped away, leaving a billowing cloud of dust in their wake.

Gradually the protective dome around them began to dissolve. Freddie looked at his backpack. The Stone had stopped glowing.

The little girl pushed herself away from him, rubbing her eyes fretfully with the back of her hand. Then, with a face alight with astonishment, she tossed back her long dark hair and proclaimed for all to hear, "That is the best king's crown I have ever seen!"

~ ~ ~

The remainder of the journey, although long and tiring, passed without further incident. Freddie couldn't believe how careless he had been earlier by not finding a safer hiding place. He had placed the whole group in danger. The North Rider had looked straight at him! There was no way he couldn't have seen him? If it hadn't have been for the Aura Stone encasing them all in some kind of invisible, protective bubble, who knows what might have happened to them?

Myla had been right. The Stone truly did possess incredible powers, much more than they originally thought. Freddie vowed there and then to protect it at all costs.

They had crossed the Plains when darkness fell, the younger children strapped still sleeping to the backs of the older ones. The little girl never left Freddie's side! He learnt that her name was Calli and that she was actually six years old, although she looked younger. For as long as she could remember she'd worked in the kitchens at Baril-Azur. That was until the day her mother and father disappeared. She didn't know where they had gone. That night, some guards had come and taken her and her little brother away, telling them that their parents didn't want them anymore.

They were thrown into the dungeon with the other children. Her little brother had died soon after. Sol had been really kind to her and comforted her as best he could. She called him Daddy-Sol!

When they reached the Great Wood,

they had stopped and dined out on the abundant fruits of the forest. Freddie had watched the children, happier now as they devoured their midnight feast. The swell of sorrow in his heart was beyond tears. The forgotten children. How many more of them were there? From what Sol had said, there could be hundreds… maybe even thousands?

Now, they were almost home. Their mission had been successful. The Aura Stone had been returned to South Tellur and, as an unexpected bonus, they had rescued some desperate children from a certain, dreadful fate. Freddie couldn't wait to see Myla again to share the stories of their daring adventure together.

As they neared the village, the rising sun only just beginning to burn away the morning mist, the rooftops of Barras came into view. Freddie half expected to see Myla and Gunda running to meet them.

The houses cast dusky, chill shadows over the roughly paved road as they approached Gunda and Hadwin's house.

Despite the early hour, the atmosphere seemed unusually quiet.

As they entered the front gate, Freddie told Seth to gather the children in the garden and wait for him. Feeling a sudden shiver of apprehension as he opened the door, Freddie stepped inside.

The living room was cold and quiet. He thought Gunda would have been up by now, as usual, busying herself with breakfast preparations and her early morning chores. They must all still be sleeping.

"Hello?.... Myla?" He stood still and waited.

No reply.

His chest felt tight and his heart began to beat with an uneasy rhythm as he hurried toward their bedroom. He swung the door open.

The three single beds were all neatly made, just as they had left them. For a moment he couldn't move, trying to work out where they might all be. Suddenly a voice from behind startled him. He turned quickly.

"Freddie? Is that you?"

Before him stood an older woman with wiry red hair, dusted with white. Her face was pale and strained and her large blue eyes were filled with sadness.

"Who... who are you?" he asked.

"I am Matilde, the wife of Aarun the Elder."

"Matilde? What... where's Gunda?" He struggled to keep his voice steady.

"Oh Freddie," she replied, moving toward him, "she hasn't returned. I'm worried about her. Where's Myla?"

Where's Myla? His head began to swirl. The question came like a blow to his stomach, knocking the breath out of him. Myla wasn't there. He struggled to gather his thoughts, his brow creased with worry.

"She....," he faltered, "she's supposed to be here... she left before us..."

Matilde weakly shook her head. "Hadwin is here, but he is badly hurt. He's in his room. I have been looking after him."

Hadwin? But, if Hadwin was here, why

wasn't Gunda? Freddie pushed past Matilde and headed straight for the main bedroom. He was about to go in when Seth appeared at the front door.

"Is everything OK?'

Freddie paused. "No, Seth. Everything is not OK! They're not here... Myla and Gunda. I'm going to talk to Hadwin. Come with me."

As they entered, Hadwin wearily opened his eyes, struggling to focus.

"The Gods be praised," he gasped, his voice barely a whisper in the stillness of the room, "Freddie, my lad, you're safe!"

Freddie knelt beside the bed and took hold of Hadwin's hand.

"Yes... but, I don't understand." He didn't know where to begin. "Where's Gunda? You left us in the Wood."

Hadwin took a deep breath, trying to steady his voice, and started to tell him what had happened. After Gunda had left him, he must have fallen asleep. He wasn't sure how long for, but he'd been awakened by the sound of voices close by. Lying there, rigid with fear, he'd listened. To his immense relief he'd recognized one of the voices and cried out. It was Aarun! He was on a night hunt with some others from Mirell. They had passed through Barras on their way to the Great Wood to drop off Matilde as she wanted to wait there for her friend's safe return from Baril-Azur.

Aarun and the men had made him as comfortable as they could and, realizing that he needed medical attention as soon as possible, had brought him back here.

"But, you should have caught up with Gunda on your way back?" Freddie was still struggling to make sense of it all.

"We thought that too," Hadwin sighed, wiping away a tear with the back of his hand. He closed his eyes.

A chilled silence filled the room.

Matilde reached over and adjusted Hadwin's pillow. "We should let him rest now. The Doctor will be here soon."

Returning to the living room, Freddie

slumped into a chair and buried his head in his hands. How could he have been so careless... so stupid? He had left Myla behind, alone. Anything could have happened to her! And now Gunda was missing too.

Seth shifted uncomfortably. "Maybe... she... Myla, might have taken a different path? She could be here any minute?"

Freddie's eyes shot up to meet his.

"We left her, Seth! We could have saved her, but we left her!" His mouth twisted with pain.

"But the Stone? She must have got out? And the horse was..."

Freddie sprang to his feet, his face flushed with anger. "Was what, Seth? Was gone? It probably just ran off! Can't you see that?" His voice rose to a cry of anguish. "None of this makes any sense, Seth! All I know is that Myla is not here and it's my fault!"

Seth's head dropped as he turned away and walked slowly toward the window. There was an awkward silence. Freddie realised that he had been too sharp in his reply. He walked up beside him and rested his hand on Seth's shoulder.

"I'm sorry," he mumbled, shuffling his feet uncomfortably, "I'm not cross with you."

Seth nodded. "It's OK, I understand."

"We must work out what we're going to do," Freddie said, "you know, how we're going to find Myla and Gunda?"

Seth continued to look out the window.

"Yes, we will... you should speak to Hadwin again to work out a plan. But first, look at all those poor kids... what are we going to do with them?"

Freddie watched as Calli busied herself in the garden collecting a bunch of wild flowers, her face alight with happiness.

Matilde bustled over to see what they were looking at.

"Mercy me!" she cried, "where did all those babies come from?"

Freddie explained how they had found the children and managed to get them out of

Baril-Azur. Matilde listened with disbelief as she learned of the reasons why the children had been imprisoned. Her eyes filling with tears, she wasted no time in taking charge.

"First we must feed the poor little beggars," she said, beginning to search through the kitchen cupboards.

"Freddie, you two must go around the village asking for help... I can't manage all this on my own.... and ask for donations of food, clothing... anything you think might be useful. We're going to have to find beds for them all too... oh my goodness!"

The response from the villagers was incredible. By early afternoon, the garden was a flurry of activity as the children, freshly fed and watered, were billeted out to homes in the village. The whole scene reminded Freddie of what he had learnt at school about evacuees in the Second World War. It must have been just like this!

Calli had insisted on staying with them. The irresistible sight of her large, pleading eyes filling with tears quickly made them realize that there was little point in arguing, so they agreed. After all, they did have a spare bed... Myla's bed. It would be alright for now, Freddie thought, just until Myla returned.

As the last of the children set off with their new families, Matilde noticed three figures on horseback riding into the village.

"It's Aarun!" she cried aloud, "... and he has the Doctor with him. The Gods be praised!" She rushed to greet them.

The three men slid from their saddles and tied the horses to the fence. Aarun stooped and kissed his wife tenderly on the top of her head. As he turned, a sudden feeling of unease gripped Freddie as he watched the old man's expression stall and grow serious.

"We must go inside," he said, in a tone that did not invite question.

Once inside, Aarun mumbled something to one of the men and pointed toward Hadwin's door. As he set off in haste, Freddie realised he must be the doctor.

Aarun then turned toward them.

"This is my brother, Joel," he said, introducing the third man, trying to keep his voice calm with an iron will of effort. "Taking his life into his hands, he managed to steal a horse and escape from Baril-Azur this morning. He must return immediately before they notice him missing"

Freddie recognized him. He was the man who had started a fight in the city courtyard, distracting the guards.

"I'm afraid Joel brings terrible news." Aarun took a deep breath, wiping the sweat from his forehead with the back of his mighty hand.

"Lord Tarin has issued a proclamation."

Freddie felt a tingling stir the hairs at the nape of his neck. He swallowed hard, nervously holding his breath.

"There's no easy way to say this so I'll be straight. Myla has been captured. Tarin has declared that if Freddie and Seth do not surrender within seven days, Myla will be executed."

Freddie grabbed hold of Seth for support as the blood drained from his face and a roaring filled his ears.

"No!" he wailed, his whole body shaking with gut-wrenching sobs. "It's not true!"

Aarun started toward him. Consumed with blind panic, Freddie grabbed his backpack and ran for the door.

"Wait! Freddie!" Aarun tried desperately to stop him, but Freddie was already outside.

Half stumbling, he raced to the gate, yanked the reins free of the fence and leapt onto Aarun's horse.

The beast reared up as he mounted, its hooves plunging into the dirt. He heaved on the reins to wheel it around and then kicked hard. The horse darted forward. Freddie hung on with all his strength as they galloped toward the Great Wood.

Aarun and Joel leapt onto the other horses and quickly gave chase. They had to stop him!

Freddie bent low over the mare's neck

to avoid the gnarled claws of overhanging branches. At full speed he raced along the narrow, uneven path, his face pulled tight against the horse's pulsing neck. Aarun and Joel remained in hot pursuit.

He had to get to Baril-Azur to save Myla. This should never have happened. It was all his fault!

With both eyes shut tight and his knuckles white from clinging to the reins, Freddie did not see the dark, swirling cloud directly ahead of him.

The horse, sensing fear as they were almost upon it, savagely dug its hooves into the soil in an attempt to stop. Freddie opened his eyes, fighting desperately to hold on. But it was too late.

The mare veered sideways, fighting the bit, and threw him from the saddle. There was nothing he could do.

With an ear-splitting scream, Freddie plunged head first into the gaping jaws of the waiting shadow.

18

Squinting as the sun broke into his eyes, Freddie lay still, staring up at the pale blue sky. A familiar voice cut slowly through the pulsing in his head.

"Freddie? Come along my duck, it's time we were getting home."

Rubbing his eyes to clear his head, he tried to focus on the figure standing over him.

"Jump to it m'lad, we've got bread to bake!" Aunt Mags broke into a wide, friendly smile.

Aunt Mags!

Freddie leapt to his feet, gasping for breath. He felt as if he were drowning!

"Aunt Mags! What are you… where…?" The shock caused the words to wedge in his throat.

She laughed. "My, you look like you've seen a ghost! You've been staring at the sails too long I think!"

Freddie's eyes darted upward at the

windmill towering over him. The pit of his stomach churned as the sudden realization of what had happened hit him.

"No! I have to save Myla! I have to save her!" he shrieked, grabbing Aunt Mags roughly by the arms.

She stepped back in alarm. "Careful, lad! What on earth has got into you?"

Freddie was distraught. How was he going to make her understand? Would she even believe him? Somehow, he had to calm down and think carefully.

"Come on now, let's get you home." She took his arm and led him back to the car.

The short journey home passed in silence. Freddie sat half dazed, his mind in turmoil. Where to begin? Even if Aunt Mags thought he was mad, he had to tell her everything! She had to believe him! He had to go back and save Myla!

Back in the kitchen, Aunt Mags set a piping hot mug of tea on the table in front of him and sat down.

"Right, get that inside you. You'll feel

better I'm sure. Touch of sunstroke I think. A nice cup of tea cures all ills."

The words started to tumble freely from Freddie's mouth.

"Steady on, slow down lad, slow down." She placed her hand softly on his arm.

His eyes filled with tears as his heart bounded into his throat.

"You have to believe me, Aunt Mags," he pleaded, "you just have to!"

Her homely face took on a warm smile. "Why don't you just start at the beginning and tell me whatever it is that's so troubling you, my love?"

And so he did. He began by telling her about the shadow at the windmill and then waking up in the Wood. How Hadwin and his sister Gunda had taken him in, and all about Myla. Myla's power… and his power!

When he struggled to keep his voice steady, his aunt just gave a reassuring nod and encouraged him to continue. Never once did she interrupt or ask any questions. As a consequence, Freddie's confidence grew, enabling him to remember even the finer details. He told her about their raid on Baril-Azur to get the Aura Stone from Tarin and Thalia… finding Seth… and how they had rescued the forgotten children. Time slipped by as his story unwound until eventually he reached a point where he didn't know what else he could say.

For a moment they sat in silence. Freddie searched her face, trying desperately to read into her thoughts.

"You think I'm making it all up, don't you?" He bit his lip, trying to hold back the tears.

Slowly, Aunt Mags eased herself out of her chair and walked over to the kitchen window. Her voice came as a whisper in the silence.

"No, Freddie, I don't. I don't think you are making it all up." She turned to face him, wiping the corner of her eye with a lace handkerchief.

Freddie simply stared at her, his mouth wide open in astonishment.

"So… so you believe me? Really?"

She met his gaze squarely. "Yes, I believe you. In fact, more than that. I know you are telling the truth."

For a moment, Freddie was speechless. She knew? How? He didn't understand.

Tears welled in her eyes choking her voice. "I… I know about Telluria. I was there myself once, long ago. I knew Hadwin and Gunda."

And then it hit him, like he'd been struck by a train. He could see it in her eyes.

"It's you, isn't it," he gasped, "you are the girl Hadwin fell in love with?"

"I was very young," Aunt Mags began, "… nineteen or twenty, I think. I'd been away at University and had come back here for the holidays. One day I was out walking when the shadow took me… just like you described."

"And then you met Hadwin and Gunda?" he asked, eager for her to tell him everything.

Aunt Mags gave a slight shake of her

head. "Not at first, no. I was very frightened. I wandered for several days until I came across a small village. Fortunately, the baker was looking for some extra help so I took a job in return for food and lodging. Hadwin was the delivery lad. Soon after that we started courting and... well, one thing led to another and yes, we fell in love."

Her voice trailed off as she once again dabbed her eyes.

Freddie struggled to find the right words. She was clearly finding this very difficult to talk about.

"But... you didn't marry him... Gunda told me that you left him?"

"The shadow returned, Freddie... the day before our wedding. It broke my heart. Even now I think about him every day and wonder what might have been. I gave up searching for the shadow long ago, hoping against hope that I might one day be able to go back... but it never came."

Freddie's heart sank. Was she trying to tell him that he would never see Myla again?

"No," he cried, his eyes overflowing, "we have to go back... we have to save Myla... and you have to be with Hadwin again!"

"Oh Freddie, I'm so sorry! I don't know what to say." He looked shattered. Heartbroken. She wrapped her arms around him as the tears once again began to fall.

For several minutes she just held him tight, until he softly pushed her away, his eyes swollen with grief.

"We can't give up, Aunt Mags!" he said. "In seven days they are going to execute Myla. We have to find a way to go back. There must be something we've missed?"

Aunt Mags gently took hold of his hand. "When I was a young girl, your grandfather used to tell me incredible stories set in a mystery land, far away... a place that could only be reached through a secret gateway."

Freddie looked up. "The shadow?"

"Possibly... I don't know. When I was about fifteen, my father started to... well, shall I say, forget things, and within a few months... he didn't even know who I was."

Freddie looked confused. "OK, so what are you saying?"

Aunt Mags took a deep breath. "Well, after the shadow brought me back, I went to visit him... we had moved him into a care home... and I just sat by his bedside and told him all about Telluria. As I was leaving, something strange happened..."

Freddie's eyes widened. "And? ..."

She continued, her voice dropping almost to a whisper. "As I was leaving, he called my name... the first time he'd spoken my name in four years. As I turned back toward him, he sat up, looked me straight in the eye and said, 'you will see Hadwin again.' And then, he lay back and closed his eyes."

Freddie was struggling to catch on to what she was actually saying. "OK, but why was that strange? So he remembered your name... but... I don't understand!"

Aunt Mags leant forward. "Well, Freddie, the strange thing is this. With everything I'd told him about Telluria, I hadn't actually mentioned Hadwin by name!"

Freddie thought for a moment. "So, what you're saying is, he must have known about Telluria?"

"Yes, exactly! And been there too!"

Freddie's heartbeat began to quicken.

"So what else did he say? You must have asked him?"

A look of sadness spread slowly across her face. "Yes, I did, I begged him to tell me more, but he never spoke another word... and a week later, he passed away."

Freddie sat back slowly, folding his arms. His mind was racing.

"I just think," she continued, "... well, it just seemed like he was trying to tell me something... that he knew that one day, I would go back. So, maybe there is a way? It's just that I've searched and searched for so long..."

Freddie didn't know what to think. It was all so odd, but, one thing was for sure... he felt a faint glimmer of hope... maybe there was a chance?

"Anyway," Aunt Mags declared,

standing up, "we must have some supper and then get to bed. It's almost ten o'clock! You must be starving… and tired out I'll bet?"

He couldn't remember when he'd last eaten. Was it in the Great Wood?

Together they set about preparing dinner. Toad-in-the-hole. It was delicious!

After they'd cleared away and washed up, Aunt Mags switched off the light and Freddie followed her into the hallway. She paused and looked up lovingly at the portrait of her father on the wall.

"Oh, Horace Cherry, my dear father," she smiled, wistfully, "what were you trying to tell me? What secrets lie behind those silent eyes?"

They both stood still for a moment, gazing intently at the image of the proud, strong man staring back at them.

"Right, young man, bed time! Tomorrow is a new day!" She began to climb the stairs.

He was just about to follow her up when something caught the corner of his eye.

"Wait!" he cried. "Look!"

Aunt Mags came back down and they both stopped still, staring at his backpack, which was leaning against the wall underneath the portrait. It was glowing!

“The Aura Stone!” Freddie gasped, “I brought it with me!”

Then something extraordinary started to happen. The inscription at the base of the portrait began to change.

They couldn’t believe their eyes! As the light from the Aura Stone lit up the portrait, some of the letters in the inscription started to glow!

Freddie began to read aloud.

“I**f our** strength fails...”

The word ‘four’ appeared to leap out at him, and it was shining!

... “at lea**st one s**tands **up**...”

Now the words ‘stones’ and ‘up’ burned brightly...

... “for pride and gai**n, or th**e card**s I** **de**al will lose the je**wel, l**eaving me lost.”

North.... side....well!

Freddie carried on reading. “I**f in d**oubt

stay calm, apply the mind."

Find map!

They stared at each other in utter amazement, then back at the inscription, their eyes on stalks! Freddie repeated the glowing words aloud.

"Four stones up north side well find map!"

Aunt Mags drew a long, deep breath. "Well knock me down with a feather, my lad! It's a clue!"

Freddie could barely breathe. "What does it mean?"

"There's an old, dry well at the bottom of the garden! I suggest we go and look."

Grabbing a torch from the hall cupboard, they raced through the kitchen and out the back door.

"Where is it?" Freddie asked.

"Follow me lad!" she replied, and they hurried off down the garden.

As they neared the bottom, the torchlight fell upon an old brick well, overgrown with years of creeping ivy.

"So, which way's north?" Freddie shouted, as they reached the well.

"Um, this side I think," Aunt Mags replied, a little out of breath, "No, wait, the back of the house faces east... so... it must be the other side."

Together they rounded the well and began to pull frantically at the ivy. Soon, rough, rusty bricks came into view. Freddie started to grope wildly at them. Aunt Mags caught his arm firmly.

"Wait, lad... four stones up... count them."

Freddie tugged at the undergrowth at the base to reveal the bricks.

"One, two, three, four.... Here it is, this one!"

Using his fingertips he began to scrape frantically at the flaky mortar surrounding the brick. Gradually it began to crumble.

"Steady on lad," Aunt Mags whispered, "mind your fingers!"

After a few minutes, he managed to scrape all around the brick. Pushing his fingers into the narrow gap, he gave it a sharp tug. The brick shifted slightly. Slowly and steadily, rocking it from side to side, he managed to pull it all the way out.

They both held their breath as he reached inside the dark, rectangular hole.

"I can't feel anything," he said with frustration, "there's nothing.... no, wait... I think I've found something."

His fingertips closed around something soft and, very carefully, he pulled it out.

Aunt Mags shone the torch on it. "What is it?"

Freddie held the object nervously in his hands. "I don't know... it's tied up... I think it's some kind of paper. I think it's the map!"

Aunt Mags stood up. "Come on. Back to the house!"

As soon as they got to the kitchen, she switched on the light and Freddie untied the ribbon, unrolled the scroll and spread it out on the table.

"It *is* a map, just like the words said!"

They both stared at it, their eyes

searching desperately for some kind of clue.

It was made of a yellow parchment, stained with age. There was an outline of an area that Freddie didn't recognize, with crisscross lines over it, like a grid. A few words had been crudely written here and there in a scratchy hand.

"It's Kent!" Aunt Mags declared, "It's a map of Kent... look, there's Shadoxhurst... and that's my house... there!" She pointed at an 'X' in the middle of the map.

Freddie continued to stare at it, hoping that some kind of secret message would suddenly appear. After a few minutes, a frown began to cross his face.

"I don't understand it," he sighed, "... the words... what do they mean?"

Aunt Mags blinked uncomprehendingly. "I don't know. Let me try..."

"Wait!" Freddie interrupted and darted into the hallway.

Quickly he returned, hurried to the table and set the Aura Stone down beside the map.

Nothing happened. They glanced at each other, nervously.

Suddenly, the Aura Stone started to glow again, casting its light over the map. As they gazed spellbound, a dark, hazy object began to appear in one corner.

"Look! It's... it's moving!"

Sure enough, what appeared to be a small, cloudy blot was creeping slowly across the map.

"Oh my sweet heavens!" Aunt Mags suddenly exclaimed in a wild, mad rush. "It's the shadow! The map is showing us where the shadow is!"

Freddie could feel the goosebumps rising on his skin. She was right!

"Where is it now?" The words almost stuck in his throat.

Aunt Mags hunched over the map and examined it closely. The shadow was moving from left to right near the top.

"Well, if that's the house," she said, pointing at the cross in the middle, "then... that must be Canterbury... so, the shadow is just to the north, moving toward the coast. That's, um, maybe twenty miles from here... and moving further away."

"Well, what are we waiting for? Let's go!" Freddie blurted.

Aunt Mags stepped back. He sensed the slight flicker of uncertainty behind her eyes.

"It's too far away. By the time we got there it would have moved out over the sea."

"But what if it doesn't come again? This could be our only chance!" Freddie felt a lump returning to his throat.

"We have to be patient, my love," she said, taking him into her arms. "And have faith! The Aura Stone has given us this wonderful gift tonight... and solved a riddle that I must have read a thousand times! The shadow will come again... and when it does, we'll be ready."

Freddie relaxed a little in the comfort of her warm embrace. She was right... again! Was it only a few hours ago that he had been full of despair? But now, there was a real chance of going back... together, to save

Myla, and Aunt Mags would get to be with Hadwin again. But when would the shadow appear again?

"Right, my love, now we must try to sleep. After all, we are going to need all our strength for what lies ahead. Come on, up we go!"

In his room, he placed the map and the Aura Stone on his bedside table and switched off the lamp. After what seemed like an age he eventually drifted off into an uneasy sleep, waking at least three times during the night to check that the map was still there.

The following day, they took turns watching it, waiting anxiously for the Aura Stone to light up the shadow. Aunt Mags had packed some food and a few other things in her shoulder bag so that they were ready to go at the drop of a hat.

By mid-afternoon, Freddie started to feel a pang of worry. He'd couldn't think about anything else but Myla, imagining how alone and frightened she must feeling, and that he only had seven days to save her… six now! And Seth? Brave Seth! What must he be thinking? He'd only just arrived and now he was on his own. And the forgotten children… what would become of them? Next time he had to be more careful… if there was going to be a next time? He knew that he had underestimated the twins, Tarin and Thalia. There was no future for Telluria under their rule. They were pure evil and they had to be stopped.

He was so lost in his thoughts that at first he didn't notice the gentle glow once more coming from the Aura Stone. Aunt Mags walked into the kitchen and stopped dead still.

"Freddie! The Stone!"

She ran over to the table and together they watched as the light grew brighter. Sure enough, after a minute or two, a small, dark cloud appeared at the left hand side of the map, moving slowly eastwards.

"There!" Freddie almost shrieked, pointing at the ghostly swirl "it's coming again. Where is it now?"

Aunt Mags perched her glasses on her nose and bent over the map.

"It's lower down this time... quick, pass me that ruler!"

Freddie reached across the table, grabbed it and thrust it into her hand.

"Now, watch closely..." Aunt Mags continued, "if I place this just there, where it appeared... in a few moments we'll be able to work out which way it's going... wait a minute, wait a minute... right, now, if I lay the ruler down like this, and...."

As she placed the ruler flat on the map, Freddie couldn't believe his eyes. It passed straight through the X in the middle of the map.

"Oh my goodness, Freddie," she gasped, "it's heading straight for us! I think it will be here in about... um," she studied the map again, "... in about... yes... twenty minutes?"

Freddie took a moment to catch his breath. Swiftly he rolled the map, picked up the Aura Stone and placed them both carefully in his backpack. He wasn't going to leave them behind, that was for sure.

He studied Aunt Mags' face. A strange, eager look flashed in her eyes. They were ready.

"Right then," she announced, trying desperately to appear calm, "let's go outside!"

The sun had begun its slide down the sky, sending pale streamers of purple and orange across the blue of the heavens. Freddie glanced anxiously around, but all he could see were a few wandering shreds of fleecy white cloud moving in a lazy procession.

"I think it will come from over there," said Aunt Mags, "we should see it any minute now." He strained his eyes into the distance to where she pointed. He could just about make out a faint dot on the horizon, but as he fixed his eyes on it, it appeared to spread and blacken as it came nearer.

"There it is," he cried. "I think it is moving quite fast."

Closer and closer it crept. Soon it

emerged through the trees at the end of the next field. They exchanged a quick glance. He could sense the message in her eyes.

"Are you ready for this, my lad?" she asked. Her eyes were alive and blazing.

The shadow was almost upon them. She reached out, took his hand and held it tight. He could feel his heartbeat thudding against his chest.

"Yes, Aunt Mags," he replied, a faint smile finding its way through the mask of uncertainty on his face, "I'm ready!"

Together they walked forward and disappeared into the blackness of the advancing cloud.

Hello Readers!

If you enjoyed this book, please let me know. I love to hear from my readers and I will always answer your emails and letters.

Why not send me some comments or a review of this book for my website? Or maybe you could draw a picture of Freddie, Myla and Seth, or a picture of one of the scenes in the book and send it to me? Just scan it as a .jpg file and email it to me. I'll put the best ones on my website!

Website: www.neilbarclay.wix.com/books

Email: nrbarclay@gmail.com

Thanks again, and I look forward to hearing from you. You can contact me through my website or simply email me direct.

Bye for now!
Neil Barclay.

To be continued…

The Tellurian Trinity

Part II ~ The City of Forgotten Souls

64627855R10124

Made in the USA
Charleston, SC
03 December 2016

PREFACE

Parsons, priests, pastors, preachers—they answer to a whole range of labels. They can be called Clerics too, or "Clerks in Holy Orders". They are "Ministers of Religion", and in former times they were often Ministers of State as well, holding high office in Government and in Royal Service. They are part and parcel of our history and heritage.

And they are also human beings, with human foibles. As Chesterfield once wrote:""Parsons are very like men, and neither the better nor the worse for wearing a black gown". The poet William Blake once wrote: "Then the Parson might preach, and drink and sing. And we'd be as happy as birds in the spring". And our own Buck's Poet, Cowper, wrote: "Oh, laugh or mourn with me the rueful jest, A cassocked huntsman and a fiddling priest". He could easily have been thinking of the Rector of Simpson, always known as Tally Ho! Hanmer, the""rollicking jolly sportsman", much loved in his parish but often forced to spend time in a Debtor's Prison.

At one end of the scale there were clergy holding high office in the church but high office also in the State—Chancellor of England for example. Henry Burgwash, Bishop of Lincoln, was one such. He grievously offended the good folk of Fingest. And let no one forget Thomas a Becket of whom Henry II said:
"Will no one rid me of this turbulent priest?". He didn't really mean it and bitterly repented ever saying it, but it led the four knights to murder the Archbishop in front of the Altar in Canterbury Cathedral.

At the other end of the scale there were devoted men of the cloth content to minister unseen in their parishes. Goldsmith wrote of one such:-

"A man he was to all the country dear and passing rich on forty pounds a year. Remote from towns he ran his godly race, nor e'er had changed nor wished to change his place".

George Herbert was another like him. Instead of the distinguished career many predicted for him, he chose to become priest of a small country parish. He was a poet as well as a priest. One of his poems contains the verse:-

"Of all the creatures both in sea and land,
Onely to Man hast thou made known thy wayes
And put the penne alone into his hand
And made him Secretarie of thy praise."

The blasphemous Slave Trader, John Newton, lived to become the faithful parish priest of Olney—an astonishing transformation which found expression in the best-known of all his hymns:-

"Amazing grace! How sweet the sound
That saved a wretch like me!
I once was lost, but now am found,
Was blind, but now I see".

The Talented **Dr William Dodd,** the absentee Vicar of no less than three rural parishes simultaneously lived it up in London and enjoyed immense popularity. He ended on the gallows at Tyburn in 1777. Like many others in this collection he has connections with the County of Buckinghamshire

These are but some of those who figure in this collection of country clerics. Their range truly justify the tag that they include "the good, the bad and the so so".

BIBLIOGRAPHY.

Browne Willis — History of Buckingham
John Aubrey — Brief Lives
John Houghton — Sanctity and Scandal
Gilbert White — Natural History of Selborne
William Cole — Blechely Diary
James Woodforde — Diary of a Country Parson.
Bernard Wasserstein — Secret Lives of Trebitsch Lincoln
Frank Markham — History of Milton Keynes & District

ABOUT THE AUTHOR

John Houghton was born in Sussex in 1916. From 1939 to 1942 he was Curate at Wolverton. From 1942 to 1973 he served in Central Africa as a Mission Priest. He was awarded the Zambian Order of Distinguished Service in 1966. He is a Canon Emeritus of Lusaka Cathedral. He returned to England in 1974 and settled in Bletchley, retiring in 1983.

THE ROYALTIES ON THIS BOOK WILL GO TO THE BUCKINGHAMSHIRE HISTORIC CHURCHES TRUST

Chapter 1.

WILLIAM COLE

BLETCHLEY'S CLERICAL DIARIST.

Many years ago I happened to overhear some one say: "You three are a fine pair if ever I saw one". I enjoyed that strange saying at the time and then forgot all about it. But it evidently lodged itself in my mind and now it has resurfaced. This is because recently my interest and reading have been particularly concerned with the 18th century. In the process I have found myself renewing acquaintance with three particular individuals and it is they who have caused that strange overheard saying from the past to come back to me. "You three are a fine pair if ever I saw one".

It is always a pity to waste a good quote and so I found myself attaching that quotation to the three individuals I was rediscovering. And they are William Cole (1714-1782), Gilbert White (1720-1793) and James Woodforde (1740-1803) This trio has so much in common. They were contemporaries, sharing the 18th century; they were all Oxbridge men, Cole, King's College Cambridge, White,Oriel College Oxford, Woodforde,New College Oxford. They were all Anglican country parsons, Cole ordained in 1745, White in 1747, and Woodforde in 1763. They all remained unmarried. Two were bachelors while one was perhaps celibate rather than bachelor. AND all of them were Diarists or Journal Keepers.

So they share immortality with other great luminaries—Pepys, Celia Fiennes, William Cobbett, Kilvert—Diarists all. To call them luminaries is apt indeed, for all of them shed light on the times in which they lived. Cole, White and Woodforde serve that office for us to illuminate the 18th century, and in this first chapter we begin with **William Cole,** Rector of St Mary's Bletchley and his "Blechely" Diary. (His spelling)

Willian Cole, 18th century Bletchley Rector and Diarist

Cole was a Cambridge man both by County and University. He was born in 1714 at Little Abington on the Essex border into a well-to-do family. His parents sent him to Eton where a fellow student was Horace Walpole. His friendship with that English man of letters, who later succeeded as 4th Earl of Orford, lasted throughout life, nurtured by regular correspondence. Both men were friends of Thomas Grey the poet, and Cole wrote often in his Diary about both of them.

From Eton Cole went up to King's College Cambridge in 1733.By then his enthusiasm for antiquarian research was already established, an interest which he maintained all through his life. His research prompted him to record meticulously a vast amount of detail about innumerable churches. He spent many hours in College libraries, saving for posterity much material which might otherwise have been lost. His Diary is, too an invaluable record of university life as it was lived in the 18th century.

His antiquarian research was almost obsessive. In a letter to Walpole he wrote:

> "You will be astonished at the rapidity of my pen when you observe that this folio of 400 hundred pages was completed in six weeks".

His self-imposed discipline enabled him to accomplish some 4000 words

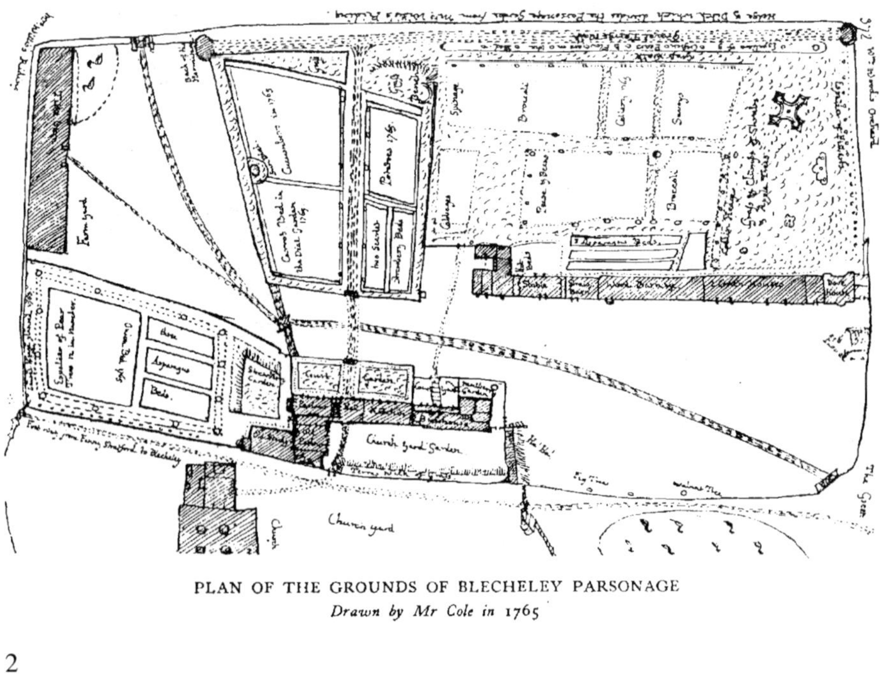

PLAN OF THE GROUNDS OF BLECHELEY PARSONAGE
Drawn by Mr Cole in 1765

and two drawings each day. In another letter to Walpole about his manuscripts he wrote:

> "They are my delight; they are my wife and children; they have been in short my whole Employ and Amusement for these 20 or 30 years. And though I really and sincerely think the greatest part of them Stuff and Trash, and deserves no other Treatment than the Fire, yet the collection which I have made towards an History of Cambridgeshire...will be of Singular Use to anyone who will have more Patience and Perseverance than I am Master of to put the Material together."

But that ambition to compile a History of Cambridgeshire was never to be realised. In 1745 Cole was ordained an Anglican priest. His duties as a clergyman did not impede his antiquarian research and in 1747 he was elected a Fellow of the Society of Antiquaries. But what did stop him from completing a History of Cambridgeshire was an invitation to become Rector of St Mary's Parish in Bletchley. He was Rector there for 14 years, from 1753 to 1767.

St Mary's, Bletchley in the 18th century

Cole left his Journals in more than one hundred manuscript volumes to the British Museum. He stipulated:

> "None of them may be inspected or looked at until 20 years after my disease, but all be put up in a large chest or box which I brought out of Portugal, locked and fastened with two iron hoops till that time be expired"

Given the asperity of some of the passages in the Diary, and the occasional near-libellous entries, that 20- year embargo might well have been too short. For instance, when King's College wanted to alter the lease of a cottage he had rented, he wrote:

> ".....yet after six years the snotty-nosed head of it, soon after his election had the rascality, with Paddon, a dirty wretch and bursar suitable to him, to alter my lease. But from such a scoundrel, and I am warranted to call him no other, with the addition of a liar and mischief-maker through life, no other than dirty treatment can be expected."

And he could be rude about his Bishop too. The County of Buckinghamshire did not become part of the Diocese of Oxford till 1845. So when Cole was Rector of Bletchley his Bishop was the Bishop of Lincoln, and about him Cole wrote in his Diary:

> "The clownish carriage and want of behaviour and manners in the present Bishop was so notorious at his last Visitation that everyone was scandalised at it, and among all my Acquaintance I never heard him mentioned but with the utmost Disrespect. Indeed, the Bishop's ungain, awkward splay-footed carriage and Yorkshire dialect is a full indication of his humble Education and mean Extraction."

He could be scathing too about Fenny Stratford, then part of his Parish. He described it in his Diary as""the sink of all that is bad". He dismissed Mr Armstead, the Apothecary of Fenny Stratford as""the mad and drunken Apothecary of F Stratford".

Yet such passages taken alone would give a false picture of William Cole whose Diary overall shows him to have been a true Pastor to his flock. And not only to those technically his parishioners. Thus, when a farmer in another parish died of smallpox, none of the neighbouring clergy were willing to bury him for fear of infection, William Cole sent a note to say he would come next day to conduct the burial.

Few other sections of that prodigious quantity of manuscripts embargoed for 20 years in "the chest or box I brought out of Portugal" have been published. So we are lucky that at least the "Blechely" Diary has emerged in print even though it covers only 2 of the 14 years Cole spent in Bletchley. One can see why Browne Willis, the Lord of the Manor wanted Cole in Bletchley. Not only were both men antiquarians—both were the same kind of Anglicans, High Church Tory with marked Catholic sympathies, and with a marked detestation of dissent and non-conformity. Certainly these two traits are frequently reflected in Cole's Diary:

> "The Discipline of our Church, thro' the practice of the Dissenters, is so relaxed as to come to nothing; there is no parleying with your parishioners in any Point of Doctrine or Discipline; for if you are rigid they will either abstain from all Ordinances, or go over to the Dissenters"

Cole was often annoyed when the Bishops seemed to be pre-occupied with what some of them saw as the danger of Papist encroachment. When the Bishop of Lincoln inquired about the number of Papists in Bletchley Parish, Cole wrote angrily in his Diary:

> "Why don't the Bishops enquire after the growth of Dissenters of multifarious Denominations? After Atheists, Deists, and Libertines, surely these are more dangerous to our Constitution and Christianity in General than the Papists whose tenets are Submission to Government and Order."

If Cole had lived, say, eighty years later than he did, he might surely have identified with the Tractarians in the Oxford Movement in the 1830s when Keble, Pusey and Newman led the revival of the Catholic movement in the Church of England. All his life Cole numbered Catholic priests among his friends and corresponded with them regularly. When he visited Paris it was in the House of the English Benedictines that he stayed.

When Browne Willis exercised his right of Advowson to appoint Cole to the Living at Bletchley he stipulated that if later on his grandson should be ordained and want the Living for himself, Cole would vacate it. There were those, legal experts among them, and many of his clerical neighbours too, who urged that Cole was not bound by this understanding and could ignore it. But Cole himself felt bound in honour to comply with the known wishes of the now dead Browne Willis. The grandson was indeed ordained and wrote to Cole to say that he intended to have the Bletchley living and would therefore expect Cole to leave. So on Lady Day 1768 Cole formally resigned the living and had indeed left Bletchley in the preceding November. He moved into a rented house at Waterbeech, 2 miles from Cambridge and found himself living in a parish""with fanatics of almost all denominations ". He wrote to his friend, Fr Charles Bonaventure Bedingfield:

> "My finances are miserably reduced by quitting the Living of Bletchley. Yet I am not disposed to engage myself in any

> Ecclesiastical matters again. Could I have my books and conveniences about me I should nowhere like better than to finish my days in a conventual manner"

In his last years Cole suffered from gout and poor health generally. He died in 1782, aged 68, with a reputation for eccentricity. To many in Cambridge he was known by the nickname "Cardinal Cole", a reference to his lifelong leanings towards Catholicism. He had survived Browne Willis by over 20 years for Browne Willis had died in 1760. The Lord of the Manor had wanted in the Rectory at Bletchley a man who was both an antiquarian and a High Church Tory priest. Cole fulfilled both criteria. The relationship between the two men was sometimes less than harmonious. Both were eccentric and both could be cantankerous. Browne Willis had wanted his appointee to work on some of his antiquarian researches and Cole did his best. Willis, just before his death had passed to Cole a manuscript in ten folio volumes of his researches into the "History of the Hundreds of Newport and Cotslow in Buckinghamshire" and asked Cole to prepare them for publishing. Cole obliged, completing the transcription but the book was never published.

The Cole Diary gives us a delightful account of how life was in the Bletchley Parish in the 1760s. Cole was writing at a time when Enclosures were a great talking point, and when the Industrial Revolution was about to begin. He had a keen eye for character and his Diary gives us profiles of so many individuals, a gallery of portraits, of notables both lay and clerical, and of humbler folk too.

Cole could be sardonic and scathing. He frequently confided to his Diary scornful opinions of others, his fellow clergy among them. The neighbouring parish of Stoke Hammond at the beginning of the 18th century had four incumbents in the space of four years. But then came an incumbent who was Vicar for several decades. He was the reverend David Timnell and of him Cole wrote in his Diary:

> "A worthy and good man, a little inclined to too much laying up of money, yet the grippingness of his little wife, Barton, made any defect overlooked. He was disordered in the head which showed itself in his daughter, a good sort of woman, unhappily married to Mr Frank from whom she parted. He

was also disordered in the head and they had a daughter who was also thought to suffer from the same affliction."

One of the most endearing aspects of Cole's character is the human interest he took in gossip, especially gossip concerning some of his fellow clergy! There is no doubt, Cole loved a bit of scandal!:

> "2nd October 1767. Mr Knapp (Rector of Shenley) told me that Mr Goodwin (Rector of Loughton) was in great affliction on account of their late maidservant who went away about a fortnight ago and has reported that Mr Goodwin offered her five guineas to lie with her, which on her refusal he offered her double to say nothing of it."
>
> Saturday 3rd October. Mrs Holt, wife of the Lord of the Manor of Little Loughton, told me of Mr Goodwin's offering the maid, soon after she came to them in November, to lie with her; that she at another time gave him a slap in the face and made it black for some time. Mr Goodwin came to dinner but said not a word. Mrs Holt said that Mr Goodwin once being in liquer had put his hand under the maid's petti coats."
>
> 17th October. Mr Eyles (Vicar of Old Bradwell) told me a great deal of scandal of other people and forgot how the world talks of him. (He had a wayward son at Cambridge). He said Mr Goodwin lay with Mrs Holt and that Mrs G told Frank that her husband lay in the same bed with her for 3 weeks together but never touched her; that Mr Knapp and his wife lived very unhappily, that they never spoke to one another or bedded together sometimes for three weeks together; that the widow Woods was a kept mistress and that Mr Pitts (Rector of Great Brickhill) said that none of his neighbours was anything of a scholar or that he could learn anything from other abundance of tittle-tattle. I told him of Mr Pitts former behaviour to me and his talk to Mrs Willis about my reputation and he seemed delighted with the acquisition".

Fascinating though the "Blechely" Diary is, an infinitely greater amount of Cole's outpourings is still only available in manuscript form—a mine of information for scholars able and willing to seek it out. Posterity owes him a great debt of gratitude because so much that he recorded longhand in folio form could have disappeared for ever. As it is the fruit of his research is still there to be harvested for any scholar who seeks access to it. In his manuscript collection of "Parochial Antiquities for the County of Bucks" there is a wealth of material on parish churches as they were in the 18th century before the Victorian era would bring in the (sometimes) destructive effects of "restoration". Cole was researching and writing of what was still largely a medieval pattern of life in North Bucks, before the effects of enclosures and the imminence of industrialisation would bring their inevitable and far-reaching changes.

Meanwhile the reader of the Bletchley Diary can enjoy the word pictures he paints of life in the 1760s in and around Bletchley. He can follow the running dispute Cole waged with that troublesome cleric, Ralph Leycester. Cole himself had appointed Leycester to be Parish Priest at St Martin's Church in Fenny Stratford, an appointment he later bitterly regretted. Leycester proved to be a thorough nuisance. Despite all Cole's complaints to the Bishop of Lincoln, and requests to have Leycester trimmed down to size, the Bishop either wouldn't or couldn't oblige. And Leycester lived to have the last word, surviving at Fenny Stratford long after Cole himself had resigned and moved to Cambridge.

The Bletchley Diary ends with the entry for the last day of 1767. By then Cole is installed in his rented cottage at Waterbeech in Cambridge. His servant Tom is still with him and Bletchley is still much in his mind as he writes:

> "Thursday December 31. St Sylvester, Pope. Thank God for his mercies of last year and pray God to prosper me in that to come. Very severe frost. Tom went out a-shooting with Henry and Edward Mason all Day till 5 o'clock when they dined in the kitchen; they only killed a Wild Duck and a Brace of Teal. Letter from Mr Willis dated at Waterhall to give me notice he was ordained at Christ's Church on Sunday 20 and sent me a copy of the Bond by which I am allowed 3 Calendar months after his Notice of 27 of this month. Yet he wants me to resign directly, and says People at Bletchley are uneasy that Service is performed only once a Day. Put up some books on the shelves upstairs."

Chapter 2.

JAMES WOODFORDE

DIARY OF A COUNTRY PARSON.

To describe James Woodforde as a "son of the manse" would be an understatement. His father, grandfather, great grandfather and great,great grandfather had all been Anglican priests too. Another ancestor had been Canon of Wells, and at least three other kinsmen were clergymen also. James Woodforde was born in 1740 at Ansford in Somerset where his father was Rector. In 1752 he went to Winchester College, and in 1759 to New College, Oxford. He graduated there in 1763 and in the same year was ordained deacon in Oxford. A year later he was ordained priest at Wells. He served various curacies in Somerset, including Castle Cary which was part of his father's living. In 1773 he resumed residence at New College, becoming Sub-Warden and Pro-Proctor.

In 1774 he was presented to the Living of Weston Longville in Norfolk, of which New College was Patron. However, he did not take up residence there immediately, but continued at New College till 1776. He completed a BD Degree in 1775. In May 1776 he moved at last to Weston Longville and stayed there till he died 27 years later in 1803.

There is an interesting coincidence in the name of his parish—Weston Longville. In North Bucks, where that other 18th century clerical diarist, William Cole, was Vicar of St Mary's, Bletchley, the very next parish was Newton Longville. Both parishes trace their origins across the centuries to the Conquest in the 11th century. One of the Commanders of William's Army at Hastings was Walter Gifford, Lord of Longville in Normandy. He was rewarded for his share in William's victory by the gift of many Manors in various parts of the Kingdom. So, centuries later the name Longville remains attached to English village names—Weston Longville in Norfolk, Newton Longville in North Bucks. There is also Longville-in-the-Vale in Shropshire.

James Woodforde was an inveterate Diary-keeper. Throughout his adult life he faithfully recorded day by day what he did, saw, or was intrigued by.

It is not known that he ever had in mind to publish his Journals. But they were all carefully preserved year after year, and after his death they all remained in his family's keeping—a huge literary treasure. The world at large knew nothing of this vast deposit until in 1924 a first volume of Parson Woodforde's Diary was published. It was followed by four further volumes, the last appearing in 1931. But these five volumes still left most of Woodforde's recordings untouched and it was reckoned that up to a dozen volumes would be needed if every entry of the 44 years were to be printed. In 1935 a condensed version of the five published volumes was made. The resulting single volume was entitled:

The Diary of a Country Parson
1758 – 1802
by James Woodforde
Passages edited and
Selected by
John Beresford.

In 1949 this volume was first included in The World's Classics, published by Oxford University Press. It has since been reprinted many times. A significant part of the interest the Diary arouses, and of its value as a mirror to the 18th century in which it was compiled, is the turbulence of the period nationally and internationally. While Woodforde was faithfully writing up his Diary, this country passed through three Wars—the Seven Years War, the War of American Independence, and the beginnings of the war first ignited by the French Revolution and stretching on into the Napoleonic Wars which were not to end till long after Woodforde was dead.

While his contemporary, Gilbert White at Selborne lived through these same conflagrations without ever mentioning them in his Journals, James Woodforde reacted to them and reflected the repercussions they made on village life. Thus he wrote in his Diary of special services of rejoicing for victory, or of services of fasting for defeats. He comments on the continuous rise of prices to pay for the war; on the anxious fears of invasion, and of recruiting for the Army and Navy, and the mobilisation of Volunteers.

James Woodforde never married. When he moved to the Vicarage at Weston Longville he was accompanied by his nephew Bill who stayed with him for two years. Then Nancy his niece arrived and stayed with him for the rest of his life. There was a period when James Woodforde contemplated matrimony. He did in fact propose to a Miss Betsy White, but she declined and married the rich Mr Webster of Devonshire instead.

Though his Diary was started in his undergraduate days, it is only after his arrival in May 1776 at Weston Longville that it truly becomes the Diary of a Country Parson. The earliest entries at Weston tell of settling in, buying household goods, hiring maid servants, employing a carpenter for domestic repairs—and a Rat Catcher who was paid 10s 6d "to destroy the rats".

He had other problems too:-

> June 4 1776. My tooth pained me all night, got up at a little after 5 this morning
> And sent for one Reeves, a man who draws teeth in this parish and about 7 he came and drew my tooth, but shockingly bad indeed, he broke away a great piece of my gum and broke one of the fangs of the tooth, it gave me exquisite pain all the day after, and my face was swelled prodigiously in the evening and much pain
> Gave the old man that drew it however 0.2/6d. He is too old I think to draw teeth, can't see very well.

Weston Longville is 9 miles from Norwich and it was to that city that Woodforde looked for his mail and for the newspapers. These kept him in touch with the wider world:-

> July 14,1789 ".....This is the day that the French Revolution first took place there last year. Pray God! Continue thy goodness to this land and defeat all the designs of the enemies to it."
> July 21 1792 "Shocking Accounts on the papers of dreadful Riots at Birmingham, Nottingham etc of commemorating the French Revolution the 14th of this month."

> Nov.28 1792 "much talking about Mobs rising in many parts of the

NORWICH. Woodforde preached in the Cathedral once, and he heard Handel's Oratorio, and saw the pig that could count.

Charles Monnet, engraving, The Execution of Louis XVI.

> Kingdom Especially in Norfolk and in Norwich"...a great number of Clubs who stile themselves Resolution Men, alias Revolution Men. Pray God however we may have Peace".
>
> Jany 26 1793. "People brought our newspapers from Norwich. The King of France, Louis 16 inhumanly and unjustly beheaded on Monday last by his cruel and bloodthirsty subjects. Dreadful times I am afraid are approaching to all Europe. France the foundation of all of it."

But Norwich was not only the source of alarming news—it was also the venue for exciting and unusual curiosities:-

> May 21 1778. "I walked up to the White Hart to see a famous Woman in Men's Cloaths, by name Hannah Snell who was 21 years as a common soldier in the Army and not discovered by any as a woman".
>
> Dec 19 1785 "After Dinner the Captain and myself went and saw the learned Pigg...it was wonderful to see the sagacity of the Animal...He would spell any Word or number from the letters and figures that were placed before him."

It was to Norwich too that he went to hear Handel's Oratorio, and to preach in the Cathedral.

At home in Weston Longville he ministered to his parish. Year after year on St Valentine's Day he recorded a quaint custom:

> Feb 14 1777 "to 36 children being Valentine's Day and what is

> customary for them to go about in these parts this day gave 3.0 being one penny apiece to each of them." (They only got a penny if they correctly recited the formula: "Good Morrow, Valentine".)

A parallel custom also recorded year after year cost the Vicar rather more. It happened annually on St Thomas Day, just before Christmas:

> Dec.21 1786. "This being St Thomas Day I gave to the poor of my parish that came to my House at 6d each 1.7.0"

The Diary gives evidence of the Parson's pleasure in gambling. It was never excessive and he always recorded his losses and gains. Sometimes it was Quadrille, sometimes Newmarket, sometimes Whist and sometimes Loo. He delighted also in hare-coursing and kept three greyhounds for the purpose.

A slightly more reprehensible practice was the Parson's smuggling! This secured for him gin, brandy, rum and tea. He usually recorded these transactions quite openly in his Diary. But one entry is rather more cryptic:

> Sept.17 1792. "I got up very early this morning and was very busy all the morning in very necessary business".

What this really signified was that he was busy hiding (perhaps by burying) his smuggled rum. And for good reason. Under the latest laws he could have been liable to a forfeit of £10 for each offence, and Informers were tempted to inform by a reward of up to £50!

Some of the entries in the Diary speak of even darker hazards...the arrival of a Press Gang which carried off a parishioner into the Navy—or the trial of "ruffians" leading sometimes to public hangings in chains. There are incidents too of violent lunacy, and of the Vicarage being broken into, and of the terrors of small pox.

The Press Gang sometimes snatched Woodforde's parishioners

In 1791 James Woodforde suffered from a stye on his eye:

> Mar.11 1791. "The Stioney on my right eye-lid still swelled and inflamed very much. As it is commonly said that the eyelid being rubbed by the tail of a black cat would do it much good if not entirely cure it, and having a black cat. a little before dinner I made trial of it, and very soon after dinner I found my Eye-lid much abated of the swelling and almost free from pain. I cannot therefore not conclude it to be of great service to a Stioney on the Eye-lid. Any other cat's tail may have the above effect in all probability. But I did my Eye-lid with my own Black Tom cat's tail".

But for the next three days trouble with the Stioney continued and he had recourse to a plaster and to bathing the eye with warm milk and water. And he was finally reduced to dosing himself with Rhubarb and taking to his bed!

James Woodforde was a wonderful trencherman! He carefully records the meals he ate and served to his guests. And 'gargantuan' is often the only word for them.:

> Sept 16 1777. "I gave them for Dinner half a dozen of my own fine Tench (taken out of my pond in the Yard), stewed. A Rump of Beef, boiled. A goose rosted. and a pudding".
>
> Sept 9 1778 "We had for Dinner some common fish, a leg of Mutton rosted, and a baked Pudding—the first course. And a Roast Duck, a Meat Pie, Eggs and Tarts—the second Course. For Supper we had a brace of Partridges rosted, some Cold Tongue, Potatoes in Shells, and Tarts."

What was the overall picture of Parson Woodforde's finances as Vicar of Weston Longville? He had the Vicarage of course, and some land where he could grow crops and sell them. There was a Stipend—not huge. And he was entitled to all the Surplice Fees, that is, the Fees he could charge for Banns, marriages, baptisms and funerals. But most important of all were the Tithes:

> Dec 3 1776 "My Frolic for my people to pay Tithes to me was this day. I gave them a good dinner, Sirloin of Beef rosted, a Leg of

> Mutton boiled, and Plumb Puddings in plenty. Received today for Tithe and Glebe of them"£236.2.0

Similar entries occur every December. All in all it wasn't a bad living. But Taxes took their toll, and they were greatly increased by the Wars:

> Nov.11 1789 "....to James Pegg this morning paid 11.2.3, that is half a year's Land Tax; 6.0.0. half a year's House Tax; 2.15.0 Window Tax; Male Servant's Tax for half a year 1.5.0; Female ditto for ditto 0.10.0. Horse Tax for ditto 0.10.0 Additional Horse Tax for 1 quarter 0.1.3. Cart Tax for Half a Year 0.1.0

When James Woodforde died in 1803 his personal effects and goods were sold for a total of £437. From this sum was taken £250 for debts owed by him.

Through the pages of Parson Woodforde's Diary we get not only a portrait of a faithful village Pastor, complete with human foibles, but also an introduction to a whole gallery of individuals and personalities. Despite the alarms and excursions of wars and occasional civil unrest, there is a tranquility in the parish and village of Weston Longville.
The very obscurity of life in so small a place suggests a continuity, an unchanging pattern of rural life, representative of a whole nation. Parson Woodforde's Diary, so faithfully recorded day by day for nearly half a century is as enchanting as it is instructive. We owe him much.

Chapter 3.

GILBERT WHITE OF SELBORNE.

Reputed to be the fourth most published book in the English language, Gilbert White's "Natural History of Selborne" is the work of another Anglican country parson in the 18th century. It is right therefore to consider it along with the Diaries of his contemporaries, also Anglican country parson diarists—William Cole and James Woodforde. Yet White's book was not in any ordinary sense a Diary like theirs. They wrote up their Diaries day by day, recording their doings, their observations on what happened to them and to those around them, and their reactions to the events of the day or the week. White's book on the other hand was almost exclusively confined to his observations on nature.

Preceding his "Natural History of Selborne" there had been two other works—"A Naturalist's Calendar" and""The Garden Kalendar". And later came his""Antiquities of Selborne". None of these excited much comment and they have seldom been published. Yet "The Natural History of Selborne", first published in 1788, has appeared in well over 200 editions and translations.

There is a further factor to consider. While it is true that Gilbert White made meticulous and enchanting observations on natural phenomena in his beloved Selborne, he also conducted a sustained correspondence with two fellow naturalists—Thomas Pennant and Daines Barrington. It was Barrington who urged White to expand his Garden Kalendar into a more general "Naturalist's Journal".

At some time in the 1770s White began to think of the possibility of turning his naturalist's journal into a book. In this he was encouraged by both his correspondents. So it came to pass that'"The Natural History of Selborne" was published in 1788. It took the form of publishing the letters he had written to Pennant and Barrington—44 to Pennant and 66 to Barrington. In addition he drew on his own naturalist journals written over many years.

He prefaced the book with an introduction:

ADVERTISEMENT

The Author of the following Letters takes the liberty, with all proper deference, of laying before the public his idea of PAROCHIAL HISTORY, which, he thinks, ought to consist of natural productions and occurrences as well as antiquities. He is also of the opinion that if stationary men would pay some attention to the districts on which they reside, and would publish their thoughts respecting the objects that surround them, from such materials might be drawn the most complete county-histories, which are still wanting in several parts of this kingdom.

Gilbert White was born on 18 July 1720 in the Vicarage at Selborne where his grandfather, also named Gilbert, was Vicar. Young Gilbert's mother was a clergyman's daughter, and many of his uncles and nephews had livings in neighbouring parishes. Gilbert's schooling was at Grammar Schools in Farnham and Basingstoke. At the age of 19 he went up to Oriel College in Oxford in 1739 and graduated there in 1743. In 1747 he was ordained. He continued in residence at Oriel for some three years as Junior Proctor. The question of parochial work naturally came up. There was no chance of his being offered the living of Selborne, for that was in the gift of Magdalen. But in 1758 he was offered the sinecure living of Moreton Pinkney in Northants, of which Oriel was the Patron. But by then he had already moved back to Selborne in 1755 and he stayed there for the rest of his life.

The Wakes, High Street, Selborne, home of the famous naturalist Rev. Gilbert White

When his grandfather had died in 1727 the family simply moved across the Plestor (as the Village Green was called) to a house called The Wakes,

which was to be Gilbert's home for the next 38 years till his death in 1793. From his home at The Wakes Gilbert White was easily able to carry out his clerical duties as Curate in neighbouring parishes. Finally, in 1784 he became once more Curate of Selborne itself. And it is there that he is buried.
His devotion to Selborne was total. He would thoroughly have endorsed the sentiment expressed by Kipling a century later. Kipling in praise of Sussex wrote:

"God gives all men all earth to love,
But since man's heart is small,
Ordains for each one spot shall prove
Beloved overall".

For Gilbert White, Selborne was that one spot, "beloved over all".

Richard Mabey, in his Introduction to the Penguin edition of White's "Natural History of Selborne" describes the village as it was in White's day, and as it largely still is today. He wrote:
"Selborne is the landscape of the pastoral dream made flesh; cosseted, balanced, endurable, a condensation into a single parish of almost every type and mood of scenery to be found in lowland England"

Mabey wrote there of the 'parish'. And White himself in the Introduction to his book in 1788 wrote of his intention to give his readers 'a parochial history'. 'Parish' and its adjective 'parochial' are evocative words. They have to do not only with geography and ecclesiastical administration, but with history and a pattern of loyalties. At root a 'parish' is the indefineable territory to which we feel we belong. Until the 9th century all England was divided into parishes. It was King Alfred who grouped parishes into Hundreds and then put adjoining Hundreds into Shires or Counties.

Gilbert White thought of life in terms of the parish. He wrote of it as a parish priest—his writing style was parochial. The parish was the context in which he studied nature, and described its phenomena in such endearing and enchanting terms. The entries in his Journals are all about the flora and fauna he saw all around him in Selborne. His many letters to Tennant and Barrington are

all about nature in the same parochial context—especially the birds and their behaviour. It is as if White thought of the plants and birds and all other natural creatures as 'parishioners' in his village. He seems to attribute to them thoughts and actions in almost human terms. Yet he contrives—just—to stop short of anthropomorphic excesses. He delights his readers with his sentiments which are never merely sentimental, and never maudlin. In a letter he wrote to Barrington in 1774 about the behaviour of house-martins we have a perfect example:

"About the middle of May, if the weather be fine, the martin begins to think in earnest of providing a mansion for his family. The crust or shell of this nest seems to be formed of such dirt or loam as comes most readily to hand...the provident architect has prudence and forbearance enough not to advance her work too fast—building only in the morning, and by dedicating the rest of the day to food and amusement, gives it sufficient time to dry and harden. Thus, careful workmen when they build mud-walls, informed at first by this little bird, raise but a moderate layer at a time. So by this method in about ten or twelve days is formed an hemispheric nest with a small aperture towards the top, strong, compact and warm, and perfectly fitted for all the purposes for which it was intended."

Many have wondered that there is so little in White's book about his human parishioners. Their absence from his pages is in marked contrast to the Diaries of Cole and Woodforde. Both of them wrote on almost every page about the folk they encountered every day. That this is not so with White implies no antipathy. By all accounts he knew and liked the farmers and squires and ordinary villagers, and they in turn liked him. Yet they are largely absent from his pages. But there ARE references to some human individuals. In nearly every such case they are curiosities. There is the mad bee-boy, and the leper, and the gypsies, and the toad-witch. Perhaps White wrote of them because they intrigued him and challenged him to study and explain them. Ordinary human beings did not challenge him in that way, so perhaps he saw no need to think or write of them as phenomena.

But there are a few exceptions. Goody Hampton, for example. He called her his "weeding woman" and wrote of her: "except that she wears petticoats, and now and then has a child, you would think her a man".

At the top of the rising ground behind The Wakes, White built the Hermitage, or Summer House. There he delighted to entertain friends to tea. On one such occasion he entertained three young ladies. White conspired with his younger brother, Harry, for Harry dressed as a Hermit to burst in on them, causing much mirth and apprehension. Later at dusk they paid a second and lamp-lit visit to The Hermitage. The young ladies were the two flighty Battie sisters and Hester Mulso. Hester is said to have been the only person to whom White had a romantic attraction. But it came to nothing and he remained a bachelor all his life. (There is a parallel here with James Woodforde. He too lived and died a bachelor though there had been a time when he wished to marry a Miss Betsy White. But she married the rich Mr Webster of Devonshire instead. William Cole on the other hand was always a celibate rather than a bachelor).

White's "Natural History of Selborne" is deservedly a classic—the fruit of his single-minded devotion to all things natural. Yet the gentle placidity of his writing is in startling contrast to the turbulent events going on in the wider world. He was born in 1720 and died in 1793. Between those dates England fought wars with Spain, Austria and Scotland; the American Colonies seceded; King George III went mad; and the French Revolution began. None of these found mention in White's pages. On the very day the Bastille was stormed, White in Selborne was happily putting on paper his observations on the nesting habits of the nightjar! From his felicitous pen we have the "parochial history" he promised his readers. And the result, in a phrase of David Elliston Allen, is that he has made the village of Selborne "the secret private parish inside each one of us."

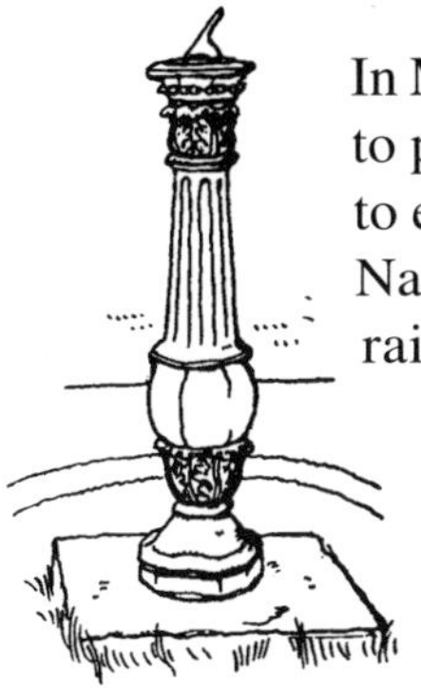

In May 1954 an Appeal was launched in The Times for funds to purchase Gilbert White's home, The Wakes. The aim was to endow it as a perpetual memorial to the Father of English Natural History. There was a good response but the money raised was insufficient both to purchase and endow the property. However, by combining the White Appeal with funds raised for a Trust in memory of Captain Oates, of Antarctic fame, The Wakes was saved as a memorial to Gilbert White for all time. So visitors can enjoy the house where Gilbert White's famous book was written. In its library are copies of nearly all the 200 editions of the book, in many languages. There are also manuscripts and some of White's own furniture. And there is an extensive collection of books on falconry, the Chase, and natural science.

The room which Gilbert White used as a study and library is where he died. In the Yard at the south end of the property is the Brew-house built by White in 1765. Here he brewed his own ale. He relates how he used to call on one of his parishioners to taste the first glass, and how the friend was never able to give a considered opinion until he had had a second glass!

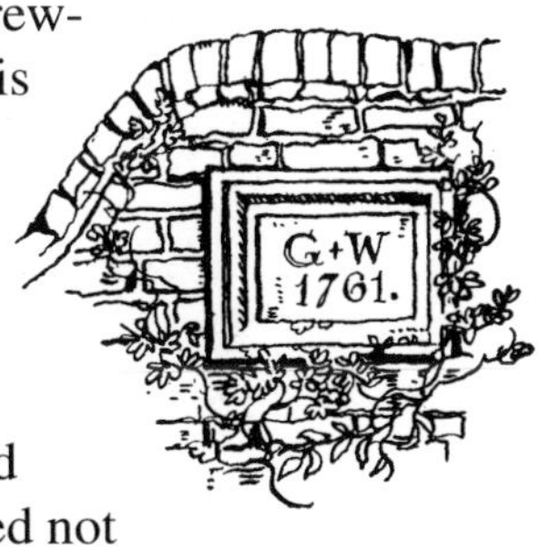

White's bird-watching Arbour is still there, reached by the little brick path he laid down so that he need not soil his shoes. The sundial he lovingly erected can still be consulted. And in the short length of wall he built, for the purpose of growing melons against it, the plaque bears his inscription: "GW.1761".

Nearby is the Church of St Mary, where his grandfather had been Rector, with its magnificent Norman pillars of the 12th century. As Curate of Selborne Gilbert White must have officiated in the church hundreds of times. And he would certainly have baptised many a child in the 800-year-old Font.

In 1920 a stain-glass window was erected in the church in Gilbert White's memory. It mentions his famous book and depicts the Yew Tree, said to be

1200 years old. About 90 birds appear in the window, and in the centre there is St Francis preaching to them. All in all, Selborne is secure in its testimony to its most famous son. Those who visit The Wakes can still climb up the Zig-zag, cut by White and his brother in 1751. And at the top of The Hanger, so closely associated with White's life and work, the magnificent panorama of surrounding countryside can still be enjoyed, as he enjoyed it throughout the 38 years of his life in Selborne.

Farming in the18th century

Chapter 4.

THE DAY THEY SHOT THE VICAR.

Who was he? George Parker was born in the village of Johnby in Cumbria in 1762, the son of a respectable yeoman. He was baptised in Greystoke Church in 1762. His schooling was at a nearby endowed Grammar School. Later he was ordained and served as Curate for several years at St.Martin's Church at Dorking in Surrey. While he was Curate in Dorking George Parker married. His wife, Mary, was seven years older than he. Surprisingly, she was unable to read or write and had probably been a servant in one of the larger houses in Dorking. In July 1799 a daughter was born and was baptised Mary after her mother.

Now that he was a family man, the Reverend George Parker felt that he needed a parish of his own. For this he needed a Patron. The Duke of Norfolk owned Greystoke Castle near Johnby, George's birthplace. But the Duke had no living of his own to offer Parker at that time. However, he used his good offices to approach his friend, Baron Foley, and by chance Baron Foley was Patron of the Parish of Oddingly in Worcestershire. That Parish was vacant and was offered to George Parker. And on May 3rd 1793 the aged Bishop of Worcester inducted George Parker as Vicar of St.James Church, Oddingly.

It was a lovely small rural Parish, 5 miles from Worcester and 3 miles from Droitwich. The Birmingham and Worcester Canal passed through Oddingly within 100 yards of the Church. The name Oddingly dates back to the 11th century and means "a woodlands clearing of the family of a man called Odda"

Lovely though it was, the Parish of Oddingly was a poor living, worth only"£150 a year. It comprised 7 farms ranging in size from the smallest, less than 60 acres, to the largest of 160 acres. None of the farms was prosperous. The local soil was poor and not suitable for wheat. To make sure of feed for their cattle the farmers relied on growing rough cereals—vetches, clover, oats or rye. Apart from the 7 farms and farm houses there were also about 25 cottages in the Parish, occupied by farm labourers. Naturally the Parish Church was by far the oldest building in the village.

The Church of St James, Oddingley

Its oldest surviving parts dated from the 15th century. But at the end of the 18th century St James Church was in a sad condition and in great need of repair.
Times were hard everywhere at the end of the 18th century. Britain was at war with revolutionary France and in wartime prices were rising. So most farmers were poor and several were in debt. A new Land Tax to help pay for the war further increased their woes. Such then was the parish in which the new Vicar was inducted in 1793. He was well received initially and most folk found him amiable, attentive and kindhearted. But as the years went by it became apparent that while the farm labourers liked the Vicar well enough, the farmers did not. Of the seven farmers only one was friendly to the Vicar. A second was fairly neutral. But that left five who were the Vicar's implacable enemies.

This all had to do with Tithes, which all farmers had to pay. Not only in Oddingly, but nationally too resentment to paying Tithes was growing. In larger towns and cities increasing numbers were non-conformist and not Anglican, so it was no surprise that the paying of Tithes to support Anglican clergy caused a growing resentment. In the little village of Oddingly the farmers and the villagers were all at least nominally Anglican. They used the Church for baptisms and burials but it has to be added, not very much for worship.

The Living of Oddingly was a poor one, worth only £150 a year and most of that had to come from Tithes. These were of two kinds—greater and lesser. Greater Tithes, at 10%, were on all field and root crops. Lesser Tithes, also at 10%, were on such things as eggs and milk. The Vicar's predecessor had agreed to an annual computation fixing the total that the Tithes should yield at £135 a year. The new Vicar felt that this was not enough and he asked that it be increased to £150 a year. He was now a family man with a child to support and also employed two servants at the Vicarage. The increase from £135 to £150 was modest enough. But the farmers refused. That angered the Vicar who was already convinced that the farmers were short-changing him and that he was not getting the 10% on either the greater or lesser Tithes. So he announced that in future he would personally COLLECT the 10% of field crops by going with his own cart into their fields. And as to his lesser Tithes, he would send his servants round to collect the eggs and milk to which he was entitled!

This was war! Such practices were unheard of and the farmers were enraged. On at least one occasion the Vicar was physically assaulted. The Vicar took his assailant to court and won his case. The farmers retaliated with threats and insults and came up with some dirty tricks of their own. They deliberately gave their labourers extra duties on Sundays so that they could not go to church! And one farmer arranged that his cows would be taken daily into the next parish to be milked so that the Vicar would not get his 10%

That was not all. Each year at the Spring Annual Church Meeting the Church's accounts were examined and by custom once a year a dinner was held to finalise Tithe Payments. The Church paid for this dinner, at which by tradition toasts were given. In 1806, ridiculously, some of the diners insulted others by deliberately drinking the Toast LEFT-HANDED! A brawl was only narrowly averted. But much more sinister was an incident next day. A

Oddingley Vicarage

bag was discovered hidden in a rick. It contained a muzzle-loaded shotgun. Some days later a carpenter named Richard Hemming, from Droitwich, claimed the gun. He said he had only hidden it because it had started to rain. The gun was returned to him, but some people were suspicious. One parishioner, a farm labourer, told the Vicar he had often seen Hemming hiding furtively in the hedgerows. "I'm surprised", the farm labourer said to the Vicar, "that you are not afraid to go out at night for fear you may be knocked on the head". The Vicar said he was not afraid. All the same his nerves were beginning to fray. Twice, late at night, the Vicar and his wife heard something like gravel being thrown against their bedroom window. The Vicar guessed it was a ploy to get him to come to the widow and be shot at as he looked out. So he wisely kept well away from the window.

The leader of the aggrieved farmers was a retired military man known as Captain Evans. His farm, called Church Farm, was right next to the Vicarage. He had a poor view of parsons in general and he positively hated the Vicar whom he regularly insulted. The Vicar kept out of his way as much as possible. But in 1806 things reached a crisis. The Vicar owned four cows, which he kept in a grazing meadow, which was part of his own Glebe Field. Every morning his servant would take the cows to the meadow and fetch them back again in the evening. But on the afternoon of June 6th 1806 the Vicar himself went to fetch his cows home. A SHOT RANG OUT. A strangled cry of "MURDER!" was heard. AND THE VICAR LAY DEAD.

The gunshot and the shrill cry of "Murder" were heard by a number of people who hurried to the scene. They found the dead Vicar with several wounds to his head and with some of his clothing on fire. In addition to the gunshot wounds it was clear that he had also been clubbed. By chance, two butchers from Worcester named Giles and Lench had been passing through Oddingly on their way to buy a cow at Hadsor. They too had heard the gunshots and cry of "Murder!". They rushed towards the scene and were just

Murdered

in time to catch sight of a man on the other side of the hedge, trying to hide something in the undergrowth. They rushed round the hedge to tackle the man, but he fled, throwing his weapon into a ditch, and they failed to catch him.

On that June day in 1806 there was no question of reporting the Murder to the Police, for the simple reason that the Police didn't exist! It would be another quarter of a century before Robert Peel, the Home Secretary would appoint any Police Force in 1829. It is true that in larger centres the office of Constable already existed as a sort of solitary law keeper, but Oddingly was far too small a place to have such an official. So the news of the horrendous incident in Oddingly that day was reported to the nearest Magistrate. He as it happens was another Parson-—the Reverend Reginald Pyndar at Hadsor House, two miles north of Oddingly. His duty was to inquire into the circumstances of the crime, to take depositions from witnesses, to compile a record of all that had happened, and to make notes of all actions put in hand.

One odd fact emerged. It was reported to the Magistrate that one farmer, named Barnett, though he heard the gunshots and the cry of—"Murder!" hid in his farmhouse and did not go to investigate the matter. The Magistrate tackled Barnett about this but got no satisfactory answer, so he made a mental note of this fact. He was already aware of the hostility shown to the Vicar by most of the Oddingly farmers and had already heard the tales about the furtive behaviour in recent weeks of the Droitwich carpenter, Richard Hemming. So he began to make plans to have Hemming arrested.

Meanwhile an Inquest was held. It could only certify that the Vicar had been killed but could not say by whom. Witnesses came forward to testify that a number of individuals had been heard to curse the Vicar and to wish him dead. Magistrate Pyndar also uncovered the suspicious connection between Captain Evans, who had led the opposition to the Vicar and the Droitwich carpenter, Hemming.

The dead Vicar was buried in St.James Church. A stone cover later placed over his grave in the chancel was carved with the words:

> Sacred to the memory of the Rev.George Parker,
> Late Rector of this Parish,
> Who departed this life June 24th, 1806, aged 43 years.

Almost none of the farmers attended the funeral. One shameful tale is told that one farmer had gone into the church before the stone was laid over the grave and had laughed with horrible glee over the dead Vicar.

Pyndar was convinced that the murderer was the carpenter, Hemming. He made stenuous efforts to have him found and arrested. "Wanted" posters were printed and widely distributed. Pyndar realised that Hemming might have fled the country. With the war with France continuing, he knew it was unlikely that Hemming would have gone there. But escape through Bristol across the Atlantic was a possibility so Pyndar sought the help of authorities in Bristol. A number of "sightings" were claimed in all sorts of places, both in this country and in America and Canada.

Pyndar did not neglect a second possible dimension to the problem, namely that some of the farmers might have""hired" Hemming to dispose of the Vicar. The years went by and several of those involved in the Oddingly tragedy died. Then, suddenly, 24 years after the murder, Hemming turned up again! But not in the flesh. He reappeared as a skeleton, discovered in 1830 under the floor of the barn at Netherwood Farm. A farmer called Clewes had rented this farm. And Clewes was one of three farmers suspected of complicity of the Vicar's murder. The other two were Barnett and Bankes. There was no doubt about the identity of the skeleton. The remains were of a short man, just 5 feet 3 inches. It was known that early in life Hemming had tried to enlist in the Army but had been turned down because he was one inch short of the 5'4" minimum. Furthermore, found with the skeleton, were Hemming's pocketknife and carpenter's rule.

An inquest was held and the three farmers were arrested. Captain Evans, who a quarter of a century ago had led the quarrel with the Vicar, might well have been arrested too. But he had long since sold Church Farm and had retired to Droitwich. He was now in his nineties, both physically and mentally handicapped, so he was not arrested.
In the trial, which now took place, yet another Parson appeared. He was the Reverend Robert Clifton and was also a Magistrate. He had induced Clewes to confess that he had helped to raise the money, with his two fellow conspirators, to bribe Hemming to kill the Vicar. The other two accused strenuously denied this.

The Trial aroused interest and excitement nationally as well as locally. London newspapers sent ten reporters to Worcester to cover the case. The London Morning Chronicle arranged for an Express train to be available each day to carry full reports of each day's proceedings from Worcester to London, a ten hour trip, so that next morning the paper would carry a full report.
It was made clear that although the three defendants were only being charged with the murder of Hemmings, if they were found guilty, then the Jury would also be instructed to enquire into their involvement with the death of the Vicar also, back in 1806, 24 years earlier. In the event, this did not happen because the Jury returned a verdict of NOT GUILTY on all three for the murder of Hemming. Wild enthusiasm and loud clapping greeted this verdict in the Worcester Court. As soon as this news reached Oddingly, 6 miles away, several villagers rushed to the Church and began to ring the bells. Hearing the bells, others came rushing to the church, bringing drinks to celebrate the event! The Vicar, the Reverend Charles Tookey, arrived back from Worcester. He was the second incumbent to have succeeded the murdered George Parker. Tookey was scandalised by the scene at the church. The Parish Clerk who was present but had made no attempt to stop the wild party was sacked on the spot. And the Vicar announced loudly that he would prosecute the offenders in the Ecclesiastical Courts. But later he thought better of it and let the matter drop.

For the first murder, of the Reverend George Parker in 1806, there can be no doubt who was responsible—it was Richard Hemming the carpenter from Droitwich. Masses of circumstantial evidence seem to make it clear that Evans, Barnett and Clewes conspired together to hire Hemming to kill the Vicar. And Hemming duly did the murder, but did it so clumsily that he allowed himself to be recognised and pursued. So, when he finally turned up again to claim his fee, the conspirators panicked and decided to do away with him. Nobody now knows in what year Hemming had reappeared.

Six years after the great Oddingly Murder Trial, in 1830 Parliament passed the Tithe Computation Act. This required Tithe Payers and their Parsons to compute the Tithes on a rate tied to the national price of grain. The Act failed to end the opposition to Tithes, but at least for some years it diffused quarrels. But alas it came a quarter of a century too late to save the Reverend George Parker from his homicidal farmers.

Chapter 5

WIT AND WISDOM.

In the first three chapters Cole, Woodforde and White gave us in their Diaries so many insights into the lives of country clerics in the 18th century. Then chapter 4 told of the sad and violent end of one particular country cleric, whose murder was plotted by his farmer-parishioners. Now we turn back to the 14th century and to that extraordinary man, **Geoffrey Chaucer.**

He was born in 1345 and died in 1400. He was the first great poet of the English race. In addition to The Canterbury Tales he wrote many other books and poems. He mastered Latin and French and had some knowledge of Italian. His career, quite apart from his writing, was varied and active. As a member of the Royal Court of Edward III he served in the wars in France, was taken prisoner and was ransomed. The King himself contributed towards the ransom payment. Chaucer later served abroad in Italy and France as an emissary of the King. Another appointment saw him working as Comptroller of Customs. Finally he was awarded a Pension and was elected a Knight of the Shire for Kent. After his death he was laid to rest in that part of Westminster Abbey which, because he was buried there, became The Poets' Corner.

Pilgrims leaving Canterbury

In the motley crowd of pilgrims who figure in The Canterbury Tales is a cross-section of the society of the time. The Tales of their Pilgrimage are a very special kind of commentary on the state of religion in the 14th century. The pilgrims include a Monk and a Friar, a Clerk, a Parson, a Pardoner, a Summoner, a Knight and a Miller. On the distaff side there are the

Wife of Bath and a Nun.
The England of that period was largely an agricultural country, with ninety per cent of the inhabitants living in villages. The Pilgrimage was from London to Canterbury to the Shrine of Thomas a Becket who had been murdered in his Cathedral in 1070. That murder made Becket's Shrine in Canterbury the magnet for pilgrims as great as those going to that other great Shrine at Walsingham. (But in Chapter 7 see how, briefly, in the 15th century the piety of the Blessed John Schorne made the tiny village of North Marston in North Bucks as popular to pilgrims as both Canterbury and Walsingham).

What does the Canterbury Pilgrimage have to tell us about the state of religion in the 14th century? The Tales make it clear that many of the pilgrims are as pleasure-bent as they are pious. Some of them are quite shameless in their motives. The Pardoner, for example, with his stock of fake relics, is clearly travelling for profit. And he can be cynical too. In part of his sermon about sin he says: "All my preaching is against avarice and such vices so as to make people give their pennies generously to me. For my sole aim is to make profit and is not at all concerned with correction of sins!!"

By the 13th century monasticism had grown in England, with foundations of many different Orders. At their best the monasteries were seats of learning and centres of arts. But by the 14th century some of the earlier virtues of monasticism had gradually eroded. Some religious houses had grown too rich and the practice of their rule had slipped.
Poverty, chastity and obedience were not as universally followed as once they were. Some of this deterioration is reflected in The Canterbury Tales and Chaucer often allows his wit to convey the falling standards. He writes of one parson who:

> ".....set his benefice to hire
> And left his sheep encumbered in the mire
> Or ran to London to earn easy bread
> By serving Masses for the wealthy dead".

Chaucer has witty comments to make also about the slackening of monastic rule:

> "The Rule of good St Benet or St Maur
> as old and strict he tended to ignore;

He let go by the things of yesterday
And took the modern world's more spacious way.
He did not rate that text at a plucked hen
Which says that hunters are not holy men
And that a monk uncloistered is a mere
Fish out of water, flapping on the pier"

Pilgrims, resting on their way to Canterbury, told each other stories to pass the time [16th century woodcut]

And Chaucer didn't spare the Friars either. He paints the Friar in The Canterbury Tales as a disreputable grasping fellow, ready to grant absolution, provided he is decently rewarded.:

"He kept his tippet stuffed with pins for curls,
And pocket-knives to give to pretty girls.
And certainly his voice was gay and sturdy,
At sing-songs he was champion of the hour.
His neck was whiter than a lily-flower
But strong enough to butt a bruiser down.
He knew the taverns well in every town
And every innkeeper and barmaid too
Better than lepers, beggars and that crew,
For in so eminent a man as he
It was not fitting with the dignity
Of his position, dealing with a scum
Of wretched lepers; nothing good can come
Of commerce with such slum-and-gutter dwellers
But only with the rich and victual-sellers"

Wit and Wisdom recorded as comment about the state of religion is a rich vein in English literature down the centuries. Chaucer was followed by many others, Betjeman among them. John Betjeman, the Poet Laureate, once wrote: "One of the joys of belonging to the warm-hearted Church of England, safely but not too folded into the cope of Canterbury, is the jokes about ourselves". The yardstick by which humorous verse about the Church must be judged is the yardstick of charity. Betjeman's conviction was that if we can laugh about ourselves we can love one another, and such "family" jokes, though they sometimes prick, will surely never wound.

Jokes about clergymen (many of them composed by clergymen themselves) are a long tradition of the church, and have been ever since the Vicar of Bray. (See chapter 8). Clerical Wit and Wisdom gently satirising the Church often takes verse form. Well over a century ago Edmund Yates gently poked fun at the celebrated Church of All Saints, Margaret Street, in London:

> "In a church which is furnish'd with mullion and gable,
> With altar and reredos, with gargoyle and groin,
> The penitents' dresses are sealskin and sable,
> The odour of sanctity's eau-de-Cologne,
> But only could Lucifer, flying from Hades,
> Gaze down on this crowd with its panniers and paints,
> He would say, as he look'd at the lords and the ladies,
> 'Oh, where is All Sinners, if this is All Saints?"

A Final Betjeman comment: "We should not be too smug or solemn, because when we have faith we can always afford to laugh. And the Saints have always been humorists."

So many others have also contributed their Wit and Wisdom about religion. William Cowper of Olney (see chapter 10) once wrote: "The parson knows enough who knows a Duke". Lord Byron once commented:""Christians have burnt each other, quite persuaded that all the Apostles would have done as they did". Lord Melbourne, the Prime Minister, after hearing an evangelical sermon, was heard to say:""Things have come to a pretty pass when religion is allowed to invade the sphere of private life".

And as we would expect, George Bernard Shaw contributed some examples of Shavian cynicism. One was: "Martyrdom is the only way in which a man can become famous without ability". And on another occasion Shaw wrote: “Christianity never got any grip of the world until it virtually reduced its claims on the ordinary citizen’s attention to a couple of hours every seventh day, and let him alone on weekdays”. Harold Macmillan, when Michael Ramsay was appointed to succeed Geoffrey Fisher as Archbishop of Canterbury, is credited with the remark: “We have had enough of Martha and it is time for some Mary”. And a contribution from P.G.Wodehouse: “The Bishop was talking to the local Master of Hounds about the difficulty he had in keeping his Vicars off the incense”

But no collection of gems of Wit and Wisdom about religion would be complete without at least a few examples from **Sydney Smith.**
Sydney Smith (1770-1845) was a priest, an essayist, and above all a wit. He was essentially an urban man, with London as his chosen base. But because the number of absentee parsons had become something of a scandal, in 1808 a Bill was passed requiring all clergymen to live in their parishes. This was an acute embarrassment to Sydney Smith because, though living in London, he was technically the incumbent of Foston-le-Clay in a remote part of Yorkshire. Required now by the new law to live in remote Foston, he tried to swap that parish with another, but without success. He did however get permission to live nearby at Heslington which was not far from York, about whose inhabitants he commented that they, “contrary to popular opinion in the south, have been converted to the Christian faith, wear clothes, and are not addicted to cannibalism”

So let this collection of samples of Wit and Wisdom end with some gems from Sydney Smith. He wrote in the Edinburgh Review: “A Curate—there is something which excites compassion in the very name of a Curate”. And to friend he wrote: “I have seen nobody since I saw you but parsons in orders, Vicars, Rectors, Curates, and every now and then (by way of turbot), an Archdeacon”. And speaking of another individual, Smith said: “He deserves to be preached to death by wild curates”. To another friend he wrote: “I am just going to pray for you at St Paul’s, but with no very lively hope of success”.
And, finally, Sydney Smith once said: “What a pity it is that we have no amusements in England but vice and religion”.

Chapter 6

A MIXED BAG — WARTS AND ALL.

As Anon so finely expressed it:

"There is so much good in the worst of us
And so much bad in the best of us
That it hardly becomes any of us
To talk about the rest of us"

In this mixed bag we meet a number of country clerics who, whatever merits they might otherwise have possessed, all fell from grace. First we meet JOHN GERVYES. He was the Parish Priest of Great Loughton in North Bucks in the 14th century. Less than three miles from Great Loughton was Little Loughton. The Parish Priest there from 1369 was Willelmum Sapcote. On June 4th 1378 one Lawrence Thetcher, walking along a country lane, came across the body of a man. He recognised him instantly as the priest from Little Loughton. He saw at once that the man was dead; the

Great Loughton Church and the village today

arrow that killed him was still embedded in his body. Thetcher reported the matter at once. An Inquest was held and the Jury found that: "Sapcote had been feloniously killed by an arrow shot at him by John Gervyes,the Priest of Great Loughton". The Records (Coroners Rolls Richard II) include the further information that the arrow was worth 1d and that the value of the bow and arrow together was 14d and: "Great Loughton is charged with this". The Records also state that John Gervyes had fled to his church immediately after the murder, and that""he had no goods or chattels".

John Gervyes, back in his church, was claiming sanctuary. In medieval England every church was considered a sanctuary. This remained the case till James I abolished the right of sanctuary for certain crimes, and in 1723 the practice of sanctuary was totally eliminated. As a priest John Gervyes would have claimed""benefit of Clergy" so that he would be dealt with in an Ecclesiastical rather than a Civil Court. The Church Courts could not impose a death sentence. So John Gervyes, at most, would only have been fined and possibly lost his parish. No one knows what caused his quarrel with his fellow priest.

Of another cleric in the 14th century it was said that he was "neither good for church nor state, sovereign nor subjects". His name was Henry Burgwash, and he was Bishop of Lincoln, no less. Other epithets heaped on him were:"'covetous, rebellious, ambitious and injurious'. Twice he was Lord treasurer, and once Chancellor of England.

How came a man of such eminence to deserve such criticism? The good people of Fingest in Buckinghamshire, at the farthest edge of Bishop Burgwash's huge diocese, could tell you. The Bishop owned the Manor of Fingest in the Chilterns. He loved to come there to enjoy the hunting and to indulge in the good life of a Lord of the Manor. In 1330, to improve the park surrounding the manor, he enclosed the common lands. The people were incensed for now they were deprived of arable lands for growing crops, and of grazing lands for their cattle. That was no way for their Father-in-God to behave! Hatred for Bishop Burgwash was intense in Fingest, and it did not cease even when he died in 1340.

Stories began to be told of ghostly reappearances of the hated bishop, dressed not in episcopal purple, but in a hunting green tunic. The green-clad apparition, it is said, begged the people to forgive him, and urged them to go to Lincoln to petition his successor to free the enclosed lands and so undo the harm that he had done. So they took him at his word, went to Lincoln to state their case, and succeeded! The villagers won back their common land. The wrong the villainous Bishop Burgwash had done was now righted.

One cleric who rather fell down on his job was Robert Dance, Vicar of Winslow. When he was examined touching his ability of learning and knowledge for the discharge of his calling in the Ministry, on October 4th 1586, he was found to be unable to answer in the Latin tongue, and was able very meanly to satisfy questions of religion in the English tongue.
In the 16th and 17th centuries numbers of the clergy were "mere readers of prayers" and were often styled "Reading Vicars" or "Reading Curates". In an edition of the Homilies republished in 1562 the Preface stated that "all they that are appointed Ministers that have NOT the gift of preaching sufficiently to instruct the people shall read plainly and distinctly one of the said Homilies as they stand in this book".

In the 17th century there was a clergyman who is very hard to classify. His name was RICHARD CARPENTER (1609-1670). He came from Newport Pagnell and originally he was undoubtedly a Catholic. On a visit to Rome, it was said, he was commissioned by the Pope to return to England and to work for the conversion of England. He was to do this under the auspices of the Benedictines. However, on his return to England he became an Anglican! But later he changed again, and became an Independent Minister! He now vigorously attacked both Anglicans and Baptists, and he preached effectively in and around Aylesbury. He died in 1670 and in the later years of his life he had returned to the Roman Catholic fold.

A contemporary of Richard Carpenter and in the same area of North Bucks there was JOSEPH NEWELL. He came as Rector of the Parish of Thornborough in 1660 and his ministry there lasted nearly thirty years. His ministry was much appreciated. The congregation admired his zeal in

Thornborough Church. For 30 years in the 17th century it had a bogus Rector. (JH)

visiting the sick and they liked his preaching and his administration of the Sacraments. In short, he did well all the things that a good parish priest does. There was only one snag—he was bogus! He wasn't a priest and he never had been. This came to light in 1688 when Diocesan authorities carried out a visitation of the Parish. When John Newell was asked to produce his Letters of Order he couldn't do so and explained that he had never been ordained! He was ordered to leave the parish and he went to live in Pottersbury where later he died.
How could such a thing have happened? The clue is probably in the date of his arrival in Thornborough—1660. That was the year when the monarchy was restored, marking the end of the long years of Puritan rule. During those years so many Parish Priests were ejected from their livings and were replaced by Puritan ministers. For a decade the Civil War and the execution of Charles I had resulted in a breakdown of most ordinary Church administration. So it could well be that when Joseph Newell arrived in 1660 and announced that he was their new Parish Priest the good folk of Thornborough were glad to welcome him.

We come next to WILLIAM DODD. Perhaps his claim to be included among country clerics could be considered somewhat tarnished because shamefully he was the absentee vicar of three country parishes simultaneously. He lived in none of them and instead paid a pittance to curates to minister in the parishes of Wing, Hockliffe and Chalgrave while he lived it up in London. Meanwhile he kept the tithes and income from the country parishes.
He was the son of an Anglican Rector who followed his father into the ministry.He was a man of undoubted gifts. He was a Doctor of Divinity and a talented author. He was a popular and powerful preacher and crowds, including Royalty, flocked to the Preaching House he had built for himself in Pimlico. The King appointed him as a Royal Chaplain. The Reverend Dr William Dodd

The Absentee Vicar of Wing, Hanged at Tyburn in 1777

was the friend and protègè of the Earl of Chesterfield who made him Tutor to his sons. Dodd was often called 'the Macaroni Parson' because of the flamboyance of his dress— 'macaroni' being the 18th century word for a dandy.

Dodd seemed to have everything going for him, but suddenly his world crashed about his ears. What went wrong? The answer is that he was living way beyond his means and was hopelessly in debt. In desperation he did a most foolish thing—he forged a Bond for £4,200, forging Lord Chesterfield's signature to it. The fraud was easily detected and Dodd was arrested and put on trial. On May 26th 1777 he was found guilty and sentenced to be hanged. On June 27th, 1777 the brilliant Dr William Dodd met his death at Tyburn. He was 48.

The Irish novelist/parson LAURENCE STERNE was born in 1713. He has been described as "a bawdy cleric". He was a great-grandson of the Archbishop of York. He was ordained in 1738 and was Vicar of Sutton-on-the-Forrest, and a Prebend of York Minster. He married Elizabeth Lumley in 1741 but sat very lightly to his marriage vows. His wife once found him in bed with the maid and tipped him out on to the floor. Soon after, she went mad and claimed to be the Queen of Bohemia!

Thomas Patch's portrait of Laurence Sterne

As a parish priest Sterne was thought to be a good preacher and he also went in for political journalism. But his real fame came through his novels. His "Political Romance" came out in 1759. It was a thinly disguised satire on the See of York. It set the scene in a backward country parish. The Archbishop of York took offence at the novel and insisted that the book should be confiscated and destroyed. So the whole edition of 500 copies was burnt.

Undeterred, within a year his novel "Tristram Shandy" came out. Its bawdiness of style seemed at first to give little offence, until, that is, the public woke up to the fact that the author was a clergyman! Even then, the Archbishop of York was delighted with "Tristram Shandy" and claimed that he read it every six weeks! Strangely enough this was the same Archbishop of York who had insisted on the banning and destruction of "Political Romance"

"Tristram Shandy" came out in a series of instalments, six of them between 1759 and 1767. Sterne also wrote "The Sermons of Mr Yorick", Yorick being the parson who figured in Tristram Shandy. The Yorick books also came out by instalments, three of them, just as Tristram Shandy had done.

Sterne loved to shock and his books featured the "indecencies" which prompted Goldsmith to attack Sterne in an Essay which he called "The Absurd Taste for Obscene and Pert Novels".

Sterne's private life continued to be unconventional. He formed an attachment to Mrs Eliza Draper, the wife of an officer in The East India Company. This liaison too was given literary exposure, for he wrote' "Letters from Yorick to Eliza", but this was not published till after his death.

Sterne suffered from tuberculosis and he died from pleurisy in 1768 leaving his familty insolvent.

A hundred years later brings us the scandalous true story of a country cleric in Bedfordshire. His name was EDWARD DRAX FREE. He was Vicar of Sutton in Beds for 22 years, from 1808 to 1830. He was a gambler, a drunkard and an incorrigible womaniser. Nowadays we often read that people with a drug habit commit crimes to finance their addiction. Edward Drax Free had no drug addiction, but he shamelessly used his position as Vicar to help him with the addictions he DID have—gambling, drink and womanising.

He virtually turned the churchyard into a farm yard. Sheep, horses, cows, roamed there at will, even into and out of the church porch. Pigs frequently dug up graves. He stripped the lead off the church roof and cut down innumerable oak trees. Fees for weddings and funerals were charged for at excessive rates. The routine services in church were conducted at breathless speed. As often as not he omitted the sermon. Sometimes services were cancelled altogether. There were periods when he locked up the church for weeks while he hid from his creditors.

He was unmarried and had a succession of housekeepers. He considered it part of their duties to comply with his wishes in bed as well as by board. No

fewer than five children were born at the Vicarage as a result.
This scandalous state of affairs would surely have to be halted. But it took 22 years for that to happen. It was the local Squire who finally took action and demanded the Vicar's expulsion. But the Rev. Edward Drax Free was not going to surrender easily. He sold the entire contents of the Vicarage and barricaded himself there with his latest housekeeper/mistress. He was prepared to shoot at any who tried to approach. It was decided to leave him to starve into submission. The villagers, led by the Archdeacon of Bedford, maintained the siege. Finally in 1830 the Vicar surrendered. His 22 years as Vicar of Sutton had been so scandalous that there could be no question of his being allowed to work in any other parish. He lived another thirteen years as a beggar. He died in 1843 after being run over by a varnish maker's cart.
A much more attractive cleric, though one not without his faults, was the Rector of Simpson, always known as "Tally Ho! Hanmer". He was addicted to hunting and dressed accordingly. He sported mahogany-coloured top boots, a square-cut riding coat, with black breeches, crowned by a peculiar black hat with a broad flat rim. He was constantly in debt and spent quite a time in a Debtor's Prison. He sponged shamelessly on his friends and neighbours, and he loved to go up to London to dine and to attend the theatre. Yet for all that, he was popular in his parish, charitable to the poor, and he could preach excellent sermons. J.K.Fowler wrote of him: "His Rectory was generally barricaded against creditors throughout the week. Only on Sundays could he walk about in its grounds, and visit his parishioners. Tally Ho! Hanmer was a rollicking jolly sportsman, a bachelor, of a type of class once very prevalent in England. For good or ill such men are no more."

This mixed bag of "Warts and All" country clerics brings us finally to the extraordinary TREBITSCH LINCOLN. He qualifies as a country cleric because for a few months in 1903 he was Curate in the Parish of Appledore-with-Ebony in Kent. He was born in 1879, the second son of a large Jewish family in a provincial town not far from Budapest. He very early on decided that he would seek his fortune in the Gentile world. Meanwhile he made a living by thieving. His speciality was watch stealing.
He travelled to England and in London he made his way to the offices of The Mission to Jews near Toynbee Hall. There he encountered the Reverend Mr Lypshytz (and stole his watch!). Mr Lypshytz assisted Trebitsch to go

to Canada under the auspices of the Presbyterian Church. But in Canada Trebitsch decided there was no future for him with the Presbyterians whom he considered"“mean”. So he switched and became an Anglican! A Canadian contact cabled to The Mission to Jews in London as follows:-"“FOUND SPLENDIDLY QUALIFIED CONVERT, DEEPLY SPIRITUAL, SEVEN LANGUAGES, SHALL I RETAIN?” The upshot was that Trebitsch returned to England, was ordained and became Curate at Appledore, where his sermons in a delicious Hungarian accent delighted the congregation. But he couldn't settle. A timely bequest enabled him to plan a new future. He married a German Protestant lady who bore him many sons, most of whom ended up badly. He now decided that he might best build his future on a Temperance ticket. He came to know the chocolate manufacturer and active Liberal, Seebohm Rowntree. Through this connection Trebitsch Lincoln (as he had styled himself since his conversion to Anglicanism) managed to become Liberal MP for Darlington. But his finances were sketchy and still needed to be augmented by thieving and a variety of frauds. So he thought it prudent to disappear for a while. He went to Romania and became involved in the oil business. In that context his travels took him to America. But oil shareholders were made restive by his claims for expenses and he was extradited from the USA to Britain. This was in the middle of World War I.

Trebitsch Lincoln tried to play German and British Intelligence against each other, offering his services to both. But the plan misfired and he was arrested as a spy and was given a three-year prison sentence.

After his release he returned to Central Europe and joined an International Counter-Revolution Group. He rose to the top of this organisation and became its official foreign affairs spokesman. He helped the Group to stage the Kapp *putsch* in Berlin in 1920. His next venture was to try to sell the secrets of the “White International” to either the Czechs or the French. In the event it was The Times that bought them.

In the 1920s several German generals went to China to offer their services to the various warlords in that vast land. Trebitsch followed them there and it was there that he “suffered” his next conversion—he became a Buddhist and styled himself Abbot Chao Kung! At this point the Japanese invaded China and occupied Shanghai. Trebitsch promptly offered his services to the Japanese. Later he also offered his services to the Nazi Secret Services! In his closing years he addressed letters to virtually every world leader, including the Pope. He invited them all to meet with him so that together they could sort out the world's problems. Nobody accepted the invitations. Trebitsch Lincoln died in 1943 aged 64.

It is hard to credit all the twists and turns in the kaleidoscopic career of this extraordinary cleric. One commentator, more charitable than most, described him as: "an impressario of charismatic charm, fantastic intuition, with a prodigious baroque sense of theatre and a quickness of intelligence which is very Jewish".

Chapter 7.

TWO HOLY MEN.

In 1290 JOHN SCHORNE came from Monks Risborough to become Rector of North Marston in North Bucks. It is said that soon after he arrived he struck the ground near the church and fresh clear water gushed out, much as Moses had done when he struck the rock in the desert. That fresh water supply in North Marston was a boon to the villagers. Associated with it was the notion that it had medicinal properties, further advancing the reputation John Schorne soon acquired for being able to cure the sick. It was also said that Master John Schorne's knees were horny from his constant long prayers for the sick and the needy.

The holy well which originally bore the saints' name derived its medicinal qualities from its chemistry and the prayers are the benedictions of John. Later it became known as the town well and consisted ofa cistern five feet four square and six feet deep with a flight of four stone steps descending into the water. It was enclosed by brick and stone walls with a wooden roof. The size would indicate that it could have been used as a bath, but according to most reports the chief benefit was as drinking water.

The Rector, John Schorne, was variously known as Master Schorne, or Sir John Schorne or as St.Schorne. Technically it was never correct to call him Saint for the Pope had never canonised him. Even so, many people in England, not only at North Marston, regarded him as a Saint. To the miracle of his creation of the well, plus his reputation for healing the sick and his manifest piety, there was also added a legend which grew up. The legend was that Blessed John Schorne possessed the ability to control the Devil—by conjuring him into a boot! It is said that there was formerly a chancel window in North Marston Church showing a representation of the "miracle" of North Marston. Browne Willis the Antiquarian, Lord of the Manor of Bletchley, said that Mr Virgin, the Vicar in 1660, told him that there was such a picture in glass of Sir John Schorne. As he described it, it showed Sir John Schorne with a boot under his arm like a bagpipe into which he was squeezing a moppet representing the Devil. It was also reported that similar pictures of the 'Saint' existed at Gately and Causton in Norfolk, which indicates how far and wide John Schorne's fame had spread. In many places too the motif of "the Devil in the Boot" was adopted as an Inn sign.

St Mary's, North Marston

John Schorne's empty shrine in North Marston Church

Incidentally, the same Vicar of North Marston, the Reverend Mr Virgin, who told Browne Willis about "the Devil in the Boot", has his own memorial in the church. In delightful naivety it depicts a hand, with the fingers pointing downwards, and the words: "He lies dust down thare".

There is other evidence also of how widely John Schorne's fame had spread. In a Poem called "The Play of the Four Pardoners" the Palmer had a line which referred to: "at St.Mark in Venice one Master John Schorne in Canterbury".

John Schorne was Rector at North Marston for 24 years. When he died he was buried, as he wished, in North Marston Church. His remains were enclosed in a shrine which rapidly attracted pilgrims to North Marston from far and wide. Indeed, it was said that apart from Walsingham and Canterbury, no shrine attracted more pilgrims than North Marston. Pilgrims came there not only from many parts of this country but also from across the Channel.

Pilgrims stayed in North Marston until the shrine was lost

But towards the end of the 15th century North Marston's days as a

North Marston St Mary'sChurch

pilgrim centre were abruptly ended. This is because in 1475 King Edward IV wished to build a new St.George's Chapel in Windsor. The King appointed the Bishop of Salisbury as Dean of Windsor and charged him with the task of getting the new Chapel built. Shrewdly, the new Dean realised that he needed a magnet to draw pilgrims to Windsor. It occurred to him that John Schorne's bones would be the answer. So from the Pope he secured permission to transfer John Schorne's shrine from North Marston to Windsor. Thus Windsor's gain meant North Marston's loss. Some might say that for this service to Royalty North Marston might at least be entitled to call itself North Marston Regis! (As a matter of fact there is a second reason why North Marston might deserve such an honour. The eccentric barrister, John Camden Neild, Patron of the Living at North Marston, astonished everybody when in his Will he left £250,000 to Queen Victoria! The Queen used some of the money to restore the Chancel of North Marston Church, and to commission a fine new East Window. The rest of the money Queen Victoria used to purchase Balmoral! So North Marston might be thought to have earned the additional "Regis" twice over!!)

Schrone College, North Marston

There was an interesting much later instalment of the Schorne saga. In the 1870s Dr S.R.James came as Vicar to North Marston. In 1874 he established Schorne College in the village. It had about ninety boys, aged 9 to 15. They were taught by various members of the Vicar's family. They published a joint School and Parish Magazine called The Schornonian. Schorne College lasted from 1874 to 1912. Ironically, given the healing miracles attributed to Blessed John Schorne almost exactly six hundred years before, it was an outbreak of cholera in 1912 which caused Schorne College to close.

The second holy man we now consider is GEORGE HERBERT (1593-1633) He was a man with good family connections. His mother was Lady Magdalen Herbert and his brother was Lord Cherbury. Educated at Westminster School, George Herbert went up to Trinity College, Cambridge. After graduating there he was appointed a Fellow in 1614, and Public Orator in 1619. In 1624-25 he was MP for Montgomery.

George Herbert who renounced his wordly ambitions to become a country parson

He was held in high regard by King James I and was a prominent figure at Court. All the signs were that he was destined for a successful worldly career, But this did not happen because in 1630, under the influence of Archbishop Laud, he turned away from "the painted pleasures of Court life" and sought ordination. He was Vicar first at Leighton Bromswold in Huntingdonshire, and then Bemerton in Wiltshire. Despite his own slender means he restored the churches at both places.

George Herbert at Bemerton

George Herbert, as well as being a priest was also a metaphysical poet. He wrote "Sacred Poems" which were published in 1633, under the title of "The Church". He also wrote a book entitled "A Priest in the Temple" and in it he gave guidance for the country parson. He thought of the Church as "Christ's comely bride to be decked with seemly ornaments". He preached the notion that holiness is to be expressed in the quiet offering of one's gifts and talents however slender they might be. One of his phrases was "The mean thy praise and glory is". One of his hymns, still often sung, has the verse:

A servant with this clause
Makes drudgery divine;
Who sweeps a room, as for thy law'
Makes that and the action fine"

George Herbert's friend and fellow mystic was Nicholas Ferrar who was made a deacon in 1625 (but never went on to become a priest). Ferrar founded a Utopian religious community at Little Gidding. Some 30 members lived in community there, combining a life of prayer and services with practical work in printing and bookbinding. It was at Little Gidding that the first edition of Herbert's "The Temple" was published in 1633.

Each in his own way, Herbert and Ferrar were setting an example of the Laudian counter-challenge to the Puritans.

George Herbert married Jane, the daughter of Charles Danvers of Baynton in Wiltshire. No children were born to the marriage. His complexion was always very fine but he was consumptive and died at 40 in 1633. The successor to the little Church at Bemerton is still there. To worship in it is evocative of the memory of that holy man who ministered there nearly four centuries ago. His writings, poetical and otherwise, are perhaps summed up in one verse that he wrote:

Of all the creatures both in sea and land
Onely to Man thou hast made known thy wayes,
And put the penne alone into his hand,
And made him Secretarie of thy praise.

St Andrew's Church Bemerton
and the footpath to Salisbury

Chapter 8

STRANGER THAN FICTION.

1

On Maundy Thursday night in 1349 the Vicar of Stantonbury, Walter de Bascheshes walked in the darkness towards his church. As he stretched out his hand to open the door he drew back in alarm. For there, on the door's central panel he saw a gargoyle so hideous that for a moment he was transfixed in horror. In desperation he hurried into the church and threw holy water from the holy water stoup on the apparition. Then he passed out!

He was found next day, Good Friday, lying insensible on the floor of the church. When he recovered he tried to explain what had happened. Asking for charcoal, he sketched a likeness of the terrible apparition he had seen. The story of this strange occurrence spread far and wide and became the basis for the Stanton Legend. The cult of the Holy Door of Stantonbury even drew King Henry V, who rode over from Windsor to see for himself the place where it had happened. Even as late as 1591 Queen Elizabeth's Court of High Commission gave orders that the old door should be pannelled on the side where the apparition was alleged to have appeared, and that in future the door should remain open.

2

The village of Fawsley is near Daventry. The Reverend Dr John Wilkins was born there in 1614. He graduated at Magdalen Hall, Oxford. After ordination he became a domestic chaplain. But mathematics and mechanics interested him as much as theology. He was one of the founders of The Royal Society. When the Civil War broke out he sided with Parliament. He was appointed Warden of Wadham. In 1656 he married a widowed sister of Oliver Cromwell. In 1659 Richard Cromwell, Oliver's son, appointed him Master of Trinity College, Cambridge. Thus far his career had prospered. But then Cromwell fell and the monarchy was restored in 1660 and the Reverend Dr Wilkins was dispossessed. However, he bounced back again and soon recovered court favour. He became Preacher at Grays Inn and

Rector of St Lawrence Jewry. From there he went on to become Dean of Ripon and by 1669 he had become Bishop of Chester! So he was a regular sort of "Vicar of Bray" character, able to accommodate himself to the changing religious views of those in power.
The original Vicar of Bray, in Berkshire, survived in his Vicarage throughout the reigns of Henry VIII, Edward VI, Mary and Elizabeth. To survive, he had twice been a Papist, and twice a Protestant. When he was accused of time-serving he was said to have replied: "Not so, neither, for if I changed my religion, I am sure I kept true to my principle, which is to live and die the Vicar of Bray". He went on to be celebrated in the song we all know:

'And this is the law I will maintain
Until my dying day, Sir,
That whatsoever King may reign
I'll still be the Vicar of Bray, Sir.'

But that wasn't the only genius of Dr Wilkins. His other genius was that he anticipated 20th century discoveries and developments way back in the 17th century. For example, in 1628 he wrote a book called "Discovery of a World in the Moon". In it he seriously discussed the possibility of communication with the moon by a flying machine! In 1640 he wrote another book called "Discourse concerning a New Planet", arguing that our earth is only one of the planets. In yet a third book, called""Mercury, or the Secret and Swift Messenger" he spelt out how man could communicate with others over any distance. In short, in the 17th century John Wilkins anticipated by about 300 years such marvels as space travel, moon landings, wireless and telegraphy.

3

Daventry is again the context for another example of truth being stranger than fiction. A Priory was founded there in 1090 by Hugh de Leycester for Monks of the Cluniac Order. Their number originally was four. The Priory grew larger and richer in later years and this attracted the attention of Cardinal Wolsey who was looking for funds to finance his plans for new Colleges in Ipswich and Christ Church in Oxford. So Wolsey hatched a plot. He incited five people to provoke a quarrel with the Monks about certain lands, intending that when the case came up for judgement it would be before him. The plan misfired and of the five people who had agreed to fake the quarrel, two killed each other; a third drowned himself in a well; the fourth, a rich man, lost all his wealth and became a beggar for the rest of his life. And the fifth man, though he went on to become a bishop was cruelly maimed in Ireland.

4

The Village of Willingale in Essex is small, population about 500. Yet it has the distinction of having TWO churches, side by side in the same churchyard. Both are fully functional and used for worship on Sundays and weekdays alike. Until 1929 the two churches were separate and distinct, each with its own Rector. They were then called Willingale Spain and Willingale Doe. The two are now united in one parish, the Parish of Willingale.

Both churches have long architectural histories, starting from the 12th century in the case of St Andrew's Church, formerly the Parish Church of Willingale Spain, and from the 14th century in the case of St Christopher's Church, formerly the Parish Church of Willingale Doe.

Willingale's Two Churches

Why "Spain" and""Doe"? The answer is that St Christopher's Church was built by Hervey D'Espania, Then in the 14th century the D'Ou family came to live in Willingale and family rivalry led to the building of the second church. That is an odd enough story, but at least it is more credible than the popularly believed story that the two churches were built by two sisters who quarrelled. The very fact that the two churches are of different periods some 200 years apart scotches the'"two quarrelling sisters " theory.

Services are held regularly in both churches—in the Parish Church (formerly that of Willingale Doe) on Sundays and greater Festivals; and on weekdays in the other church, (formerly the Parish Church of Willingale Spain.) And on Palm Sunday both churches are used in the course of the one service—the Palms are blessed in Spain Church, the procession then goes to Doe Church where the Eucharist is completed.

5

The small village of Molland-Bremley on the edge of Exmoor has a beautiful church with an interesting history. The legendary figure of the Reverend John Froude, the incumbent at nearby Knowstone often preached here. Many stories are told of this rather lawless character who, it is said, organised bands of thugs to burn or otherwise destroy the property of anyone who offended him. Not surprisingly, he became known as "Wicked Parson Froude". He died in a fit of rage, being unable to revenge a young farmer who had removed a shrub growing in front of his parlour window. Parson Froude was the character upon whom R.D.Blackmore based""Parson Chowne" in his novel, "The Maid of Sker" (1872). The real but legendary figure of the Reverend John Froude, was the Incumbent of Knowstone for almost half a century. It is said that his ghost walks the lanes at night in Knowstone.

6

RICHARD NAPIER was the parson of Great Linford in North Bucks from 1590 to 1634. He was a pupil of Simon Forman the astrologer and inherited all his papers. Apart from astrology Napier was also well-known for his medical skill and he was formally licensed to practice medicine in 1604. He was a person of great abstinence and piety and spent two hours in prayer every day. People who were sick, in mind or body sought his help. Invariably he would retire to pray for the patient. From his papers it is clear that Napier would lay the needs of the patient before Raphael the Archangel, and that he would then be guided by Raphael's response. He kept careful "case notes" and these frequently record in the margin the letters: R.Ris. This meant Responsium Raphaelis (Raphael's Answer). Raphael would tell Napier whether the patient was curable or incurable. The problems about which Napier consulted Raphael would include not only medical matters, but also more general queries, some of them in astrological contexts. Thus in 1621 Napier felt able to tell John Prideaux DD that in 20 years time he would be a bishop. And so it came to pass, for in 1641 Dr Prideaux became Bishop of Worcester.

Richard Napier
1559-1634

Parson of Great Linford (Bucks) from 1590-1634. He was a pupil of Simon Forman the astrologer (whose diaries have recently been published) and he inherited Forman's papers. He was equally well known for his medical skill, and was formally licenced to practice in 1604.

One religio-philosophical query on which Napier consulted Raphael was the question: Do evil spirits out-number good spirits, or vice versa? Napier's papers record the verdict:-The Good Spirits. And in the margin alongside is written; R.Ris.
Napier gave the poor most of what he earned for treating the sick. It would be very natural for Napier to give thought to his own health and expectations about the future. For the record it can be said that he foretold his own death to a day and an hour. And on that day and at that hour he did indeed die, praying on his knees. It was 1st April 1634 and he was 75.
To this day there is in existence the well-known Church organisation called the Guild of St Raphael and very many parishes have local branches of it to promote prayers for the sick.

Guild of St Raphael

7

It was Christmas Eve, 1753. Or was it? That is what many hundreds of people were wondering, crowded into the Rectory garden at Quainton in Bucks. There was excitement and much pushing and shoving. Then as midnight approached the hubbub died down and lanterns were raised even higher, as people pressed forward to get a better view.

Quainton Church and Almshouses. In the Rectory garden in December 1753 something odd occurred

Why were they there? What did they expect to happen? To answer those questions you must go back twice into the past. First, into the very recent past—just to last year, 1752. In that year by Statute 24 of George II it was decreed that Britain would change its calendar to bring these islands into line with the continent of Europe. The old Julian Calendar would be dropped and the Gregorian Calendar would henceforth be followed. To make the change over it was announced that 24 September 1752 would be followed next day by 14 September.

There was consternation everywhere. People thought they were being cheated out of eleven days of their lives—that their life-spans would be shortened by nearly two weeks! And would it not mean that they were being cheated out of eleven days' pay? There were near riots in many places and the cry went up all over the land—"Give us back our eleven days!"

Quainton was as much affected by all this furore as anywhere else. History doesn't relate who first suggested that Quainton had its own special contribution to contribute to the argument. To know what that special contribution was means going back into the past—a long way back this time, to AD 63 in fact.

In AD 63, so folklore and fable said, Joseph of Arimathea came to Britain, and so brought the Christian faith. He settled in Glastonbury. And he did not come empty-handed. Folk-lore said that he brought with him the Holy Grail, the very cup that Christ used at the Last Supper. He also brought his staff and planted it in the soil in Glastonbury. Miraculously, the staff took root and grew into a tree. And the tree miraculously budded and flowered every Christmas in honour of Christ's birth. It was widely believed that the Glastonbury Thorn flowered at midnight on Christmas Eve and that the blossoms lasted just the one day, the day of the Saviour's birth.

And Quainton comes into the picture because in the Rector's garden there was a tree said to have been grown from a cutting from the famous Glastonbury Thorn Tree. That is why the crowd was there. They hoped that their own local descendant from the Glastonbury Thorn would settle their doubts once and for all. They would trust nature to decide for them whether tomorrow, 25 December 1753 (new style) was Christmas Day or not. If the thorn tree in the Rector's garden budded on 24 December (new style) they would accept that both by the Law of the Land and by the law of nature next day really would be Christmas Day.

Came midnight—and no buds appeared. The crowd waited for a while, to give the tree a chance. But no buds appeared.—"That's it, then" they said, "tomorrow isn't a true and proper Christmas Day, no matter what the King and his Parliament may say". And they all went home.

So on Christmas Day 1753 (new style) nobody went to Church in Quainton. Instead, eleven days later people kept Christmas on the old date, 5 January. In time of course the fuss died down. The new Calendar was gradually accepted by everyone and Christmas Day was accepted to be December 25. But for the record, 5 January, which on the Julian Calendar is Old Christmas Day, has for centuries been called Twelfth Night. It is the eve of the Twelfth Day after Christmas. And that Twelfth Day is the Feast of the Epiphany which celebrates the coming to Bethlehem of the Three Wise Men. So, whether in Quainton or anywhere else, the Christmas Festival neatly spans the eleven days that everyone got so worked up about nearly two and a half centuries ago.

8

Finally, here is a touching true story which well illustrates that truth can be stranger than fiction. In the parish of Brackley in the late 18th century John Moore was the curate. Curates are often poor and John Moore was poorer than most. Also in Brackley there was a rich business man named John Watts. He and his wife worshipped at Brackley church. They befriended the poor curate and often invited him to dine at their house. On one occasion John Watts lent the poor curate £10. When the curate was unable to repay the loan he felt too ashamed to continue to enjoy the business man's hospitality, so he went no more to the rich man's house for dinner. The rich man learned why the curate stayed away and persuaded him to resume his visits for dinner.

Later, the curate was appointed to a good living. From that moment onwards his progress was steadily upwards. In fact he rose so high that eventually he became the Most Reverend John Moore, Archbishop of Canterbury!

Meanwhile the business man's affairs in Brackley were moving in the opposite direction. The plumbing business which had been the foundation of his success suddenly failed. He and his wife found themselves almost paupers.

Archbishop Moore learned of this and promptly sent money to help his old friend. From then on he paid Mr and Mrs Watts an Annuity. When Watts died, the Archbishop continued the Annuity to his widow.

Then Archbishop Moore died. But the Archbishop's widow continued paying the Annuity. And when the Archbishop's widow died, her son continued to pay the Annuity. And this went on until, in 1821, Mrs Watts herself died, aged ninety-six.

Chapter 9

MISADVENTURES OF FOUR COUNTRY CLERICS

1.

The Rev. Anthony Tyringham.

Almost invariably the House of God is found adjacent to the house of the Lord of the Manor. By the power of Advowson the Lord of the Manor had the right to appoint the priest for the parish. It often happened that a member of the family of the Lord of the Manor would be ordained, in which case he could take the Living. Such was the case of the Rev.Anthony Tyringham who had served as Priest of the parish since 1611 in the Valley of the Ouse where Tyringham Manor stood.

Here is the fascinating but shocking contemporary account of what happened to him in 1646. It was written soon after the shameful affair took place and was first published in a small Royalist book called "Mercurius Rusticus". The spelling and phraseology are of the period. Where necessary an explanation appears in italics and in brackets.

Master Anthony Tyringham, Parson of Tyringham in Buckinghamshire, having businesse at Maids Morton at his returne came to Buckingham, where he met two of his nephews. The Uncle and his Nephews glad of so happy a meeting, after some stay to congratulate the good chance, and to refresh themselves, set forward in their journey and passed in peace without danger untill they came neere to Stony-Stratford, where a partee of Dragooners coming from Ailesbury surprized them; and instantly, scarce asking them from whence they came, searched and disarmed them, which was no difficult achievement, there being but one sword amongst all three. The Rebells take from them their Horses, their Coats and money; superfluous things as they conceived

for men destined to captivity; for having spoyled them of their Horses, Money and Garments, they send them with a strong guard prisoners to Ailesbury, while the rest of the Partee, lurking about Stony-Stratford, stayed there to expect some fresh booty. And that in this we doe not slander these great Champions of the Subjects Liberties and Properties, the issue will acquit us. For presently after (to show that all was Fish which came to Net) they seized upon a poore Bone lace man and a shoemaker, robbed them of what they had, and in the same manner sent them away prisoners to Ailesbury. (*A 'lace' man was an intermediary between local lacemakers and the markets. The qualification' 'Bone' signifies that he dealt in bobbin lace rather than in needlepoint lace.)*

The guard of Dragooners having brought their three prisoners about a mile and a half on the way towards Ailesbury, commanded them againe to alight. And they first commanded Master Tyringham to pull off his cassocke, who being not sudden in obeying the command, nor over hasty to untye his Girdle to disroabe himself of the distinctive garment of his Profession one of the Dragooners, to quicken him, cut him through the hat into the head with the sword taken from one of his Nephews, and with another blow cut him over the fingers. Master Tyringham wondering at so barbarous usage without any provocation, came towards him that had wounded him, and desired him to hold his hands, pleading that he was a CLERGIEMAN, a PRISONER, and DISARMED. The cowardly Villaine either fearing the approach of a disarmed man, or willing to lay hold on any advantage to expose the Prisoners to the fury of his fellowes, cryed out: "Shoot the rogues, for they intend to resist". The word was no sooner given but a Musquet was instantly discharged at one of Master Tyringham's Nephewes; but the Musqueteere missing his mark, another of the Rebells with his sword aymed righter, and ranne him into the shoulder. A Musquet was presented to the other Nephew, but God's Providence restrained the murtherous intention of the Rebell that he did not give fire. Thus exercising their pleasure upon disarmed wounded men, they rob Master Tyringham of his Cassocke, rifle all their pockets, and take from them what they please, and to palliate their cruelty, they send two Dragooners back, to tell their Captains and their Companies that the Prisoners committed to their custody and conduct made resistance. Upon this false alarm given, presently the Captains and their Companies make up to them, to assist a strong guard against three disarmed, and of them two wounded men, being come where they were, they encompasse them about, and without any examination of the businesse, presuming the suggestion to be undoubted truth, one of the Rebells, Captain Pollard by name, with a full blow strikes at Master Tyringham, and with his sword cuts his Arme and Cubit -bones crosse the elbow almost asunder. Master Tyringham (almost three-score yeeres of age within two) bore this barbarous usage with undaunted courage, and hearing this bloody villaine called Captaine Pollard, in a pleasant indignation, expressed the sense of the injurie thus: "That now he has made him a Pollard indeed", a metaphor easily understood by Woodmen, who usually call a Tree whose limbs or branches are lopped off a Pollard.

Master Tyringham's arme thus miserably wounded and hanging dangling from his shoulder, without any government from the nerves or sinews, one of his nephewes having a mourning Riband, tendered it to his Uncle to bind up his arme, but the Rebells will not permit it, but they remaine inexorable, and having rendered them so farre unable to resist, that some were hardly able to sit the jades on which they were mounted, they again set forward for Ailesbury. *(Jade—a poor or tired horse)* The horses being tyred, made the way very tedious, especially to Master Tyringham, who lost much blood on the way as they went. The prisoners were again commanded to alight at a towne called Whitchurch, within two miles of Ailesbury. Here they fall on Master Tyringham afresh, and plunder him as eagerly as if he had been new come into their hands, and not touched by them before. They pluck off his boots, and take from his Jerkin, his Hat and Cap, all the fences provided for cold and weather, and the usual fortifications against the injuries of wind and raine, and so make a Patterne of the man wounded Between Jerusalem and Jericho. *(The Parable of the Good Samaritan. St Luke chapter 10).*

At last they arrived at Ailesbury in cold and darkness. The Chyrrurgions (*Surgeons)* viewed and dressed the wound but concluded unanimously that they must cut off his Arme next day, or else it would Gangreene and infallibly kill him, which next day was done accordingly. Master Tyringham bore the losse of his Arme with incredible resolution and courage, as knowing the justice of that cause for which he suffered, and as willing to lay down his Life in testimony of his Loyalty, as his Brother Master Edward Tyringham, one of the Gentlemen of the King's Privy Chamber had done before him, who had the last Winter being employed in his Majestie's service, and set on by a Partee of Rebells fought valiantly but oppressed with multitudes, received so many wounds that he dyed of them. But it hath pleased God so to blesse the means used for this Gentleman's recovery, that there are great hopes he will survive these maimes, and (as himself undauntedly told the rebells to their faces): "Lived to see them hanged. Amen"

Anthony Tyringham made a remarkable recovery. He continued at his post as Rector of Tyringham until his death on 19th August 1659 at the age of 81, and was buried at Tyringham. While he may not have fulfilled his prophecy to see his attackers hanged, he probably outlived many of them. And he certainly outlived Oliver Cromwell who died a year earlier in 1658. Saddest of all, he did not live to rejoice in the Restoration of Charles II to the Monarchy in 1660.

2.
THE PARSON AND THE BEAR.

A second example of shameful mistreatment to a country cleric also occurred during the Civil War. It illustrates all too graphically the disturbed state of the country and the general insecurity of life and property at that sad time. On this occasion the victim was an elderly country parish priest in Wellingborough, Northants.

A gang of thugs and ruffians was roaming the countryside intent on mischief. They attacked a barber and stole his Dancing Bear. Continuing on their way, beating the bear as they went, they looked to see what other "fun" they might have. By sad mischance they came across the old country priest and set upon him with glee. They seized him and tied him onto the back of the tormented bear, expecting it to turn and savage the old man. But instead, as soon as the frightened old man was on its back, the bear instantly became utterly docile. Deprived of their fun, the ruffians pulled the old man off the bear's back and one of their number took his place on the bear's back. At once the bear became vicious and savaged its tormentor to death.
Still more angry, the gang made its way into Northampton. There they handed over the frightened old priest to the authorities who put him into prison where he died. But this shameful story does not end there, for the local 'Mayor' gave orders that the old parson should not be given a proper Christian funeral. Instead, he ordered that the priest's body should simply be put in a grave and that the only words spoken should be:

"Ashes to Ashes, Dust to Dust
Here's the pit, and in you must"

3.

THE ODD SHILLING.

We move now into the 18th century. The background to the story is as follows:- Browne Willis, the autocratic high church Tory antiquarian was Lord of the Manor of both Bletchley and Fenny Stratford. He exercised his power of Advowson to appoint a Rector for the ancient parish church of Bletchley. He could not do the same for Fenny Stratford because there had never been a parish church in Fenny. Browne Willis was determined to build such a church. He begged for donations far and wide and the building of the church began. By 1725 when the walls were up to ten feet, more funds were needed. Browne Willis drafted an Appeal and got leading Fenny Stratford citizens to sign it. The Appeal was sent to the Newspapers and also to a number of parishes. It met with a fair response, some 21 parishes replying. Among them was the Parish of Wappenham in Northants, where the Rev.Mr Wheeler was Rector. When he received the Appeal in 1725 his mind went back to a great indignity he had suffered in 1710—in Fenny Stratford, no less!. A lesser man might have thrown the Appeal on the fire. But not Wheeler! He decided to send a Donation but to use the occasion to administer a rebuke.

So what had happened to him all those years ago? Well, as he rode through Fenny on that day in 1710, he had sand thrown in his face! He decided to send a donation of one guinea and in his letter he wrote:

"Twenty shillings is towards the building, and THE ODD SHILLING is towards cleaning the Chapel when finished of chips, dust and rubbish and in remembrance of my cleaning my own face when dashed with grains as I was passing through the place." And his letter went on:""A rudeness like this having not anywhere met with in my whole life, I cannot easily forget; nor my resentment at such treatment done to a CLERGYMAN!".

No doubt feeling better having got that off his chest, he concluded his letter in calmer vein. "Religion teaches civility and good manners towards man, as well as piety and devotion towards God, and I hope the erecting of this Chapel among them may in good time have this visible effect upon the inhabitants, as in both respects to reform them."

4.

THE VICAR AND THE HIGHWAYMAN.

Three down, one to go. The fourth and last misadventure befalling a country cleric happened in 1766. It happened to the Rev.Mr Risely, Rector of Tingewick. It caused him to be put on trial for manslaughter.
Mr Risely had been riding his horse one day near Stony Stratford. He happened to witness a highwayman holding up another traveller. The Rector went at once to the assistance of the victim. The two together then chased after the highwayman, calling on him repeatedly to stop. The Rector, either by a remarkably good shot, even as he was galloping, or more likely by chance, hit the fleeing highwayman, shooting him dead.

That was the affair that brought him into court, charged with manslaughter. The Duke of Grafton, as Magistrate hearing the case, had no hesitation in acquitting him. More than that, he was so impressed by the Rector's prowess, that he offered him a better Living at Ashton in Northants.

Chapter 10

THE OLNEY POETS.

One of them was a country cleric and the other was the son of a country vicarage. A sensational headline for the first might be:
"The Slave Trading Vicar". And for the second: "The Suicidal Poet". Providence brought them together.
One of the dictionary definitions of Providence expresses the notion that God foresees human needs and contrives to help men to meet those needs. We can surely see Providence in that sense in the coming together in one place, Olney, of two remarkable men, Cowper and Newton. One inevitably brackets them together for the obvious reason that they were great friends, that they lived for many years in the same place, that they shared a strong evangelical faith, and that they both loved to write. All these are factual dimensions of their association. They exemplify all that they had in common and show the ways in which they resembled each other. Yet in so many ways they were different. They truly were an odd couple. They came from such different backgrounds; their separate lives before they met had been so dissimilar.

John Newton-Slave Trader turned Vicar.

Anyone who knows anything about John Newton knows that he had been a slave-trader and that he later became a priest. The story behind that metamorphosis is truly astonishing. It never ceased to astonish John Newton himself. He himself painted on the wall of an attic in Olney Vicarage (and the words are there to this day) a quotation from Deuteronomy: "But thou shalt remember that thou wast a bondsman in the land of Egypt and the Lord thy God redeemed thee"
He was born in 1725, the son of a sea captain. His mother died when he was six and he was packed off to a boarding school where he suffered both from the brutality of the teachers and from the bullying of older boys.

John Newton, the former slave-trader, who became vicar of Olney.

These experiences were curiously paralleled by William Cowper. He also lost his mother when he was only six and was also sent off to boarding school where he was most unhappy. But thereafter their paths were different. Newton left formal schooling when he was only ten, while Cowper continued his education at Westminster School till he was eighteen.

At the age of eleven John Newton went to sea in one of his father's ships. He served on several voyages with neither pleasure nor enthusiasm. Relations with his father were always strained and Newton in his' 'teens was obviously an awkward and rebellious character. A friend of his father offered to set young Newton up with a job on a plantation in Jamaica. This would have taken the seventeen year old John Newton abroad for the next five years, a prospect he did not relish.

He paid a visit to friends of his late mother, the Catlett family in Chatham. There he met for the first time Mary, the fourteen year old Catlett daughter and fell instantly in love with her. That further increased his reluctance to go to Jamaica. So, wilfully, he stayed away from home, deliberately delaying his return till he was sure that the ship must have sailed without him.

His father, not best pleased, at once arranged for him to join a ship sailing for the Mediterranean. He served as an ordinary seaman and on that one year's voyage, herded in the forecastle with the crude uncouth sailors of those days, he became as crude and uncouth as the company he kept. As soon as he landed he went to Chatham to visit the Catlett family. Their welcome was as warm as ever, but her parents made it plain that they did not regard a common sailor as a suitable match for Mary.

At this point John Newton's life took a dramatic twist—he was pressganged and found himself an unwilling sailor in the Royal Navy on the warship HMS Harwich. The ship was to sail in convoy to the East Indies, but had to put into Plymouth for repairs. The love-sick John Newton jumped ship in Plymouth, intending to make his way back to Chatham. He was arrested and taken back to his ship in irons. There he was flogged, stripped of his rank as midshipman and made to serve as an ordinary seaman again.

His resentment and self-pity made him a rebel. The Captain of HMS Harwich determined to get rid of him as a nuisance and a trouble-maker. The means to this end were ready to hand. It was the custom in those days that any Navy Captain could rid himself of any troublesome members of his crew simply by swapping them for an equal number of ratings from a merchant ship. So when HMS Harwich reached Madeira Captain Carteret made a

deal with the skipper of a merchant ship. He handed over John Newton and another sailor and in return received two ratings from the merchantman.
And that was John Newton's introduction to the slave trade, for the merchantman on which he now found himself was a Slaver. The nineteen year old Newton soon made himself a leader below decks. Soon his morals were as scandalous as any of his new shipmates. He found special delight in blasphemy and in ridiculing all things religious. Towards authority he was obstreperous and unco-operative—all in all a trouble maker.
By chance the ship carried a passenger, a man named Chow. Chow was heavily involved in the slave trade, working from an island base off the coast of Guinea in West Africa. As a way of getting free from his wretched life on the ship, young Newton persuaded Chow to offer him a job. John was later to regret that move. Chow treated him almost as a slave himself, added to which he suffered greatly from fever on that malarial island.
Relief came unexpectedly. Another white trader arrived and set up business on the island and Newton managed to secure employment with him. Then, one day a trading ship, The Greyhound, put into the island. Newton was astonished to learn from its captain that his father had learned of his whereabouts and of his plight, and wanted him to take passage on The Greyhound and to return to England. So he sailed home a free man, with renewed hopes that he would see Mary again.
But he was no longer the innocent youth he had been when he first met Mary. Now he was often drunk, always blasphemous, dissolute and depraved. The Greyhound ran into a violent storm in the Atlantic and might well have gone down. The whole crew battled to save her. For eleven hours Newton lashed himself to the wheel and steered the ship through the gale. It seemed impossible that The Greyhound could survive, but she did. She finally drifted into Lough Swilly off the coast of Donegal.
This escape from death greatly affected John Newton. After this there was no more blasphemy, no more mocking at God or religion. He didn't turn saint over night—his drinking and general debauchery continued, so did the coarseness of his language. But at least blasphemy was a thing of the past.
He was now 25 and was offered command of a sailing ship, The Brownlow, another Slave Trader. But he did not feel ready yet for a command and agreed to serve as First Mate. Before sailing he visited Chatham again where he found Mary, now nineteen, as attractive as ever. But there was no talk yet of making her his wife.

The Brownlow was active in the so-called Triangular Trade—carrying trinkets and trade goods to Africa for the purchase of slaves, then ferrying the slaves to the West Indies or America, and then returning from there to England loaded with produce from the plantations.
Newton made at least three voyages on The Brownlow and then, on 12 February 1750 he married Mary Catlett in Rochester. Three months later he sailed again, this time on a ship called The Duke of Argyle, another Slaver. After one voyage on her he was given command of his own ship, yet another Slaver, called The African on which he made two round trips.

By now he was a completely changed man, a reformed character. No doubt his marriage to Mary in part accounted for this, but much more significant was his conviction that he had been saved from illness, hardship and death for a purpose.
He was later to express this conviction in perhaps the best known of all his hymns:

"Amazing grace! (how sweet the sound!)
That saved a wretch like me!
I once was lost, but now am found,
Was blind, but now I see

'Twas grace that taught my heart to fear,
And grace my fears relieved;
How precious did that grace appear
The hour I first believed!

Through many dangers, toils and snares,
I have already come;
'Tis grace has brought me safe thus far,
And grace will lead me home.

The earth shall soon dissolve like snow,
The sun forbear to shine;
But God who called me here below,
Will be for ever mine".

But long before he was to write that hymn in Olney there was another crisis to be survived. In 1754 at home with Mary he was preparing to sail yet again, on another ship, The Bee. Suddenly he collapsed and for over an hour he was insensible. He recovered just as suddenly but the doctor ruled that his sea-going life was over.
He needed then to find a job and succeeded in doing so. He became a Tide Waiter at Liverpool. A Tide Waiter was a Customs Officer who boarded and inspected incoming ships. For the moment let us leave him there while we take up the story of William Cowper. Neither yet knew, or had even heard of the other. But Providence was about to make their paths converge.

William Cowper.

William Cowper, poet and friend of John Newton

William Cowper was born in 1731, so he was six years younger than Newton. His father was Rector of Berkhamstead and he was born in the Rectory there. His mother was Anne,daughter of Roger Donne, of Ludham Hall in Norfolk.
William's infancy and earliest years were ideally happy. But when he was only six his mother died soon after giving birth to another son, John. She was only 34. William was shattered by his mother's death. Very many years later he was to express his grief in these words:

"My mother! When I learned that thou wast dead,
Say, wast thou conscious of the tears I shed?
Hovered thy spirit o'er thy sorrowing son,
Wretch even then, life's journey just begun?
Perhaps thou gavest me, though unfelt, a kiss;
Perhaps a tear, if souls can weep in bliss-
Ah, that maternal smile! It answers-Yes.

I heard the bell tolled on thy burial day,
I saw the hearse that bore thee slow away,
And, turning from my nursery window, drew
A long, long sigh, and wept a last adieu."

There is a sadly significant phrase in that poem. It is the line in which Cowper describes himself as:"Wretch even then life's journey just begun". Remember that he is speaking of himself as he was at the age of six and is implying that even at that tender age he had already started to know depression and melancholy—those parlous states which in later life were to bring him to the depths of despair, and cause him on at least two occasions to attempt suicide.

When he left Westminster School at eighteen he began to study law, taking Chambers in the Temple in 1752. He made little progress in the profession and was lucky to procure an appointment as Clerk of the Journals of the House of Lords. But later he lost that job because he couldn't qualify at the Bar.

In 1756 his father, the Rector of Berkhamstead died. Young Cowper had to leave the Rectory and the countryside he knew so well. The result of all this was the first of what were to be frequent attacks of depression. In despair he went through the motions of trying to take his own life. He was taken to the Asylum Insanorum of Dr.Cotton at St Albans for treatment. He recovered in four months but he stayed on there for another year.
He decided to try to find some quiet rural retreat where he could be at peace and write poetry. He chose Huntingdon, partly because it was near Cambridge where his younger brother John was. So he found himself living once more in a Rectory, the Parsonage of the Reverend Morley Unwin. There he became as he said: 'almost like an adopted son'.

The tranquility of that safe haven was rudely shattered when Morley Unwin was thrown from his horse and killed. Always William Cowper found the deaths of those close to him more than he could bear. First his mother, then his father, and now Morley Unwin, almost his second father. Later would come the death of his brother John, and the death of William Unwin, Morley's only son. Much later still would come the death of Mary Unwin, Morley's widow. She meant so much to Cowper At one time they even

contemplated matrimony. For many years she was his faithful companion. Each of these deaths had plunged Cowper into despair and depression and unhinged his mind. Four times he was to know melancholia of the most acute kind.
Now Providence took a hand. Someone suggested to the Vicar of Olney that he should go over to Huntingdon to visit the recently widowed Mary Unwin and to visit the depressed William Cowper. That Vicar of Olney was, of course, the Reverend John Newton whom we last left as a Tide Waiter in Liverpool. We need now to resume his story.

In Liverpool John Newton derived increasing comfort from religion. He went to hear all the best evangelical preachers and was much moved by the sermons of Whitfield when that celebrated evangelist visited the city. Newton even began to preach himself, at first to his own household. The notion that he should seek Holy Orders seized hold of him. He was now 33 and was determined to be ordained. But would any Bishop take him seriously? It seemed not, and John Newton was almost diverted in another direction—he was invited by a Presbyterian church to become their minister. Once more Providence took a hand and brought Newton to the attention of Lord Dartmouth. Lord Dartmouth was impressed by Newton and offered him the Living of Olney, of which he was Patron. The Bishop of Lincoln agreed to ordain John and so Olney had a new Vicar, the one-time slave trader, now a priest.

It was early in his ministry at Olney that a friend urged him to ride over to Huntingdon to comfort the widowed Mrs Unwin and the melancholic Cowper. Newton urged that they should come to Olney where he undertook to find them a house. So they moved to Olney in 1767. While the house, Orchard Side, was being made ready they stayed at the Vicarage with John and Mary Newton.
Orchard Side was to be the home of William Cowper and Mary Unwin for the next

Orchard Side House, Olney, the home of William Cowper for 19 years and now his museum. (JH)

nineteen years. Early during that period Newton was very worried about Cowper's mental health and distressed at his friend's fits of depression. As therapy he urged Cowper to concentrate on his writing. One splendid outcome from this was that Newton and Cowper later compiled The Olney Hymnbook, the first of its kind ever published in England. It came out in 1779. It contained 348 hymns of which 280 were Newton's and 60 were Cowper's. Many of them are seldom sung today. But others are classics and continued to be sung regularly. From Newton we have:

*"**How sweet the Name of Jesus sounds**"*
"Glorious things of Thee are spoken"
"May the grace of God our Saviour"
"Amazing Grace, how sweet the sound".

To Cowper we owe:

*"**O for a closer walk with God**"*
"Hark, my soul it is the Lord"
"God moves in a mysterious way"
"Jesus, where'er Thy people meet".

In 1780 John Newton left Olney to become Rector of the Parish of St Mary Woolnoth in London. His departure was a great blow to Cowper. Their friendship continued but their daily companionship was over. Cowper and Mrs Unwin stayed on a further six years in Orchard Side. In 1786 they moved to Weston Underwood and lived there nine years. In 1795 they moved finally to Norfolk and there in 1796 Mary Unwin died. Her death, like all the deaths of those close to him, left Cowper shattered. This time there was no real recovery from his depression. His last years were very sad and his health both physical and mental deteriorated. He died on 25 April 1800 and is buried in East Dereham.

For much of his life Cowper knew deep personal distress, hovering between religious mania and despair. Yet at other times he could write with delicious humour, wit and charm. We shall never fully know how much we (and Cowper) owe to the influence Newton had on his improbable friend. But certain it is that it was Providence that brought them together.

And it was Providence too that brought Newton to London to be of such enormous help to William Wilberforce in his long struggle to secure the abolition of slavery and the slave trade. Newton died in 1807 at the age of 82 and was buried in London. But in 1893 he and Mary his wife were re-interred at Olney in the Churchyard of the Parish where for so many years the improbable friendship of John Newton and William Cowper had flourished.

St Peter and St Paul's, Olney

Olney is not only famous because of Newton and Cowper. Ever since 1445 it has been the venue for its Shrove Tuesday Pancake Race. This originated because in the Middle Ages traditionally housewives were taught to use up dairy products and eggs before Lent began. So the annual Olney Pancake Race was instituted. It covers the 415 yards from the Market Place to the Parish Church. Only Olney housewives are allowed to compete. During the Race each competitor must toss and catch her Pancake three times. The winner gets a Prayer book and a kiss from the Sexton. Following the Race a Shrove Tuesday Service takes place in the Church.

The Olney Pancake Race

Chapter 11

WATER STRATFORD'S ARMAGEDDON THE OBSESSION OF JOHN MASON.

Actually, he had two obsessions, one after the other. The dictionary defines obsession as "a persistent idea or impulse; a persistent idea or feeling, sometimes akin to madness".

John Mason came to Water Stratford as Vicar in 1674 and stayed there till he died in 1694. Both he and his wife were popular. The Vicar loved hymn writing and the villagers appreciated the fame that his hymns earned for the parish. Parishioners are often pleased if their vicar has any special gifts and share in his reflected glory.

John Mason was a great student of the Bible, a very proper interest for any incumbent to follow, and one of which the parishioners of Water Stratford at first approved. But only later did it emerge that in John Mason's Bible study lay the seeds of his first obsession. He was convinced that through the chronology of Scripture he could determine the whole history of the world and trace it back to the exact date of creation.

He wasn't the first to have such ideas. Before there had been James Ussher, an Anglican Bishop of the Church of Ireland. He too believed that by taking the individuals and events recorded in the Bible, and assigning dates to them, you could by working backwards from the end of Revelations, arrive finally at Genesis Chapter1, Verse 1, and so be able to state with authority exactly when God created the world. And that date, declared Bishop Ussher, was precisely the year 4004 BC!

Bishop Ussher died in 1656, eighteen years before John Mason became Vicar of Water Stratford. Mason undoubtedly knew of Bishop Ussher's work but he didn't agree with his findings. So he worked on his own and reached his own conclusions. His labours were truly obsessive. At last he announced his results. And he was shattered when nobody took any notice! The Church rejected his theories and his findings. So all those years of study had been in vain. He was heart-broken and mortified. Coincidentally, his wife died just at that time. John Mason's world collapsed about him. He suffered nightmares and horrifying dreams. He carried on as Vicar of Water Stratford but in a sort of daze. The double blows he had suffered had driven him into a sort of madness.

His first obsession, trying to establish how and when the world began, was now abandoned. And his mind now turned in the opposite direction. His second obsession took possession of him. He would study the matter of the END of the world and discover when and how it would come about. He worked as frenetically on this anticipation of the coming day of Judgment as once he had worked on tracing the origins of the world and its creation. He reached some astonishing conclusions! Not only did he feel able to announce precisely when the Day of Judgment would come, but also, more astonishingly, he was able to state categorically that when Judgment Day came only Water Stratford would be saved and all the rest would be lost! Hellfire preaching along these lines drew crowds from far and wide. So effective was this preaching that people from faraway sold their property and moved to Water Stratford, determined to be in that one small place which the Vicar said would survive the Day of Judgment.

Browne Willis, the antiquarian Lord of the Manor of Whaddon in Bletchley, and author, wrote about this strange Rector of Water Stratford in his "History of Buckingham" published in 1755. He wrote:

> *"In the year 1693 and 1694 this place was much resorted unto on account its Rector, Mr John Mason, who taught publicly that he had seen Christ, and that He had at this place begun his Personal reign on earth; which enthusiastical Prediction occasioned great resort hither from many parts of the neighbourhood insomuch that all the Barns and Houses hereabouts were filled with his followers, many of whom were so infatuated that they sold their estates, being persuaded that this World was at an end; and so took up their abode and dwelt here some years after his death".*

We have an interesting contemporary comment on all this in the shape of a letter written in 1694 by a gentleman who lived near Water Stratford to his brother in London. He wrote:

> *'Brother, I have here according to your desire sent an account concerning Mr Mason, Minister of Water Stratford. I have heard some of his hearers say that they did believe they should see Christ appear, but in what manner they would not be positive. Some of them would say VISIBLY APPEAR; others say His appearance in the clouds and his reign in the clouds. Further I have heard them say that those who did not believe this, and did see his appearance would live one*

thousand years, and all that while without sin; and likewise that the fulness of the Gentiles has come in. They call Water Stratford SION and count Mr Mason a prophet in whom alone the revelations of St John will be revealed. They do conclude their reign will begin about Ascension Day next; and that all that believe this must dwell at Water Stratford and there they will be preserved; and neither Magistrate can meddle with them, nor any other hurt can befall them, and that they shall stand upon Mount Sion, and see all the wicked round about them be burnt up. They have had Musick and Dancing and singing of hymns and clapping of hands, about 6 weeks night and day. The week before Easter several families moved to Water Stratford to live, carrying all they had thither. They sold houses and land for what they could get. They did, last winter, lay in at Stratford 20 quarters of wheat, 10 quarters of malt and 20 or 30 hundred weight of cheese. This spring they have laid in several fat bullocks and hogs.

On Easter Monday night Mr Mason declares he saw Christ and on the next Lord's Day following some of our neighbours went to hear and see how the people went on; and being a great multitude of people gathered together round the country, more than the church could contain, they stood in the minister's Yard, and he out of his chamber window, declared unto the multitude that on the Monday night before, he being in bed and awake, lying on his left side, he turned himself to his right and saw Christ sitting in a chair, and a candle lighted in a candlestick standing on a stool; and that Christ was clothed in a purple robe, dipped in the blood of his enemies. He confirmed this with an oath, saying by the eternal God that what he said was true, and that himself was neither in a dream, nor mad or drunken and neither was affrighted.

He hath not given the Sacraments these last 2 years and now they do not read nor pray only 4 or 5 of the last words of the Lord's Prayer, which is in the praise of The glory of God. They say all is done and there is nothing to be done, only to Praise God. There may be about 40 that are constant but there are sometimes about 500 or 1000 to see their fashions and actions in dancing.

Your brothers and some other young men went last Saturday night to see them and stayed all night. The dancing is in no order but after an antic manner, sometimes 3 taking hand and jumping round; others leaping from one end of the room to the other, catching over their heads with their hands, and clapping them, saying, sometimes, appear, appear, appear, while others say glory, glory, glory.

There is one dancer among them with a wooden leg and he makes great noise among them with his leg when he cuts capers. Mr Mason will not dispute with any divine concerning his opinions but will only say all is done; they that are righteous let them be righteous still; and they that are filthy let them be filthy still. Mr Croft talked with some of the hearers, in particular the man with the wooden leg. Mr Croft said that the heavens must retain Christ until the restitution of all things The man said all things ARE restored, but our minister answered they are not all restored, because he had not got his good leg restored again.
We do hear that within the past two days some of the saints of this new-named Sion have left it and go about their employment again. I know no more at present, but when I am further satisfied of their proceedings you shall know of it. Yours etc

What were the Church authorities doing about all this? They were naturally alarmed but were at a loss to know how to handle it. They decided to send a senior clergyman to look into the matter and report. The man they chose was the Reverend Maurice, Rector of Tyringham. Maurice had been a friend of John Mason for the past 20 years. So it was thought that he would be welcomed, and yet sufficiently detached to make a mature assessment

Maurice was astonished and appalled at what he found. All over the village, but most of all in and around the church, he found crowds, dancing, singing, clapping, in a state of high hysteria, determined to be ready when Judgment should come. He made his way to the Vicarage and things there were even more chaotic. People were swarming in and out of the house and up and down the stairs. The noise of their singing and chanting was deafening. Some of them danced and sang so exuberantly that they dropped exhausted. But others took their place and the frenetic singing and dancing continued unabated.

Meanwhile at the very top of the house in an attic, the Vicar lay dying. His sister who was at his bedside explained to Maurice that her brother had been struck dumb. He could hear but not speak. She begged Maurice not to distress her brother by questioning him about recent happenings in the village. That was all very well, but Maurice had been sent to assess the situation and would have to give a report to his superiors. He tried to question others in the house, but no real dialogue was possible. People simply told him that he was damned and should leave.

A month later, in 1694, the reverend John Mason died. He had often told people that though he might die, he would be resurrected after three days. It was said by some that this had actually happened, and that they had seen him. The Church authorities sent a replacement for John Mason. The new Vicar, a man named Rushworth, cannot have relished his appointment. Faced with those repeated tales about a resurrected Mason having been seen, Rushworth opened up the grave to demonstrate to all that the body of the dead John Mason was still in it..

The crowds gradually dispersed and life in Water Stratford returned to a semblance of normality. But a few people who had come from elsewhere stayed on. Some of them were still there 16 years after John's death.

Long before that Maurice had reported back to his superiors. It was a fair and charitable report. Maurice stressed his conviction that John Mason had genuinely believed that his village and parish had been specially set apart by God. And Maurice had tried to find an explanation for this delusion. And he was satisfied that he had found one. John Mason's delusion, he said, had been brought about by his addiction to tobacco! Whenever he had visited his friend over the years he had always found him enveloped in clouds of smoke. Clearly, he concluded, this had over heated John's brain. But perhaps the poet, Alexander Pope, would have been nearer the mark with his line: *"A little learning is a dang'rous thing"*.

Water Stratford Church
scene of astonishing events in 1693. (JH)

POSTSCRIPT.

Preoccupation with Armageddon, and prognostication about the likely date for the end of the world certainly did not cease with the death of John Mason in 1694!
In 1872 in America a 'Pastor' Charles Taze Russell launched a new organisation known at first as Millenial Dawn. It foretold that the world would end in 1914. It didn't. But the organisation was able to rationalise its failure and survived. Its name and its leadership have varied over the years and currently the body is best known as Watchtower or as Jehovah's Witnesses.
The original leader, Russell, was followed by 'Judge'Joseph Rutherford. He in turn was succeeded by Nathan K Knorr in 1942 and by Frederick W Franz in 1983.
The prophesied date for the end of the world has inevitably been revised from time to time. It was confidently announced that the world would end in 1975. It didn't.

At the end of November 2001 a half-page Advertisement appeared in The Times. It was paid for by "The Lord's Witnesses" and it gave a London address. The advertisement did not say or claim that the Lord's Witnesses are the same as, or the successors of the Jehovah's Witnesses/
The advertisement claimed that Sir Isaac Newton spent many years studying the Bible and that he concluded that the world would end in 1948. It didn't. Sir Isaac Newton himself died in 1727.

The Lord's Witnesses in their 2001 Advertisement ventured a new prophecy. It is based, they say, on the study of Revelations chapter 17 with its references to 10 Kings. The Lord's Witnesses say that they like Sir Isaac Newton, are convinced that the Bible has a symbolic code which needs to be decoded. From their own decoding they have reached certain conclusions which enable them to prophesy confidently that:
THE UN SECURITY COUNCIL WILL ACCEPT 5 NEW PERMANENT MEMBERS ON DECEMBER 5th 2001. IT WILL EXPAND TO 10 PERMANENT MEMBERS, 10 'KINGS', ON THAT DAY. THE UN WILL TAKE OVERALL POLITICAL CONTROL OF THE WORLD ON DECEMBER 5th 2001, THE SAME DAY, BECOMING THE 8th KING OF THE WORLD IN BIBLICAL TERMS.

While various dates have been named for Armageddon, ranging from John Mason's "next Ascension Day" in 1694, and Isaac Newton's 1948, and Russell's 1914, and Rutherford's 1975, it is noticeable that the Advertisement in The Times on November 28th 2001, though it was specific on what the UN would do on December 5th 2001, gave no firm date for the end of the world. Indeed, the Advertisement specifically said that this was their final advert and their final prophecy on this matter.

A belated acceptance perhaps by the Witnesses on their part of something that John Mason had overlooked, namely that Jesus had said:
"About that day and hour no one knows, not even the angels in heaven, nor even the Son, only the Father".

Chapter 12

A PANORAMA OF PARSONS.

This could well have been the subtitle of this book instead of "A Collection of Country Clerics". A Panorama is an overall view. In the foreground and middle distance—lots of detail; in the far distance the detail is obscure and only an outline of shape is suggested. The same could be said of our panorama of parsons. Many a parish can trace the list of its parsons going back to the 12th or 13th century. We can look at their names on the board at the back of the church and wonder about them. For most of us search in archives is not easy, but as we come nearer to our own times other sources of information are more readily available. There are references in history books, and sometimes in diaries, and quite often in Church Guides, many of which are excellent.

Sometimes, in a long list of rectors whose names mean nothing to us, we suddenly come across one about whom we know quite a lot. It is as if a column of men is passing by in the darkness, and then suddenly a spotlight comes on and picks out one of them. John Schorne of North Marston whom we have already met is a good example.

The tiny village and parish of Milton Keynes provides other examples. Centuries after the village began its name was chosen to be the title of the great new town of Milton Keynes which began to be created in the 19 sixties. Walter de Keynes wasn't its first parson but we know he was Rector in about 1290 and probably built the chancel of the church. But there followed him some 17 parsons about whom we only know their names. Then, in 1559 there came Francis Babington. He was Rector of Lincoln College, Oxford, Rector of Milton Keynes, and also of Adstock. We do know a little more about him because, being a Roman Catholic, and not willing to become otherwise, he had to flee overseas to save his life.

Four incumbents later we come to a Rector who is much more than just a name. He was the Reverend Lewis Atterbury. Two things make his name familiar. The first is that he died in tragic circumstances. He fell off his horse and was drowned in 1693 while riding back from London to Milton Keynes. The accident happened as he was passing over the bridge at Newport Pagnell during a great flood. He had a son born in the Rectory at Milton Keynes who became famous, or as some would have said, infamous. He was the Reverend Francis Atterbury. He was educated at Westminster and did brilliantly at Christ Church, Oxford. After ordination he became the leading preacher and controversialist of the High Church and Tory Party. He became in turn Dean of Carlisle, Bishop of Rochester, and Dean of Westminster. He officiated at the coronation of George I, but it was known that his sympathies lay with the Stuarts. In 1720 he was arrested and accused of plotting with the Jacobites. Stripped of all his ecclesiastical appointments, he was banished from England in 1723. He died in exile in France in 1732, but in a way he had the last word, for his body was brought back to England and privately buried in Westminster Abbey.

Keach of Winslow.

From 1660 to 1668 Benjamin Keach was Pastor of the tiny Baptist church in Winslow. He was the child of Anglican parents and had been baptised in the parish church of Stoke Hammond. But in his teens he came under the influence of a Baptist preacher and was baptised by him. Those were days of religious intolerance when dissenting ministers were often persecuted. Keach was arrested both because of his preaching and his writing. His spoken and written words were deemed to be "to the great displeasure of God and the King's peace" He was fined twenty pounds, sent to prison for two weeks, and made to stand in the pillory at Aylesbury and also at Winslow. In both places Keach used the pillory as a pulpit, preaching even while he was being ridiculed and stoned. The little Baptist chapel in Winslow where he ministered is the oldest nonconformist place of worship in Buckinghamshire.

Keach's Meeting House, Winslow. (JH)

Keach in thestocks, still preaching!

Enter the Wesleys.

In the 18th century the Church of England was badly in need of a shake up. At Oxford University in 1729 a group of pious Anglican students tried to do something about it. They formed The Holy Club, concentrating on worship combined with works of charity. The leaders were John and Charles Wesley. The Holy Club only lasted till 1735 but its influence continued through the ministry of the two Wesley brothers both of whom were ordained in the Anglican ministry. The name 'Methodist' was coined because John Wesley urged that Christians should live according to the method of life given in the Scriptures. This is the origin of what became the Methodist denomination, separate from the Church of England. But John and Charles Wesley remained priests in the Church of England until they died. They still hoped to wake up the established church from the inside, but were frustrated by the opposition of the bishops and many of the clergy. They travelled extensively all over the country, preaching to large crowds—in the open air because they were denied access to church pulpits.

John Wesley

John Wesley preached often in Stony Stratford and he visited Bedford no less than 32 times, preaching there for the last time at the age of 88, when he had to be helped into and held up in the pulpit by two men.

Norman Guest.

Not every parson gets to have a Pub named after him. It happened to the Reverend Norman Guest. There are many who still remember him, for he was truly an eccentric man. He was an Irishman and was Vicar of St.James Church, New Bradwell from 1909 to 1946. He invariably wore an old pair of what he would have called plimsolls (trainers). He rode an old bicycle which would not have been out of place in a museum and he could be seen riding it with his feet up on either side of the front mudguard when he

St James, New Bradwell

coasted down hill.

His church, St James, was a Victorian building erected in 1860 to meet the needs of the workers in Wolverton Railway Works. The building had been provided by the London and Northwestern Railway.

Ecclesiastically it took the place of the ancient parish church at Stanton Low, about a mile away. (A Norman arch from the old Stanton Low Church has been built into the west wall of St James Church)

Nobody had thought, in 1860, to make sure that the new church was properly licensed for marriages. It was just assumed automatically that the pastoral responsibilities of the old parish at Stanton Low had devolved on the new parish, including the administration of the sacrament of Holy Matrimony. Unfortunately, and technically, this was not so. This awful realisation surfaced soon after the new Vicar was appointed. A frantic examination of the parish registers revealed that between 1860 and 1909 a total of 434 marriages had been solemnised at St James Church. In the eyes of the Church all these couples had been properly wed. In the eyes of the State they had not.

Never one to waste a good opportunity to 'make a drama out of a crisis', the Reverend Norman Guest astonished the congregation at Evensong one March evening in 1909 by telling them that more than 800 people, married in

The Victorian church of St. James, New Bradwell, has a Norman arch from the ancient church of Stanton Low at its west end. The Vicar caused a sensation in 1909 when he said that more than 400 weddings solemnised there had been invalid.

St James Church up to that time, had not, in one sense, been married at all! So they had all been living in sin! And all their offspring were therefore illegitimate! Sensation—embarrassment—anger! The Vicar hastened to add that action would be taken to put matters right. The appropriate action was taken—by the Home Secretary. The Government passed a Provisional Order in Council declaring retroactively that all those previous marriages could be regarded as valid, and all the offspring resulting from them were thereby legitimised.

Fr Guest has long since gone to his reward. He certainly left many memories behind him. A Pub, called The Jovial Priest, survived for some time in Bradville and a Play all about him was produced some years ago in Stantonbury Theatre

Long Service Medals.

Nicholas Bloddington was presented to the Parish of Moulsoe as Rector in 1223 by the Prioress of Goring. David Morgan-Evans was presented to the Parish of Moulsoe as Rector in 1938 by Lord Carrington, father of the former Foreign Secretary. He retired in 1985 but Lord Carrington said that he could continue to live at the Rectory. He died there, aged 93, in 1992.

His official tenure as Rector, therefore was 47 years, from 1938 to 1985. In his last years as Rector he had the distinction of being the oldest serving clergyman in the Church of England. You might suppose that in the long line of Rectors of Moulsoe, from Nicholas Bloddington to Morgan-Evans, the latter's tenure would be the longest. Not so. His '47 not out' is handsomely exceeded by Richard Cautley who put in no less than 56 years as Rector before dying in 1842.

David Morgan-Evans was ordained priest in 1930, so he celebrated his Golden Jubilee in 1980, and his DIAMOND Jubilee in 1990. His first 9 years in the ministry he spent as Curate in the parish of Llanryst in St David's Diocese. His duties there included the Chaplaincy at Gwydyr Castle, seat of the Marquess of Lincolnshire. So it came about that when Lord Carrington, kinsman of the Marquess, needed a Rector for Moulsoe he offered it to David Morgan Evans.

Moulsoe, now in Newport Pagnell Deanery is only in Oxford Diocese by a whisker. Its population is about 300,its church basically 13th century with alterations, and its Rectory Georgian and enormous. The parish has not been spared the changes common to most villages. The days of a dozen or more in the choir and sixty plus at Evensong are gone. So many other changes too. Morgan-Evans commented; "There used to be just three cars in the village—mine and two others, Now there are about 200".

If you've been Rector of a small village for half a century you can be forgiven if you sometimes indulge in nostalgia. "You see that two-acre paddock just beyond the lawn—I used to put that down to potatoes, and I loved to be out there working at five in the morning. First, you'd hear the cuckoo, then the School bell, and then the sound of the hammer on the anvil at the smithy". There are no potatoes planted now—no school bell and no smithy, but the cuckoo can still be heard in that lovely countryside on the northern edges of Buckinghamshire, looking across to the Brickhills. And David Morgan-Evans in his nineties, looked back across the length of years.

Things are ordered differently nowadays. Parsons move, or are moved, much more frequently. The days of a parson's freehold are over. It is no longer the case that an incumbent appointed to a parish can stay there for as long as he wishes. His appointment will nowadays be for a set number of years. But one aspect of the parson's job does remain unchanged. He continues to be a parson even if he doesn't stay for years in one parish. And he is still a parson even when he retires. *"Thou art a priest for ever after the order of Melchisidec".*

Chapter 13

"CHERISH YOUR HERITAGE".

A few years ago there was an Art Exhibition in Central Milton Keynes devoted to African Art. While the Exhibition was on it had its own resident poet. He was a West African poet named Kwahu Akuhoka. In fine calligraphy on the walls of the Exhibition there was a copy of one of Kwahu's poems. It said:

> "Cherish your heritage. It is a noble one. And remember your history. For a man who forgets his history deserves only one thing—the pity of a man who has lost his memory".

That West African poet was saying at the end of the 20th century something that had already been said in different words 200 years earlier in the 18th century by Edmund Burke. He once said: "People will not look forward to posterity who never look back to their ancestors".

And both of them, Kwahu in the 20th century, and Burke in the 18th century, were saying in their words something that had been written more than 2000 years ago by Ecclesiasticus. He wrote: "Let us now praise famous men and our fathers who begat us". Most people know that quotation, but perhaps not so many know those other words of Ecclesiasticus in the same book, which might be paraphrased as:-

> "Let us also praise the common man. He puts his trust in his hands and becomes wise in his own work. Without the common man the city cannot be inhabited.
>
> You may not find him in the Councils, and in the Assembly he may not mount up on high. He may not sit in the seat of the Judge, but the common man will maintain the fabric of the world".

As we seek to "cherish our heritage" and also "remember our history", there are two areas to cover. They are""people and places". Or put another way, they are "flesh and blood" and""bricks and stones". The concern of this book has been to focus on clerics—priests, pastors, parsons and preachers, and to see them in the context of the places where they lived and worked. And we have found them to be Good, or Bad, or usually—"So So" . They have been famous, or infamous—saintly, or full of human foibles much like ourselves. Some were so famous or saintly that shrines were set up for them to which pilgrims flocked.

In 596 Pope Gregory I sent Augustine with some 40 followers, to England. They established themselves at Cantwareburh, the 'fort of the people of Kent', in other words in Canterbury. There the little chapel of St Martin was built. It is there still, the oldest continuously used church in England. In due time Canterbury Cathedral was built nearby. After the murder of Archbishop Thomas a Becket, Canterbury became the main goal of English pilgrimages. But Christianity had also arrived in England both earlier and by a different route. St Cuthbert was made Bishop of Lindisfarne. After his death the monks of the island, threatened by Viking raids, took Cuthberts's body from Lindisfarne and sought a place where they could lay him. That place was on a high rocky peninsula above the river Wear. There a monastery was created around the shrine of St Cuthbert in what became Durham Cathedral.

From such beginnings there developed over time a Christian church which spread throughout England. It spread, nurtured and fostered by and through the work of the monasteries. Initially these were Benedictine, but later a wide range of monastic houses of other rules were established.

The priests or clerics were of two kinds. There were those known as Major Orders, but there were also a wide range of men in Minor Orders—clerks, accountants, doctors, lawyers. The Major Orders, created by 'ordination', were divided into two classes. First there were the monks, living in seclusion and subject to the "regula" of a religious order and therefore known as regular clergy. But other priests, also created by ordination, were not secluded in a monastery, but lived in the world (in seculo) and hence known as secular clergy.

Gradually the church grew and spread and 'parishes' were formed till notionally the whole country was divided into parishes. It was Alfred the Great who in the 9th century grouped these parishes into' 'hundreds' and then grouped the 'hundreds' into what became counties or shires.

Among the earliest places or worship there was the Saxon Chapel founded by St Aldhelm at Bradford-on-Avon in the late 7th century. It is there still. At Greensted-juxta-Ongar in Essex there is the only surviving log church in the country, dating from about 850. It is there still and it once sheltered the remains of St Edmund.

Besides the monks there came also the Friars. They too were 'religious', living under a rule, but not confined or secluded in monasteries. The Friars,

Above: Saxon chapel, Bradford-on-Avon, Wiltshire. Founded in the late seventh century by St Aldhelm, this tiny church was once used as a school and cottage.

Above: Greensted-juxta-Ongar, Essex. The only surviving log church in the country, with nave timbers which may date from 850, once sheltered the remains of St Edmund.

like the' 'secular clergy', lived in the world, but they were less restricted than the secular clergy—more—'free range', you might say. There were four main orders of Friars, usually known by the colour of their mantles. Thus, the Carmelites were the white friars; the Fransiscans were the grey and brown friars; the Dominicans were the black friars. It has to be said that the relations between the secular clergy and the Friars was often far from peaceful.

These, then, were the clerics—monks regular and monks secular, and the Friars, who in the Middle Ages created the Church in England. They included some undoubted saints, not a few sinners, and many others who were certainly "so so". The time would come when the Church in England would become the Church"**of** England. But that state of affairs awaited the 16th century with all its religious upheaval, and the 17th century with all its civil turmoil.

Meanwhile, this all too fleeting survey of the Middle Ages cannot omit the mention of two clerics whose places in our history make them UTTERLY UNIQUE.

The first was a man named Nicholas Breakspear. He was born in 1100 in Abbots Langley near St Albans. His father was a civil servant who later became a monk. Nicholas too later became a monk in the Monastery of St Rufus near Avignon. In 1137 Nicholas was elected the Abbot there. He exerted such strict discipline that he was reported to Rome. The Pope was so impressed by him that he appointed him Cardinal Archbishop of Albano in 1146. In 1152 he was sent as Papal Legate to Scandinavia to reorganise the Church there. He earned fame as "the Apostle of the North". Finally, in 1154 Nicholas Breakspear was elected Pope! As Pope he chose the name Adrian IV. He died in 1159—the only Englishman ever to have been Pope. So the lad from Abbots Langley in Hertfordshire had done very well—uniquely well!

By a coincidence, the second utterly unique"cleric" also has a St.Albans connection. He was a Romano-Briton named Alban living in Verulamium (now St Albans). He joined the Roman Army. One day a fugitive Christian priest was on the run, being hunted down by the Roman Army. Alban took him in and sheltered him, a most risky thing to do. While Alban kept the fugitive priest hidden he was much impressed by him and he decided that he wanted to be a Christian. So the fugitive priest baptised him. But the hunt for the fugitive was still on and the fatal day came when the authorities arrived to make the arrest. There was just enough time for Alban to make an incredibly brave offer. He insisted that he and the fugitive should change clothes and when the soldiers arrived Alban surrendered to them, purporting to be the priest.

Bede, writing 400 years after the event, relates the story as he understood it. He says the Judge asked Alban to recant but he refused. He was then asked to sacrifice but again he refused. So the Judge ordered that he should be flogged and finally he sentenced him to be beheaded. All this happened in June 304.

Bede goes on to say that a small church was built on the site of the martyrdom. This was superseded by the Abbey Church of St Albans which was built by the Mercian King Offa in 793.

There is an ironic postscript to this story. When, later the Danes were invading this country, the Monks of St Albans sent Alban's body to the Monks of Ely for safe keeping. But when the danger of invasion passed, the Monks of Ely refused to return the body to St Albans. The Monks of St Albans then claimed that they had only sent a duplicate body to Ely and that they still possessed the original! True or false, this benefited nobody, because both sets of remains, genuine and spurious alike, were destroyed by Henry VIII at the Reformation. But in any case St Alban himself remains utterly unique, as England's PROTO-MARTYR.

The Royalties on this book about the clerics who have figured in our heritage and history. so many of them particularly part of Bucks history, will go appropriately to The Buckinghamshire Historic Churches Trust.

Chapter 14

UPHEAVAL IN THE 16th CENTURY.

"From lightning and tempest, from plague, pestilence and famine, from battle and murder and from sudden death—Good Lord deliver us".

So runs one petition in the Litany in the old Prayer Book. Every century of our history has featured all this catalogue of ills from which we seek deliverance.

Other than war, it is hard to think of two greater disasters that have afflicted mankind in past centuries than fire and plague. Few towns or villages escaped them. Yet there was one moment in history when these two scourges almost coincided with beneficent effect. That was in the two succeeding years 1665 and 1666. 1665 had seen the worst pestilence the country had known for centuries—the Great Plague in which thousands died in London.

"Bring out your dead": the Great Plague of London in 1665

A year later, in 1666, occurred the worst conflagration the capital had ever seen-the Great Fire of London. Both were disasters on a massive scale, yet the effect of the Great Fire was in a sense to sanitise and disinfect the streets of stricken London. Perhaps those who survived the successive calamities were in no mood to count their blessings, but the fact remains that the Great Fire helped to snuff out the Great Plague which had preceded it.

the Great Fire of London in 1666

Some three hundred years before the Great Plague of London in 1665 there had been the horrendous plague which swept across Europe—the Black Death. It came from Asia and ravaged Europe between 1348 and 1351. It reached England in 1348 and carried off up to a third of the population. It was called the Black Death because of the dark skin haemorrhage which accompanied it. Because it was invariably accompanied by coughing and sneezing it is thought to have inspired the nursery rhyme:

"Ring a ring o' roses
A pocket full of posies
A-tishoo! A'tishoo!
We all fall down."

The 'ring o'roses' meant the red rash which was usually the first sign of the onset of the disease. The 'posies' were sweet-smelling flowers and herbs used to detract from the stench of the dead. And even though this is a children's nursery rhyme, the'"all fall down" meant that the plague had claimed another victim! Though the years 1348 to 1351 marked the beginning of the Black Death, there were periodic repeat variations at intervals thereafter. London suffered again in 1361-62, and in 1379, with the worst visitation being the Great Plague of 1665 already mentioned.

This repetitive pattern was seen all over the country. Fenny Stratford for example suffered at least six serious outbreaks of plague between 1500 and 1665 with over 100 deaths in that latter year.

Though the Plague was no respecter of class or profession, it is a matter of observation that clergy of all kinds were decimated by it. One bishop wrote: "The contagious nature of the present pestilence has left many parish churches, and consequently the people, destitute of curates and priests". A St Albans monk noted: "The plague being so violent, the living were scarce able to bury the dead". In Luton the Vicar died of the Plague in 1349. The priest sent to succeed him died before the year was up. The next replacement was so scared that he ran away. By 1350 a clerk only in deacon's orders was all that could be found to take over the parish.

The Prior of St Albans died of the plague, along with 47 of his monks, three-quarters of the complement of the Abbey. Markham in his History of Milton Keynes wrote that the Black Death was at its fiercest from May to September 1349 when half the clergy in North Bucks fell to it. At Bradwell Priory the Prior and many of his monks died. This so reduced the Priory that no new recruits were forthcoming and even the election of a new Prior was impossible and the Priory's buildings deteriorated for want of monks to maintain them.

Some Religious Houses lost all their inmates and ceased to exist. Other houses almost disappeared. The secluded Meaux Abbey in Yorkshire lost its Abbot and 32 monks out of a total community of 50. The Cistercian foundation of Newenham in Honiton lost 23 of its 26 brethren

The Victorian writer, F.A.Gasquet calculated that some 25,000 priests and monks died of the Plague. Old documents reveal that two-thirds of the parish priests in the West Riding of Yorkshire died of the disease, along with 17 of the 21 parish priests in York. It could be argued that priests by virtue of their duties to minister to the sick and give absolution to the dying were particularly exposed to infection. But there is also evidence that some priests fled their parishes rather than share their fate with their parishioners. To escape the plague in London many fled to the countryside, which served to carry the infection still wider. A sad example of this concerns the tiny village of Gibralter in Buckinghamshire. To escape the plague a group of Londoners walked all the way to the village where one of their number had relatives. But they carried the infection with them, with the result that 40 of Gibralter's 80 inhabitants died Bubonic plagues were not the only intermittent scourges to afflict people. Cholera epidemics also exacted a fearful toll from time to time. Once more the little village of Gibralter provides a sad example. 48 people died there of cholera in a few hours in 1849.

The tiny village of Gibralter, near Dinton, lost half its population to cholera in 1849. Earlier, in 1665, forty villagers had died in the Great Plague

Just as many places experienced repeated outbreaks of plague, so too many places suffered repeated outbreaks of fire. Stony Stratford for example had major fires in 1703, 1725, 1736 and 1742. In one of those fires the church of St Mary Magdalen was burnt down, though the tower survived, and still does. The town of Buckingham lost almost a third of its houses by fire. Woburn, Luton, Northampton and Olney all had disastrous fires, and so did many villages, Great Horwood for example. Sundial House in Stony Stratford has an attractive sundial affixed to its wall. It bears the inscription: TEMPUS ET IGNIS OMNIA PERDUNT. "Time and Fire consume all things". It says much for human resilience that new homes and houses always appear, Phoenix-like from the ashes.

St Mary Magdalen's Church, Stony Stratford. It was burnt down in the 18th Century but the tower still survives.

Of the ills for which the Litany prays for deliverance some, like lightning and tempest, plague, pestilence and famine, may be thought of as threats from nature itself, or even as 'acts of God' for which Insurance Companies might claim exemption! But "battle, murder and sudden death" which the Litany also mentions are in a different category altogether. They speak of upheaval and turmoil, and it is upheaval that we see unfolding in the 16th century

UPHEAVAL.

Henry VIII came to the throne in 1509 and reigned for 38 years, dying in 1547. It was one of the most momentous reigns in English history. The first 20 years were marked by domestic peace and tranquility. Peace was made with France in 1514 and Henry' sister married the French King Louis XII. Louis died and was succeeded by Francis I. With great pomp and ceremony in 1520 Henry VIII of England and Francis I of France met on "the Field of the Cloth of Gold".

But thereafter the reign of Henry VIII descended into upheaval stemming from separate yet interlocking crises—Henry's matrimonial affairs, the dissolution of the Monasteries, and the Reformation.

The nation watched with astonishment as Henry married no less than six times in his passionate need for a male heir.'"Divorced, Beheaded, Died; Divorced, Beheaded, Survived" is the popular mnemonic which helps us all to keep track of what happened to Henry's six wives! At last, after two daughters, Mary and Elizabeth, a son was born to Jane Seymour, the future King Edward VI.

One obscure individual who had taken much interest in Henry's matrimonial affairs was George Taylor of Newport Pagnell. He was foolish enough to say publicly: "The King is but a knave and liveth in adultery, and is a heretic and liveth not after the laws of God. I set not by the King's crown and if I had it here I would play football with it". He was arrested and put on trial and at the Buckinghamshire Assizes held at Little Brickhill he was condemned to death.

Jane Seymour died ten days after giving birth to Edward. Henry had at last achieved a male heir, but he was a sickly child and his reign was all too short—he died in his teens. Who would succeed him? Would it be Mary, the daughter of Catherine of Aragon? Or Elizabeth, the daughter of Ann Boleyn? But both had been declared bastards following the divorces of their respective mothers. There was one other possibility—Lady Jane Grey. She was the granddaughter of Henry VII and was therefore a genuine Tudor. So plots were hatched to make her queen when the young Edward VI died. The Grey family of Bletchley Manor were naturally excited at the prospect of a kinswoman of theirs becoming Queen. But Mary Tudor acted swiftly, urged by Sir William Dormer of Wing she was proclaimed Queen, thus frustrating the Grey's family who had intended to proclaim in Aylesbury Lady Jane as Queen. In nine days it was all over and the unfortunate Lady Jane Grey and her young husband were both sent to the Tower and executed. William, Lord Grey of Bletchley was made to suffer for his temerity in supporting the cause of Lady Jane grey. He was arrested and sent to the Tower. He escaped execution and was even pardoned, but only at the expense of having all his honours and estates forfeited. But all came right later. Queen Mary only reigned for 5 years and was succeeded by her half-sister Elizabeth. And Queen Elizabeth restored all William Grey's honours and estates.

In the wider scene, while Henry VIII was desperately seeking a male heir, he set to work to dissolve the Monasteries. Between 1536 and 1540 some 8000 monastic houses were suppressed and their properties transferred to the Crown. More than 5000 monks were pensioned off, in addition to 2000 nuns and 1600 friars. Many of the monks and friars became parish clergy. But one, Robert Hobs, the last Abbot of Woburn, was not so lucky. Hobs had been outspoken in the matter of Henry's matrimonial entanglements and he had publicly denied the King's supremacy in Church affairs. So Abbot Hobs wasn't just despatched into the world to fend for himself—he was despatched at the end of a rope from the branches of an oak tree just outside Woburn Abbey gates.

In general, it was recognised that the immense wealth of the monasteries should be transferred to more deserving hands. Most reforming clergy would have welcomed the transfer of monastic wealth to the endowment of charitable, religious and educational enterprises. Instead, while the King used the dissolution to enhance royal finances, Parliament welcomed the changes to avert the unpopularity of increased taxation. And the landed gentry naturally welcomed the chance of enlarging their estates through the gains they enjoyed from the share out of former monastic holdings.

The King himself diverted some of the proceeds from the dissolution by creating six new Dioceses, one of which was Oxford.

The dissolution has also to be seen in the wider context of the Reformation. There was a continental dimension to the Reformation, as witness Martin Luther in Germany, and Calvin in Switzerland. In England itself a series of Acts were passed, all aimed at the reform of the Catholic Church in general, and in severing Papal claims in England in particular. The Acts included the suppression of Annates (the payments to the Papacy of first fruits). See in the next chapter what happened to them. Other Acts abolished appeals to Rome; the Act of Supremacy naming the King as "supreme head" of the English Church; and the Act of Uniformity which authorised the replacement of Roman Missals by Prayer books in English.

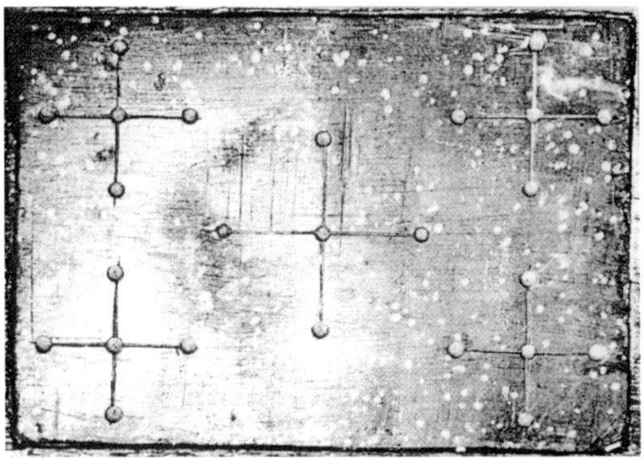

The Super-alter lost for 300 years at Addington.

How some individual clerics reacted to all this upheaval is illustrated by some interesting examples from North Bucks. The parish priest of Addington couldn't bring himself to accept the changes or to obey the law which said that all Roman Catholic Missals and Prayer books must be destroyed. So he hid his six Catholic books in the walls of his church. And with them he also hid the small'"super Altar", made of stone, on which the Chalice and Paten were stood in the Mass All these remained hidden for nearly 300 years and only came to light in 1857 when part of the church was being rebuilt. When that restoration was carried out the "super Altar" was returned to its place on the Altar.

Exactly the same happened at Granborough. There the parish priest hid in the walls of his church a small leaden casket measuring 2x2x2 inches. Inside the casket were three round receptacles. It was a Chrismatory—the three containers for Holy Oil used in the Catholic Church for anointing at Baptism and Confirmation, and for Extreme Unction for the Sick. The discovery was only made centuries later when restoration work was being done in the church. Also in Granborough a small alabaster panel of the Crucifixion, with the fugures of St John and the Virgin Mary, was discovered, improbably built into the gable of a house in the parish.

The upheaval of the Reformation was marked most horribly and dramatically by the persecution of both Catholics and Protestants. Between 1581 and 1588, the year of the defeat of the Spanish Armada, at least sixty-four clerics, eighteen laymen and two women were executed for their adherence to the Catholic faith. On the other side, some three hundred Protestants perished in the fires of Smithfield and elsewhere during the reign of Queen Mary. One notable individual to come to a violent end was The "Nun of Kent". Elizabeth Barton, was a visionary and a prophetess. She had spoken out against Henry's divorces. She was arrested and tried for treason and was hanged, together with four clerical associates. One Welsh writer claimed that'"over 5000 men were hanged in the space of six years".

The 16th century, then, had been one of upheaval. The changes it wrought in state and church affairs had been monumental, and their effects remain with us still. As the 16th century gave way to the 17th century we shall see in the next chapter how upheaval gave way to turmoil.

Chapter 15

TURMOIL, CIVIL WAR, And "THE GLORIOUS REVOLUTION"

Queen Elizabeth died in 1603. She was the last of the Tudor monarchs and was succeeded by James I, the first of the Stuarts. The Stuarts almost exactly cover the 17th century, starting with James I in 1603 and Anne, the last of the Stuarts who inherited the throne in 1703.

Charles I who lost the civil war

The 17th century was to see two major plots, the execution of one king, the exile of his successor for 11 years, a civil war, the turning of England into a Puritan Republic, the restoration of the monarchy, the fall and exile of another king, the peaceful invasion of the Kingdom by William and Mary, and what was claimed to be "the Glorious Revolution".

Oliver Cromwell who won the civil war

In short, the 17th century was marked by turmoil, by revolution and counter-revolution, and in the end by a pragmatic settlement. But other countries on the continent were passing through even more troubled times. As Macaulay was to write in the 19th century: "Englishmen are different from others. Because we had a preserving revolution in the 17th century, we have not had a destroying revolution in the 19th century".

Elizabeth I never married, so who should succeed her? The answer was James VI of Scotland who became James I of England. He was the son of Mary Queen of Scots, a kinswoman of Elizabeth who nevertheless ordered her execution. So it is ironic that Elizabeth should be succeeded by James, also her kinsman. His accession brought the whole of the British Isles under the rule of one sovereign for the first time.

How would James be received as King in England? To answer that question it is necessary to recall what had happened under the last three monarchs of the Tudor dynasty. Under the young Edward VI Protestantism which had been triggered off by the Reformation was rendered still more Protestant both in style and content. But then came Mary I who promptly made England Catholic again! Her reign was short, only five years. She was succeeded by her half-sister, Elizabeth who was determined to avoid both the Protestant extremes of Edward's reign, and the rigid Roman Catholicism of Mary. Elizabeth sought a middle way, determined to avoid the persecution and execution of both Protestants and Catholics. In this she was partially successful. She tried to achieve a settlement which would give her kingdom a church with which the majority of the population would be happy—a church which some could think of as'"Catholic without the Pope"

That was the situation James I inherited when he became King. Though the great majority of the people might be reasonably satisfied with the Elizabethan "settlement", that still left two diverse elements in the population who were profoundly unhappy. They were the Puritan element on one side, and the Roman Catholics on the other. Both elements pinned their hopes on what King James would do for them.

The Roman Catholics soon realised that the new King was unlikely to favour their cause, so plotting began to get rid of him.

In the very north of Bucks, only 3 miles from each other stand the two great houses of Gayhurst and Tyrringham. Both have connections with the Gunpowder Plot of 1605. At Gayhurst was Everard Digby—young, active, intelligent. He had acquired Gayhurst Manor by marriage to Mary Mulsho. He had been completing the enlargement of Gayhurst, including in the building secret passages, a priest's hiding place, and a discreet small chapel where Mass could be said. It was here that some of the plotting was planned. Guy Fawkes, Everard Digby and Robert Catesby, a kinsman of the Tyrringham family, conspired to blow up Parliament, together with the King and his family, in one big bang. But the plot failed and all the main plotters were put to death.

Gayhurst Manor where the Gunpowder Plot was hatched. (NK)

So James I escaped death in the 1605 Gunpowder Plot. But he had already been in peril twice over before because in 1603 there had been two other plots, in both of which Lord Grey de Wilton of Bletchley had been involved. In July 1603 what became known as the BYE PLOT was hatched. It was an unsophisticated affair—simply a plan to seize the new king and to try to force him as a prisoner to grant religious toleration to Catholics. But there was also what was called the MAIN PLOT, a more complicated affair aiming to depose James and in his place to put the young Arabella Stuart on the throne. The plotters were Sir Walter Raleigh, Lord Cobham and Lord Grey de Wilton of Bletchley. Both plots failed. The principal plotters were arrested. Lord Grey of Bletchley was sent to the Tower and spent the remaining eleven years of his life a prisoner there. He died in the Tower in 1614. All his estates were forfeited to the Crown and in 1616 the King made a gift of them to his favourite, George Villiers. So the Manors of Water Eaton, Bletchley and Fenny Stratford all passed to George Villiers and thus the power of the Grey family which had lasted for some fifteen generations in North Bucks came to an end.

James I died in 1625 and was succeeded by his son, Charles I. Charles believed firmly in the Divine Right of Kings. "The King can do no wrong". Within four years of his coronation he had quarrelled with Parliament over matters of finance, religion and foreign policy. He dissolved Parliament in 1629 and for eleven years ruled the country without it. But a threatened rebellion in Scotland, and his need for finance, forced Charles to recall Parliament. From then on the battle was joined between King and Parliament, turning into outright civil war which lasted from 1642 to 1649.

The contemporary woodcut reproduced above shows Puritan iconoclasts (the word means, literally, image-breakers) smashing Laudian church furnishings, including an altar-cross and altar-rails.

Buckinghamshire was one off the first counties to join in an association for mutual defence on the side of Parliament. The Bucks MP, John Hampden became a national hero for his leading role in this. No part of the kingdom escaped the effects of the seven years of the Civil War in which over 250,000 people were killed. The Civil War, besides being between King and Parliament, was also a war between families and religious loyalties. There was wanton pillage and destruction perpetrated by both sides. One in seven of all the clergy in Buckinghamshire were ejected from their livings, among them the incumbents of Stony Stratford, Shenley, Moulsoe, Newton Longville, Great and Little Brickhill, Winslow and Beachampton.

No really great battles were fought in Bucks itself. There was a fair sized battle at Aylesbury and there were skirmishes at Fenny Stratford, Newport Pagnell and Olney. Incidentally there was a young eighteen-year old trooper in the Parliamentary Garrison in Newport Pagnell who was destined to make a name for himself later. He was John Bunyan.

In North Bucks support for both sides was fairly evenly balanced. Aylesbury was firmly held by Parliament which also held the strategic ridge of the Brickhills. Perhaps the most moving individual episode of the Civil War to impinge on our local history was the death at the Battle of Edgehill in 1642 of Sir Edmund Verney of Claydon, the Royal Standard bearer who lost his life in that battle.

So many deaths and so much other suffering flowed from that coronation in 1625 of a King who believed so firmly that his coronation conferred on him Divine Right to rule. And it led to his execution on a cold January morning in Whitehall in January 1649. That execution was carried out because 26 men signed the Death Warrant. Nine of them came from Bucks.

In 1660 the monarchy was restored and Charles II ascended the throne of

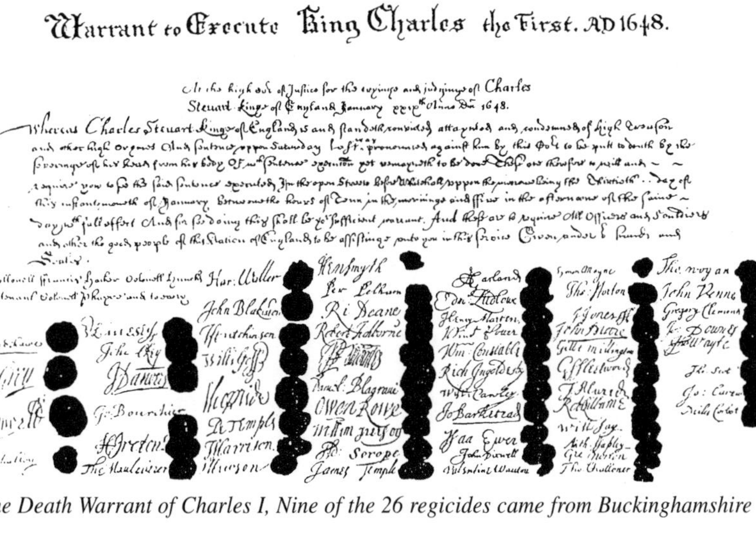

The Death Warrant of Charles I, Nine of the 26 regicides came from Buckinghamshire

his late father. At once the hunt was on for the regicides. Some had already died and others had fled the country. But nine were arrested, tried and executed.

THE COMONWEALTH OF ENGLAND

This is the term usually applied to the eleven years from 1649 to 1660 when Cromwell ruled as Lord Protector and England was a Republic. It was a time when the Book of Common Prayer was proscribed, the observance of Christmas Day was abolished, all travel on Sunday was forbidden. All Catholic priests were hunted down. Anglican clergy were forbidden to preach or teach. Many of them were ejected from their parishes and replaced by Puritan ministers. The Press was censored and a whole plethora of Puritan laws were imposed on every aspect of daily life. For the time being at least, all that the great "Elizabethan Settlement" had aimed at was no more.

One very good local example of how all this worked out in practice is seen in the case of John Gibbs. He was Vicar of Newport Pagnell in the 1650s during the Protectorate of Oliver Cromwell. There is no evidence that he was ever ordained episcopally or that he had received ordination through Presbyterianism. Throughout the 1650s he conducted a double ministration, simultaneously in the Parish Church and in the fostering of gathered congregations in and around Newport Pagnell. When the Monarchy was restored in 1660 the Convention Parliament passed an Act: "For Confirming and Restoring of Ministers". The Act identified four categories: First, Ministers occupying Livings from which the legal incumbents had been ejected, must hand them back to the original ministers if still alive. Second, ministers who had secured livings by keeping out legitimate applicants for those livings must make way for those they had displaced. Third, ministers who had petitioned for the execution of Charles I, or had opposed the restoration of Charles II must be ejected. Fourth, ministers who had publicly denied the validity of infant baptism must be ejected.

It was on that fourth point that John Gibbs was ejected. He left the Vicarage and took up residence in the High Street, renting a small house behind which there was a barn. And in that barn the Newport Pagnell Gathered Church met for worship with John Gibbs as their Minister. Very much later, in 1820, repairs were being made to the house which John Gibbs had rented. In the course of the work a hidden cupboard, four feet square, was discovered. The only way into it was by a trap door concealed in the chimney breast of the room below. The Nonconformist's "priest's hole" was found to contain some coat buttons, two small tobacco pipes, and a few silver coins!

For a poet's comments on these events as he lived through them we can quote Charles Cotton. He was born in 1630 and died in 1687. In a poem which he called'"The Litany" the opening three verses tell us what he thought of Cromwell and the Commonwealth!

1.
From a ruler that's a curse,
And a government that's worse;
From a prince that rules by awe,
Whose tyrannic will's his law;
From an armed Council board,
And a sceptre that's a sword,
Libera nos.

2.
From a kingdom, that from health
Sickens to a commonwealth;
From such peers as stain their blood,
And are neither wise, nor good;
From a gentry steeped in pots,
From unkelleners of plots,
Libera nos.

3.
From a church without divines,
And a presbyter that whines;
From John Calvin, and his pupils,
From a sentence without scruples,
From a clergy without letters,
And a free state bound in fetters,
Libera nos.

The eleven years of the Commonwealth under Cromwell had truly represented a revolution. It had marked so great a swing that it might have been expected to be followed with a counter-revolution when the Monarchy was restored. But that in fact did not happen immediately. The Prayer Book was reinstated, the ejected Anglican clergy came back into their own, both literally and metaphorically. But the Puritans were still a force to be reckoned with. Charles II was at pains to accommodate them as far as he could. He issued what he called "A Declaration concerning ecclesiastical affairs" in which he undertook to appoint a Commission of "learned divines of both persuasions" to revise the Prayer Book and to make concessions to meet some of the Puritan demands. One can see here an attempt by Charles II to recover something of the comprehensiveness at which Elizabeth had aimed. He convened the Savoy Conference to discuss all these matters which were then sent to Convocation, the Church's own Parliament, and then to Parliament itself.

Out of all this activity came the 1662 Prayer Book, which in a sense is an Act of Parliament as well as a Prayer Book. Up to this point the Cromwellian revolution had not yet produced a counter-revolution, but at least Charles had gone as far as he could to accommodate the Puritans. But that left only the Catholics as the frustrated and aggrieved element in the population. Their time was to come.

When Charles II died he was succeeded by his brother, James II. Charles himself, though himself a secret Catholic, had ruled the country largely through Anglican Squires and Parsons. His brother James, openly a Catholic, would seek to rely on Roman Catholics.

Aware of this danger, Puritans and Cromwellian survivors joined together in The Rye House Plot in 1683. The plot took its name from Rye House the home of Rombold at Hoddeston in Hertfordshire. Rombold was a die-hard Cromwellian who feared that when the self-avowed Catholic James II succeeded his brother Charles the 'closet' Catholic, all would be lost. So a number of people who shared Rombold's fears gathered round him to strike a blow for the Protestant cause. The plot hatched was a simple one. Charles II was at Newmarket with his brother James. They plotted to murder them both on their journey back to London when they passed through Hoddeston. The plot failed for the simplest of reasons—the Royal brothers left for London a day earlier than expected! When the failed plot became known arrests were made and some executions followed.

When James II came to the throne in 1685 Roman Catholics were readmitted to the English Army. In 1687 he received the Papal Nuncio in London.

Alarm spread. Was England to be turned into a Catholic State again as it had been under Mary? Rombold and his friends had failed to prevent it. Now others took a hand. A group whom history has named—"the immortal seven", seven English Lords, invited Willliam of Orange to come from Holland to take over the Kingdom with Mary his wife as Queen. So the

Glorious Revolution of 1688 took place. James II abdicated and fled to France where he died in 1701.

William III, a portrait after W. Wissing in the Nation Portrait Gallery

His daughter Mary had married her cousin William, the Stadtholder of the United Netherlands in 1677. Mary had therefore a right of succession to the English throne. Her husband, William of Orange, landed in Torbay and marched unopposed on London in 1688.

A year later, in 1689, the Toleration Act was passed, allowing all Nonconformists freedom of worship in England. This stopped short of allowing them full religious and civil freedom—they were only to obtain those in the 19th century. Nonconformists continued to be barred from public office unless they were prepared to communicate once a year in their Parish Church. Roman Catholics meanwhile cont-inued to be discriminated against in every way.

Mary II, the Queen who reigned as joint-sovereign with her husband

Many other Acts were passed. These included the public statement that Mary II was Queen, not by traditional divine right, but by the invitation of Parliament and People. Other provisions were that Parliament must be summoned at elections at least every three years and that taxation except by Parliament was illegal.

The last Stuart monarch came to the throne in 1703. She was Anne, another daughter of James II, and half-sister to Mary II. Very early in her reign, in 1704, Queen Anne set up a Fund which became known as Queen Anne's Bounty. The Fund was for the relief of the poorer clergy of the Church of England. It was created out of the moneys from the First Fruits or Annates. The Annates in pre-reformation times had been the payments made to the Pope of a year's income on the appointment of every bishop and other high ecclesiastic. These payments to the Pope had been stopped at the Reformation in 1534 and transferred to the Crown. In 1704 Queen Anne decreed that these moneys should be made over for the relief of the poorer Anglican clergy. Subsequently the Fund set up by Queen Anne was increased by Parliamentary Grants. Finally in 1948 Queen Anne's Bounty was merged with the Ecclesiastical Commission to form The Church Commissioners who still today administer the finances of the Church of England.

The final settlement usually described as'"The Glorious Revolution" of 1688 can fairly be called a victory of pragmatism and human reason.

In January 2002 history was made when the Queen invited the Cardinal of Westminster to preach in Sandringham Church. He was the first Cardinal to be so invited since the "Glorious Revolution" of 1688. The Queen's invitation marked the beginning of her Golden Jubilee and reflected the culmination of years of careful friendship-building between the Monarch as Supreme Governor of the Church of England and the Roman Catholic Church. In accepting the invitation Cardinal Cormac Murphy-O'Connor said:'"It is a clear sign of the Queen's willingness to promote ecumenism".

Cardinal Cormac Murphy-O'Connor and Canon George Hall after the service at Sandringham Church

There had been earlier signs of this ecumenism. In 1982 when Pope John Paul II visited England the Queen invited him to Buckingham Palace. In 1995 the Queen attended Vespers in Westminster Cathedral, the first monarch since the Stuarts to take part in a Roman Catholic service. And in 1999, when Cardinal Hume was dying of cancer the Queen appointed him to the Order of Merit.

POSTSCRIPT.

A Poet's salute to the country cleric.

In 1830 Winthrop Mackworth Praed wrote a poem which he called, simply, The Vicar. It makes a fitting Postscript to this book. In its five verses it is almost as if he was thinking one by one of some of those we have met in these pages.

His talk was like a stream,which runs
With rapid change from rocks to roses;
It slipped from politics to puns,
It passed from Mahomet to Moses:
Beginning with the laws which keep
The Planets in their radiant courses,
And ending with some precept deep
For dressing eels, or shoeing horses.

John Wilkins of Fawsley in 1628 wrote books about "Planets in their radiant courses" and he anticipated 20th century marvels by some 300 years. (See page 49)

He was a shrewd and sound Divine,
Of loud dissent the mortal terror:
And when by dint of page and line,
He 'stablished Truth, or startled Error,
The Baptist found him far too deep;
And the lean Levite went to sleep,
And dreamed of tasting pork tomorrow.

William Cole, Rector of St Mary's, Bletchley, with all his strictures on nonconformists, was often "of loud dissent the mortal terror". (See page 5)

His sermon never said or showed
That earth is foul, that heaven is gracious,
Without refreshment on the road
From Jerome, or from Athanasious:
And sure a righteous zeal inspired
The head and hand that penned and planned them,
For all who understood admired,
And some who did not understand them.

One thinks of Wesley and the thousands of sermons he preached "without refreshment on the road" as he travelled all over England.. (See page 80)

He did not think all mischief fair,
Although he had a knack for joking:
He did not make himself a bear,
Although he had a taste for smoking;
And when the righteous sects ran mad,
He held, in spite of all his learning,
That if a man's belief is bad,
It will not be improved by burning.

Does that remind you of Tally Ho! Hanmer of Simpson, of whom J.K. Fowler wrote that he was "a rollicking jolly sportsman", popular in his parish, charitable to the poor, and a very good preacher? (See page 41)

And he was kind, and loved to sit
In the low hut or garnished cottage,
And praise the farmer's homely wit,
And share the widow's homelier pottage;
At his approach complaint grew mild;
And when his hand unbarred the shutter,
The clammy lips of fever smiled
The welcome which they could not utter.

One can think of no less than four country clerics who have been written of in this book who deserve the praise in this final verse of Praed's poem. And they are: James Woodforde of Weston Longville (See page 9); Richard Napier of Great Linford (See page 52); John Schorne of North Marston (See page 43); and George Herbert of Bemerton . (See page 46).

INDEX